SILVER MOON

GREAT NOVELS
OF
EROTIC DOMINATION
AND
SUBMISSION

NEW TITLES EVERY MONTH

www.smbooks.co.uk

TO FIND OUT MORE ABOUT OUR READERS' CLUB
WRITE TO;

SILVER MOON READER SERVICES;
Barrington Hall Publishing
Hexgreave Hall
Farnsfield
Nottinghamshire NG22 8LS
Tel: 01157 141616

YOU WILL RECEIVE A FREE MAGAZINE OF EXTRACTS
FROM OUR EXTENSIVE RANGE OF EROTIC FICTION
ABSOLUTELY FREE. YOU WILL ALSO HAVE THE
CHANCE TO PURCHASE BOOKS WHICH ARE
EXCLUSIVE TO OUR READERS' CLUB

***

NEW AUTHORS ARE WELCOME

Please send submissions to;
Barrington Hall Publishing
Hexgreave Hall
Farnsfield NG22 8LS

Silver Moon books are an imprint of Barrington Hall Publishing
which is part of Barrington Hall Ltd.

Also by Francine Whittaker;

In Silver Mink
The Connoisseur
Punishment Bound

In Silver Moon
Amber in Chains
Slave Path I
Slave Path II
Slave Path III
Bad Blood (with Sean O'Kane)

The Whipmaster Series
The Whipmaster
Pleasure Control
Bridled and Bound

In Silver Mistress
Mistress Blackheart
Lady Nightshade

***

All characters in this book are fictitious, and any resemblance to
real persons, living or dead, is purely coincidental.

BAD
BLOOD

by

Francine Whittaker

and

Sean O'Kane

CHAPTER ONE

❝You bitch!"

The words bubbled up in her throat and were spat out before Vanessa could help herself. The blonde cow was tall and leggy but still had plenty of tit to flash at the guy she was sitting next to. And the guy she was sitting next to was none other than Alex Mayfair.

Alex!

Her Alex!

Alex who she had slept with for the first time only two months ago and who now regularly gave her the best seeings-to she could remember. Alex whose good looks and gentle manners she had been cooing about to her girlfriends all that night. That and the size of his cock! She had told them all that he was hung like a horse and how it had made her eyes water and her insides quiver rapturously.

Vanessa stood stock still and glared at the blonde apparition who was staring back, quite cool and collected. Not that her butter-wouldn't-melt looks fooled Vanessa for one minute. Alex didn't even seem to give a damn and leaned back in his seat, a slight grin on his face. Around the frozen trio the club thundered on, lights swirled, couples danced, drank and pushed past. One of her girlfriends took her arm and tried to pull her away but she wouldn't have it. She shrugged the girl off and took a step forwards, not really knowing what she was going to do; only certain she was going to damn well do something.

The blonde saw her coming, smiled lazily and crossed her legs, revealing an impossible length of pale thigh as the pink, triple-layered mini skirt rode upward. Then she sat back next to Alex and as Vanessa watched in sick horror, she reached out to Alex's groin and rubbed her hand slowly up and down the front of his trousers, using her thumb and forefinger she outlined the column of his towering erection. The gesture was strangely and heart-stoppingly emphasised for the watching Vanessa by the jangling of the silver and pink pearl charm bracelet which hugged the bitch's wrist as she rubbed Vanessa's nose in her humiliation.

Alex grinned again and shrugged his shoulders helplessly, then reached out to the blonde and pulled her treacherously angelic face to his, kissing her with bruising strength on her pink-glossed, parted lips.

"C'mon luv," Alison behind her pleaded. "It's you the bastards'll throw out if you start anything!"

Almost numb with shock and trembling with rage, Vanessa followed Alison to the bar. As she walked, the beads of her own cheap, multi stone, glass and plastic bracelet rattled in time with her steps.

"The bitch! The bastard! The fucking pair of fucking bastards!" she found herself repeating in a dazed mantra as her friends closed ranks around her. Vaguely she heard them run through the usual platitudes, 'not worth it', 'he's the loser, he just don't know it yet!', 'what a tart!'

Strangely though she began to calm down and eventually her thoughts focused on the one simple idea; if he can do it, so can I. She would show him that she was better than that candy-flossed little tart! With the unbidden picture of the two of them lingering in her mind, she determined to show him what he was missing, and that if he didn't want her, there were plenty of others who did! She was a girl on a mission and directing her anger towards her new goal she pursed her lips, tossed her head and flicked her long, sleek, mahogany-rich hair over her shoulder.

She glanced around and saw a presentable enough guy swigging down a bottle of beer just along the bar. Before her friends could stop her she had sashayed up to him and was standing directly in front of him. Her fleshy-lipped, wide mouth smouldered a pouty smile.

"If you've got a girl with you I'll piss off. If not, you've pulled." Staggered at her own audacity Vanessa realised she had had more than she ought to drink and almost giggled at the startled look the guy threw her. But she was not too drunk to notice that he recovered himself quickly and took a quick inventory of what was on offer. And it was a good offer!

She was an attractive girl with good legs which she had left bare; their nice sheen was due entirely to the liberal use of baby oil. Her denim bum scarf was slung low on the hips and left virtually nothing to the imagination. All the girls were wearing them these days for the round holes punched at intervals around the short wavy hem, each one about the size of a ten pence coin and decoratively ringed with metal studs. Every now and then an onlooker could catch a tantalising glimpse of bare flesh through the holes. The brown leather belt she wore with it was about a third of the width of the skirt. Above it was an expanse of creamy bare flesh with a pretty little belly bar piercing her navel, the red stones catching the light. Above it her cropped, lightweight and short sleeved top was a pretty, ivory colour that almost matched her skin tone, and had a deeply scooped neck which helped her bra display her generous, perfectly formed tits to their best advantage. She glanced down as she saw his eyes fix on them and proudly pushed the straining mounds towards him.

He smiled. "My name's Darren," he said. "Drink?"

Out to prove she was more of a woman and a whole lot more fun than that silly, fluffy bimbo Alex had hooked up with would ever be, she turned down her usual Bacardi Breezer in favour of a pint of lager.

Later, she would never remember if she saw Alex and his tart leave or not, though she did remember her friends trying to drag her off with them. But by that time she had become so enamoured by her mission that she wanted only to get Darren between the sheets, so they left her to it. He took her over to one of the bench seats at the back of the room.

Within moments he was getting his hands pretty well wherever he wanted to put them. It really wasn't too much of a problem with her skirt, and the denim-look thong with its heart-shaped motif was easily twitched aside. She quivered slightly as his fingers swept tickling-sweet across her carefully trimmed pubes, the cheeky arrow design copied from a feature in one of her magazines. Lifting her glass to her lips, she ignored the bitter taste of the liquid and concentrated instead on his fingers as they bypassed her clit and pushed their way inside her startlingly wet pussy. Without considering whether anyone was watching as she opened her legs wider to ease his access, she lifted her hand to her mouth and used her fingers to wipe the froth from her lips and then put her glass on the table and held it tightly as Darren's fingers swirled inside her, sending little ripples of agitation through her belly. Her cunt muscles clenched involuntarily around his unfamiliar digits and bolts of arousal zinged through her, stiffening her nipples. Even as she bit her lip to stop herself from moaning her pleasure, she wished he would give some attention to her throbbing clit. Nevertheless, she thought she would die with pleasure as her vaginal muscles twitched in sheer delight. Raising her glass she took another slug of the bitter liquid and inwardly she smiled at the thought that people might be watching her practically giving herself to a virtual stranger, and for the first time she experienced the heated excitement of exhibitionism. She gave a little cry of discomfort as his fingernail briefly stabbed the wall of her delicate insides. Words of complaint formed in her brain but drifted out again before she had spoken them. Reality began to ebb and flow, until a certain haziness had her staring fixedly at some point ahead. Nothing mattered but the rhythm of Darren's probing fingers, and her heart beating in time. She was suddenly aware of the changing sound of her breathing and, glancing at her own fingers as they clutched the glass in mid air, she noticed her hand was shaking and the liquid sloshing in the glass. Trying to maintain an air of nonchalance, she lifted the glass and poured a fair quantity down her throat. His fingers changed from swirling to plunging in and out rapidly, then swirled inside her again before continuing with the in-out as his lust increased. Adjusting her pose she slouched on the bench and opened her legs wider, so wide that the elastic of the thong was cutting into her quite uncomfortably. And all the while his fingers stirred her juices up inside her and she began to respond in an automatic sort of way, while feeling herself moisten even further, at the same time as she sullenly slugged her way towards drunkenness.

Eventually Darren guided her out into the night and she tottered unsteadily on her heels in the fresh air. She could feel that the gusset of her thong was still askew and, coming to an unsteady standstill she spread her legs where she was so she could get one hand up inside her skirt and twitch the thong across then wriggle herself back into comfort.

"What a whore!" a gravely voice said from her right hand side.

"Yeah." That was Darren's voice. "But she's tight and juicy, believe me."

"Okay, get her in."

Vanessa found herself grabbed by strong hands and thrown forwards. Fuzzily, she was aware of landing lying across the laps of several men sitting in the back of a big car. She stifled a giggle.

Doors slammed and the car moved off. Alarm bells belatedly began to ring in Vanessa's drink fuddled brain. Unable to find purchase, her hands slipped on trousered thighs and knees as she tried to lever herself up but a strong hand on her head forced her down again.

"Get down and get used to it, darlin'," another voice said to general laughter.

Now she knew something was wrong. She tried flailing about but all that achieved was hands holding her down by gripping her thighs, thick, coarse fingers digging deep into her soft flesh. Other hands reached over her shoulders and one reached a bit further and took a handful of her breast. She felt her skirt being wrenched up and hands trailing across the soft globes of her buttocks.

Slowly, through the alcoholic mists in her mind, the realisation dawned on Vanessa that she was about to get gangbanged.

***

The drive wasn't a long one and fairly soon the car bumped over rough ground and then halted. Vanessa was starting to feel queasy and the fresh air let in by the car doors being opened was a welcome relief. Someone reached in and grabbed her under the arms, hauling her roughly out into the chill night air. Standing unsteadily with her head like cotton wool, she was hardly aware of the way her heart was pounding in fright, glassy-eyed she looked around her, shaking her disarranged hair out of her eyes. When her vision finally focussed she saw that the car stood in the middle of a scrapyard. Around it were precarious stacks of rusting and half-flattened wrecks. On the ground someone had scattered some old rear seats with foam bursting out in places, looking unpleasantly as if it had exploded from within a skin.

"Here's your fucking-ground, darlin'," a male voice whispered malevolently in her ear and she was shoved forwards violently.

The chunky beads at her wrist clunked and clanked noisily as, with her arms windmilling wildly, she fought for balance on the rough ground in her high heels. She staggered towards the seats and was just able to make it, falling face down on one and immediately pushing herself up onto her elbows to get her face away from the stink of mildew and other things. She felt a sudden weight on the centre of her back and craning her head round saw

Darren with his foot on her. Slowly she became aware that her heart was thumping rather too loudly, reverberating through her as panic tried to make itself recognised through her stupor.

"You can either strip yourself, or we'll do it for you," he told her.

Mentally grappling to maintain control of her already demolished dignity, a last streak of defiant pride flickered into life inside her and she shook her hair back proudly.

"I'll do it," she said and tottered back up to her feet.

Despite her swaggering, plucky display her fingers just didn't seem to want to comply and she fumbled and fiddled with her buttons for some seconds before she had any success. But once she got her top off she smoothed her hair back and as she reached behind her and fumbled again to unfasten her bra she was able to see that five men stood before her, all stripped to the waist and grinning menacingly at her. Vaguely the thought occurred to her that she had no idea what having five men take their pleasure with her would feel like. But as she brought her arms forwards and discarded the bra in what she hoped was a sexy, teasing manner and let the heavy orbs of her breasts swing free on her slender chest, she could clearly see the straining bulges at the fronts of their trousers. A strange thrill swept through her body as she realised that no fewer than five, hard, lovely big cocks just couldn't wait to get inside her. That thought set her heart beating to an excited, choppy rhythm. She grinned back fiercely at the men, carried away by the exhibitionist high as she threw her belt aside and unzipped her skirt, stepping out of it quickly so that suddenly only her thong hid her quim and her long thighs gleamed palely in the gloom.

She spread her legs and put her hands on her hips.

"Okay boys. Come and get it."

In the days that followed she came to think that her moment of bravado had been a bad idea but once her black eye had calmed down and the welts on her bottom and back had faded and the bruises were yellowing, she had to admit that it had had the effect of producing a gangbang that she was quite proud of having endured.

Darren had gone first, stepping out of his trousers before pushing her down onto her back on one of the seats once she had stepped out of her thong in her turn. He had knelt between her legs and suckled and licked at her nipples until they were really hard and her breasts felt full and tight, then he sat back and slapped them to and fro. In the exciting and faintly unreal situation in which she found herself it didn't hurt and she even giggled along with the men as the heavy mounds swung and rippled ponderously. Then he started doing it harder, really hitting them and suddenly it was all too real after all, and it hurt.

"Ow! Please, Darren!" she had protested and then he had slapped her face equally hard and with belated caution she realised that it was safest to keep quiet. At last, with her tits feeling as though they were on fire, he tired of that game and instead stretched out on top of her. She pushed her pelvis up at him to encourage the hardness she could feel at his groin and he drove in. She scrabbled with her feet to get some grip so she could arch her back and extract the last few inches of penetration from him and grip with her vaginal muscles. Their perspiration-bathed bodies pressed together and she felt her breasts flatten uncomfortably under his rigid chest as he settled down to a good steady rhythm, pushing deep inside her and pulling out almost to the point of disengagement, fetching anxious whimpers from her as she felt herself emptied.

"Once she's got it up her, she don't like losing it, does she?" gravel voice observed.

Vanessa's befuddled brain was beginning to clear but still, Darren was definitely a good shag, he wasn't on a short fuse, that was for sure. She felt herself begin to spiral up towards orgasm and increased her tempo. He grinned down at her and retaliated. Groin to groin they smacked together, grunts filled the sordid yard but Vanessa's whole world had come down to the few inches of her vagina and the several inches that filled it, rather deliciously she thought. She yelled in triumph as her first climax exploded inside her. She hardly felt Darren empty himself into her before he had rolled clear.

Vanessa dragged in a couple of good lungfuls of air and then with no warning, a youth sporting a gelled and spiky haircut was on top of her and the blunt roundness of his helm was already pushing into her sperm-slippery entrance.

She didn't orgasm that time nor the next.

But when gravel voice was ramming himself to ecstasy inside

her and nearly crushing her ribs under his bulk, she managed to catch up enough to grind herself against him sufficiently to reap her orgasm at about the same time as he spurted his thick jism up her and was still spurting as he slid out and the fifth man turned her face down, then hauled her hips up and sank into her to the hilt from behind. She was so full of spunk by then that she felt a sudden wash of hot, unadulterated shame as her vagina emitted a sound that was very much like a loud fart as she was penetrated. For some reason that seemed to bring down the floodgates. It was as though it reduced her to a collection of holes to fuck in their eyes and she ceased being any kind of person at all. They had all got their initial lust satiated and from then on they became much more inventive. She was exhausted and once the fifth man had had her from behind she collapsed forwards and lay panting on the filthy plastic seat. Behind her she heard the sounds of cans cracking open and beer being chugged, slowly she raised herself onto all fours, estimated the distance to the gates and - to hell with being naked – prepared to make a break for it. The fresh air and the orgasms had cleared her brain enough for her to realise that despite the orgasms, this was not a healthy place for a girl to be.

"Time to go, Vanessa," she whispered to herself.

She jumped up and tried to run but stepped straight on a stone and fell before she had made three yards. Darren was onto her immediately and hauled her up by her hair and a handful of tit.

Before she knew any more one of the men hauled off and fetched her a blow to the face that made her teeth rattle and finally finished the job of clearing her head. She knew she was in real trouble now.

She felt like a rag doll as she was thrown forwards and landed face down on another old seat. Before she could move she felt a sudden pressure on the back of her neck and wriggled fiercely until she could get her hands up behind her and realised someone was bloody standing on her neck and her naked arse was waving in the air! She heard a Crack! and for a moment wondered what had happened but then a burning pain ignited in her bottom and she realised that she had been beaten with something or other. Screaming into the stinking plastic she wriggled even more in a vain attempt to escape and heard the men laughing in delight. She took another stroke and another, she tried to flatten herself by parting her thighs and squatting but that just resulted in her taking a heavy stroke right between the legs, right along the length of her already burningly abused pussy. She couldn't believe that they would do that and she almost succeeded in dislodging the foot on her neck, such was her outrage. That only encouraged them and she felt hands pulling her feet apart and from then on anything went.

Eventually they stopped whipping her with what she finally saw was a heavy belt and began fucking her again. They seemed to love the way exhaustion made her sag and go limp as they grabbed and pawed at her then slammed their cocks into her, or stood over her and wanked their thick, slimy spend over her face and tits. She didn't get any respite. As soon as one finished another was on her, or so it seemed. And when they got bored of using her cunt, they started on her arse and mouth. She had only done anal once or twice, but now she was expected to take one after the other up her tight, narrow channel. She tried screaming but got a suffocating mouthful of cock for her troubles. She didn't dare think about which of her holes it had been in previously and just sucked for her life. Self preservation was the name of the game by that time and she stroked the thick, hard shafts of cock even as she sucked at their bitter tasting slits, waiting for yet another load of spunk to erupt into her.

They started whipping her again; this time while she was taking two up, one from behind and one in her mouth, but the pain in her arse and back and the burning in her cunt dulled it to simply a series of bruising impacts that shook her as she presented every hole to the seemingly unending procession of cocks.

She never saw them go.

There was just a time when she came round and found herself alone. Cold, fucked stupid, filthy, naked. And dimly, beneath the tumultuous images of the last couple of hours, she remembered the club. She remembered the club and Alex and that fucking blonde tart. It was all her fault. And that was the last thought she had before exhaustion claimed her.

CHAPTER TWO

Breeze from the open window whispered across her naked flesh. Full wakefulness loitered within her grasp as, with her head cradled in the hollow of her pillow, Vanessa screwed up her eyes in protest. She did not want to wake yet! Shaking her head in denial of the pain which tugged at her consciousness, she was unable to ignore the brass band thumping away just above her right eye and marching down toward her ear. Except it wasn't only the din of trumpets, cornets and drums which woke her so heartlessly but the bells of St. Hilda's. Semi-comatose she realised that if the bells were ringing then it must be Sunday morning.

Feeling returned with a vengeance and she became aware of an ache between her legs. It was so bad that it felt as if she had been booted in the crotch. But that was ridiculous she told herself as her hand wandered from its resting place to cup her mound protectively, she hadn't been kicked at all, just fucked! But she was so bloody sore down there! Why? It was true that Alex was a bit of a stud, a man who could keep going half the night, but she had never been this sore afterwards previously. It must have been one helluva fucking, she mused sleepily and reached out to touch him. Her fingers came in contact with the empty space beside her, and in her sleep-befuddled brain, she concluded he had gone to the bathroom. But the funny thing was, she didn't remember going home with him. In fact, she didn't remember much at all.

Still clutching her vulva with one hand, once again she patted the space beside her. Slowly it dawned on her that she was alone. A slight uneasiness crept into her consciousness as she realised that she didn't actually remember being with Alex at all last night. So if she hadn't been with Alex, who the hell had she been with? And if she wasn't at his place, then where was she? The uneasiness grew, and with it the reluctance to open her eyes for fear of what she might discover. Instead, she searched her memory in an effort to remember what had happened last night to make her feel so utterly wretched.

Leafing through the blurred, spattered pages of memory she recalled the night out with her mates. Alex was there, she had seen him......and then with the force of a thunderclap she remembered he had been with someone else......that fucking blonde tart! But not just any blonde tart, she realised with a jolt, but one with whom she had once been well acquainted. That it was bloody Rae Carroll, or Rae Camel as she had called her at school on account of her long legs and natural ability to give Vanessa the hump, made it a thousand times worse! Of all the girls Alex could have chosen to two-time her with, why did he have to pick her, the girl she had first encountered during school days? She hated that bitch!

And then, for the briefest moment Vanessa recoiled into the warming glow of a distant, hugely satisfying memory of Rae sprawling face down in the dirt on the athletics track. They had been about sixteen at the time, and both girls had been hugely competitive. On that faraway day, Rae had blamed Vanessa for sticking her foot out as she had come alongside but nobody had seen any offending foot and just for once, Vanessa had triumphed over her rival.

Yet even as her lips curved into a smile as she recalled lifting the trophy above her head, Vanessa's brain demanded that she concentrate on more recent events. It was imperative, her brain screamed, that she remember how she came to be in this painful condition. Still keeping her eyes closed, she pictured the scene at the night-club, and saw herself spiting Alex and Rae by picking up someone else. Except now she really thought about it, there had been several someone elses! As the recognition of pain stole across her body, slowly she opened her eyes. However, one of them just didn't seem to want to and continued to pound at her brain with messages of urgent pain. It took several seconds for Vanessa to focus with her good eye, and she realised that she was in her own bedroom. She glanced around and was relieved to see no evidence of anyone else there.

During the seconds which followed, horrific scenes suddenly leapt into her now wide-awake consciousness and played out in lurid detail seemingly in the centre of her forehead. She saw herself, tossed about like a rabbit by a pack of dogs as the men had taken it in turns to violate her. Yet even now she didn't completely trust the recollections. Surely the gangbang hadn't been real? She moved her leg, and gave a cry as her normally supple, well-toned body objected. Her horrified expletive echoed around her bedroom.

"Shit! It really fucking happened!" But if that was the case, how did she get back here, to her own flat? She was not lying in the bed she realised but on top of the duvet. She moved her head on the pillow and saw her clothes, or what was left of them, stashed on the floor in the corner. Somehow she must have staggered home and dragged herself as far as the bed before collapsing upon it.

She put all her effort into getting up off the bed and lurched her way to the kitchen......coffee, that's what she needed. Without bothering to draw fresh water she switched on the kettle, reached for the Nescafe and swung her gaze around in search of a mug. It was only when she stretched her arm to reach the top shelf for the only clean mug in the place that she noticed the huge bruise on her wrist. There was another on her upper arm. In fact, as she looked down at her naked body, she realised that she had bruises everywhere, and she couldn't help noticing the crusting of sperm around her upper thighs and in between her breasts, her heart sinking she stroked her cheek, yes, she had some on her face too. She glanced towards the shiny metal kettle and saw the mess that someone had made of her eye.

"Oh no!" she groaned out loud as suddenly another pain that had been struggling to make itself heard finally broke through. Her hand flew behind her and she realised there was another good reason why the walk through the flat had hurt her entire genital region. She'd been buggered as well as fucked.

When her coffee was made she added milk and sweetener then, mug in hand, she padded slowly across to the balcony, where the curtains were open. Ignoring her naked state she opened the door and stood with her belly against the railings. From her position she could see most of the small town, with the new Thornycroft housing estate to the far left. Almost next to it was the town centre itself, with the Spire of St. Hilda's rising from its centre. She could not see where the night-club was located but she had an almost uninterrupted view of the road which passed through the small village of Langley Feldon. And she couldn't quite see the great Lewington House, where local legend had it all manner of debauched happenings went on. It was as she stood there, looking out across the town as the sun threw its rays across the rooftops and glinted on the windows of the office buildings to her right that she allowed herself to fully recall the terrors of the previous night. She remembered there had been about five of them......

animals, that's what they were, animals! And yet looking back, if she was completely honest it wasn't so much the horror of the gangbang itself that made her feel sick, she realised, nor even the filthy surroundings in which the abominations had taken place that really turned her stomach. What really pissed her off was that it was all bloody Rae's fault! If it had not been for that long-legged, big-titted lump of shit, she would never have gone off with Darren in the first place! And God help her......if she ever set eyes on the cow again, she'd bloody well kill her!

Such was her distress that she felt no shame in standing naked on the balcony as she sipped her coffee. Nor did she feel joy in the glorious sunshine. She continued her survey of the area and flipped her gaze to farther on her right. Over there, somewhere between the railway station and the Bulliver Building, where she was a popular member of the workforce, was the place where the gangbang had taken place, the dump! And all because of Rae bloody Carroll.

She had ruined much of Vanessa's school life. They had both been keen sportswomen and had been competitors in gymnastics, hockey, tennis...just about everything. And Alex wasn't the first boyfriend she'd stolen, either; there was Peter Perkins. At thirteen, the young Vanessa had been devastated when blonde, long-legged Rae, without an ounce of puppy fat, had waltzed in and stolen Peter from under her nose. She had gone on to "steal" Vanessa's place in the County Swimming Team.

Sighing, she made her way back inside and towards the bathroom where the full extent of the damage became plain. For the life of her she couldn't actually recall being beaten but right across her bottom and her back was an entire ladder of dull red stripes........although there was a brief vision of Darren lying on his back under her with his cock stuffing her divinely and there was a stinging pain across her shoulders, and there was male laughter in the background. She sighed again, soaked a flannel in cold water and got on with nursing her hurts and her resentment in equal proportions.

***

Vanessa walked into the office the next morning, fifteen minutes late as usual. But instead of the daily lecture from her supervisor, an efficient, middle-aged woman whose sour demeanour was probably due to her dried-up cunt, Vanessa surmised uncharitably, her late arrival met with uninterrupted indifference. There was none of the familiar, Monday morning banter, "Hi Vee, did you do anyone special over the weekend?", "Did you get laid, Vee?" or "Alex still flavour of the month?" as she made her way to her work station. There weren't even the expected remarks about her black eye or her miserable attempts to camouflage it. In fact, no-one was sitting at their work stations. Instead, they were all clustered noisily around the workstation by the window. What was going on? Ah yes, she thought as she took her seat and switched on her PC, the new girl was supposed to be starting today. Although quite what all the fuss was about, she had no idea. To her mind, it was taking the whole "must be able to work in a team" a bit too far when the whole "team" gathered round like it was a major event. It was only a new employee after all! It was with unnecessary vehemence that Vanessa typed in her password: sexnbooze.

After another five minutes or so, the giggling and general friendship was beginning to grate on her. She was just about to go and complain that she was the only one doing any work when a shadow loomed over her. Her heart plummeted still further. If there was one thing she didn't need right now it was a visit from the lecherous head of department, Nigel Pickett, or as Vanessa called him, never-get-well-while-you-pick-it. Her flesh crawled as he stood on the other side of her desk, facing her.

"What's going on?" he said quietly, more concerned with Vanessa's breasts than with the lack of work. He leaned across the computer screen toward her.

If he touched her again, like he had last week.......and the week before.......she would have him up on a sexual harassment charge! she told herself resolutely. She raised her head and flicked her eyes from her computer screen to his ruddy-cheeked face.

"I think they're all saying hello to the new member of staff," she said.

"Then that gives us a few minutes to say hello after the weekend," he smirked, extending his hand. He used his thumb and forefinger beneath her chin to tilt her head slightly backward. "My! That's quite a shiner you have there," he whispered. "What have you been up to?" Leaning closer, the forefinger of his other hand hooked back the opening of her low-cut blouse. "Deary

~ 21 ~

deary me! You seem to have a nasty bruise on your tit! Come through to my office and we'll see if we can't find something to make that better."

"No, it's okay, really," she smiled, cursing herself for not having the guts to report him, "it doesn't hurt. I'd just as soon get these reports done if you don't mind."

"But I do mind," he said with a grin, "I mind very much, my dear, that you won't allow me to help you. Come on now," he withdrew his hand and with pressure beneath her chin encouraged her to stand, "let's go and see what we can find in the First Aid box. Or would you rather I called in Social Services to talk to you about how you got into that state – or maybe you'd rather talk to the police?"

She shook her head dumbly. It was easier to let him have his thrills than go back over her own stupidity and that fucking cow's treachery. After all, he couldn't get up to much here at work! Of course, there had been that time in his office when he'd cornered her and felt her up beneath her skirt, but he wouldn't dare do that again. As she followed him back to his office, she heard the group breaking up behind her and the girls returning to their own desks.

"Hey Vee, come and meet the new girl! She's really nice. I know you'll like her," her friend called after her.

"Mr Pickett wants to show me some sales figures for my report," she called without looking back.

It was an hour later when Vanessa returned to the spacious, open plan office in which she worked. Her boss had indeed found something to rub on her bruised tit, though it had certainly not come from the First Aid box. The wet patch on her blouse adhered to her breast and she would have to go to the Ladies and clean up, or else she'd stink of spunk all day. She felt everyone's eyes on her as she walked briskly through the office toward her desk, clutching the bogus files to her chest. She glanced toward the window, but there was no sign of the new girl. Perhaps they'd sacked her already for being too disruptive, Vanessa thought as she dropped off the files on her desk on her way to the Ladies.

Once inside the toilets, she dashed into one of the cubicles, pulled off a long trail of loo roll then made a bee-line for the row of washbasins. She ran some water, then removed her blouse and bra. Leaning forward over the hot water, she dipped the toilet tissue into the water and then used it to wash away the spunk. Behind her inside one of the cubicles, the toilet flushed. Mild panic set in. The last thing she wanted was to be caught with her tits out! Still, there was nothing she could do about it now. The blouse was ruined, of course. She would have to go home at lunchtime to change. The door behind her opened and she glanced up at the mirror above the basins.

"Oh fuck! That's all I need!"

"Hello Vanessa," the voice oozed sweetly, "fancy seeing you here! And so soon after the other night."

"Bloody too soon for me, you fucking whore!" Vanessa swung round to confront her bête noir. "Listen Rae, you may have that lot in there fooled," she jerked her head toward the door to indicate the office as Rae washed her hands beside her, "but I know the real scheming, lying, bitch of a whore behind that candyfloss façade. I know you for what you are. And it's far from nice!"

It was true, of course. Beneath the soft, sweet exterior which she displayed so readily to the world at large, Rae had a heart of stone and a tongue like a viper. Having been spoiled as a child by parents who sacrificed everything for their only daughter, Rae had grown up believing that all she had to do to get her own way was smile prettily. And it usually worked! She was also highly competitive and, despite her big tits and long legs, like Vanessa herself, Rae had kept her body in shape. Not that either girl had the muscle-bound body of a bodybuilder, more the toned, powerful thighs of a runner and the suppleness of a gymnast. Now Rae's baby blue eyes bored ice holes in the other girl's face.

"You call me a whore? But Vanessa, which one of us has her tits out?"

Ignoring the remark, Vanessa's tone was a harsh undertone as she went on warningly, "You keep your hands off my Alex........."

"Your Alex?" Rae's sweet, little glossed mouth twisted into an ugly sneer. "Listen, you sad excuse for a woman, a man like Alex Mayfair doesn't belong to any woman, least of all you! He said you're like a leech he can't shake off."

"You lying bitch!" What was left of Vanessa's world collapsed around her ears. First Alex had cheated on her at the night-club, then there was the gangbang, now this. And Rae was at the root of it all. "That's not true. He'd never say that! He loves me. You keep your filthy hands off or I'll......"

"You'll what? Go off with Darren and his nasty little mates again? Oh, don't look so shocked, we saw you. If I remember correctly," she turned away from Vanessa and, leaning across the wash basin, she wet her middle finger before smoothing her eyebrow, "you always did like to play with the boys. What was the chant they made up about you at school?" She repeated the process with the other eyebrow. "I remember, yes......... 'Vanessa, I've bed her, no need to wed her.' "

It was the final straw. Still with her breasts hanging freely Vanessa lunged at her, raising her hand to strike that slutty, sweet little face. But Rae was too quick for her and grabbed her arm, just as the door opened and Annie, one of the other girls walked in.

"Rae? Vee? What's up?"

Rae released her grip.

Vanessa let her hand drop. Soundlessly she mouthed "next time!" before turning back to the basin. The water had dried on her skin and she pulled on her bra. "Nothing's up," she said brightly. "I just thought I saw a bit of black fluff in Rae's hair. Must have been a root," she said cattily.

"Yes, that's right," Rae smiled pleasantly, her demeanour one of innocence and sincerity, "and I was just telling Vanessa that I have some perfume in my bag that she might want to borrow.... I'm sure I can smell semen!"

Angrily, Vanessa pulled on her blouse as Rae giggled sweetly and headed for the door.

Annie laughed when she had gone. "Oh Vee! You didn't tell us you knew her. Isn't she great? Sooo pretty. Witty, too. She was telling us all about some girl at the night-club on Saturday. Apparently, she was a right slut, tried to butt in between her and her boyfriend...."

"Her boyfriend?"

"Yes. According to Rae, the girl was a right slut. Sat with her legs wide open, sucking some bloke's hand right up her pussy, and sloshing beer down her throat like there was no tomorrow. When the bloke tried to shake her off by saying he was meeting his mates outside, the slut said she'd give them all a blow job in return for another beer. The last Rae saw of her, the girl was staggering along behind them, making a nuisance of herself. Oh

Vee, it was so funny the way she told it. You'll have to get her to tell you the story."

Vanessa was seething. "Yes, I'll make sure of it!"

CHAPTER THREE

Vanessa pointedly ignored her for the rest of the morning. Settling down at her workstation after lunch, she strained for the necessary enthusiasm needed to immerse herself in her work; she needed the sales figures, monthly projections and quarter end report as a balm to her tormented heart. But she couldn't put thoughts of recent events completely from her mind. In all honesty, she excused herself as she screwed up a scrap of paper and with perfect precision tossed it into a waste bin on the other side of the room, it was a hurdle too far when one took into account the close proximity of Rae. It was exactly the same as it had been all those years before.... the bitch still attracted attention as she did then; males and females alike were attracted to her the way a picnic attracts wasps. And, as Annie and the rest of them buzzed around Rae on her return from lunch, a two-hour lunch she noted sourly, Vanessa's blank expression as she stared into space instead of at her screen was noted by Maggie Huffer, her supervisor.

"Are we keeping you awake, Vanessa?" the woman asked sarcastically as she hovered vulture-like beside her. "If you haven't got anything to do, I'm sure I could find you

something." There was a malicious edge to her voice as she went on. "I hear the post room is understaffed."

Vanessa picked up on the threat at once and swivelled her chair round. She jerked her head up to face the woman. "You wouldn't dare!"

"Try me!"

"What about her?" Vanessa jabbed her thumb over her shoulder in the general direction of Rae, who was currently holding court by the drinks machine. Even from here she could hear the sugar-toned bimbo giggling her way through another story of her conquest of Alex. It really was too much!

"That bitch hasn't done a stroke of work all morning and I doubt you'll get much out of her this afternoon. She didn't even appear at her workstation until after three o'clock and it's......"

"Half past. Not that it's any of your business! Unlike some I could mention," Miss Huffer went on tersely, "Rae actually arrived back early from lunch and..........."

"Oh yeah! Miss goody fucking two shoes would get back early, wouldn't she? Trust her to make the rest of us look bad! But you tell me this, Miss Huffer.........if she got back early, where the hell's she been until now?"

Vanessa noted the slight hesitation before the other woman answered, and she was quick to note the unaccustomed quiver in the brittle voice as her supervisor tried to maintain her professionalism.

"Rae's been in with Mr Pickett since she got back," she said primly.

Bloody hell! The old biddy was jealous! Surely to God she wasn't sweet on him, not Pervy Pickett?

She went on, "He spotted her potential this morning......."

"I bet he did!" Vanessa laughed bitterly, and wondered why the knowledge was like the twisting of a knife in an already bleeding wound. After all, she should be made up that Rae's arrival had diverted Pervy Pickett's attentions away from herself so why wasn't she delighted that he had found a new toy to play with? Her own voice was laced with resentment. "With tits the size of hers, it would be hard for him to miss it!"

Miss Huffer chose to ignore the remark.

But Vanessa's rancour, bitter as it was uncommon thanks to everything she had gone through of late, made her unaccountably cruel as her gaze fastened on the other woman's androgynous figure. "Mr. Pickett likes them big-titted. 'Something to get hold of,' he says."

There! That struck a chord! Yet Vanessa felt no satisfaction at the very obvious signs of hurt that crossed the older woman's face. Nor did she feel triumphant as Miss Huffer turned on her heel and marched down the office. Instead, she felt ashamed. As much as she disliked her supervisor, she had never set out to hurt her before. They had had their arguments, of course, but it had never been malicious on Vanessa's part before. And she did not like the change within herself.

Putting her supervisor from her thoughts, she dwelt once again on the fact that everything that had happened was Rae's fault.

She swivelled her chair back round to face her screen, just in time to see Kieren, the guy with the nice bum and extremely lickable cock that she had once had the pleasure of sampling, walk past her desk toward Rae's. A wayward thought flitted into her mind and she momentarily smiled as she imagined the scene in the scrapyard, except this time Kieren had replaced Darren!

Suddenly she felt the bile rise. How could she even think such a thing? Just then she heard him laugh at something the blonde bimbo had said, and she forced herself to look at the screen in front of her, where the patterns which swirled from corner to corner proved just how long her attention had been diverted from her job. She reached out and touched her mouse. At once the swirling blues and reds were replaced by rows of figures. If only it were that easy to replace the thoughts which swirled around her head. They were hardly suited to the workplace. On the contrary, they were most disruptive.

For up until that fateful night when she had been too drunk to recognise what Darren and his mates had planned for her, and then had been too stupid to do anything to try and save herself when the light had finally dawned, she had always considered herself to be in control. She would be the first to admit that at times she could be a bit wild, everyone knew that and that was part of her charm, or so she believed, but she had always remained firmly in control. In any case, up until Saturday night, she had been a girl who was relatively happy with her lot in life and had not been bothered by who was fucking who, or the other, equally petty issues of the workplace. But all that had changed; she was a different girl now.

But the thing that really bothered her was that on one pathetically stupid level she was actually glad that it had happened. Of course, she would never forgive Rae for being the spur that had driven her towards her self destruction, but in all honesty...... and she was being honest now...... when all was said and done and however much she argued otherwise...... she had actually enjoyed the scandalous abuse she had been subjected to. Looking back, she recognised that at the time she had revelled in the shame and, God help her, had even got off on the pain.

And that knowledge was bad enough. But worse still, even more frightening than that knowledge was the additional fact that now she was drowning in guilt. Not guilt at having let it happen but guilt for enjoying it! Guilt was a feeling Vanessa was unaccustomed to. And because that guilt that was tearing her apart, the feeling that made her despise herself, she blamed Rae.

She managed to get through the next morning without incident by steering well clear of Rae but at lunchtime Annie called across.

"Hey Vee, fancy a drink at The Pipe and Tabor?"

"Yeah, great." Without looking away from her screen, she told her friend, "You've no idea how much I need a drink! I'll just finish these figures and then we can go."

"Okay. Great." Annie resumed her journey down the office, then suddenly stopped as if she had just remembered something. She turned her head and called back up the room. "Vee and I are going for a drink in about ten minutes. Coming, Rae?"

Vanessa's right hand stopped mid air on its journey to the half empty plastic cup on her desk, her heart clunked to a stop and the fingers of her left hand remained stationary on her keyboard as with bated breath she listened for Rae's reply.

Rae looked up, her eyes shining brightly and her glossed lips smiling sweetly. "Oh, thanks. Love to."

Vanessa stared unseeingly at her screen as her fingers gripped the cup. Taut with a sudden anger, she crumpled the cup, splitting it down the side and spilling cold coffee over the figures printout. Fucking, fucking shit!

***

Not wanting to lose face in front of her work colleagues, Vanessa had not backed out but instead walked with the other two girls as they made their way out of the office. Seemingly oblivious to the simmering emotions of her colleagues, Annie chattered happily in the lift down to the ground floor. Or maybe she was just uncomfortable with the hostility which Vanessa positively oozed from her pores and decided to act as peacemaker, for she managed to squeeze between Rae and Vanessa and, linking her arms through theirs, she steered them towards the pub.

Situated directly across from the Bulliver Building, The Pipe and Tabor was the watering hole of most of the staff. And that particular lunchtime it was positively heaving as the three girls, forced into single file with Vanessa in the lead, shoved and squeezed their way through to the bar. Or to be more accurate, it was Vanessa who barged through in front without as much as an "excuse me", her lack of manners motivated entirely by her displeasure. Annie followed her through, turning first this way and that as she tried to keep up with her friend. But unseen behind them, Rae stopped and, while smiling innocently, slipped her bag onto her shoulder and fluttered her spread fingers at her sides. As she walked between them she smiled first this way and that, letting her fingers close over the fronts of the trousers of two men from the third floor who stood chatting together with their pints raised. She squeezed their cocks into firm bulges.

"Excuse me, please," she said with syrupy sweetness.

"Anytime, gorgeous!" they said in almost perfect unison as they stepped apart to let her through.

And so it went on, on her entire journey to the bar, squeezing the cocks of all the men who parted like the Red Sea to let her through. When she reached the bar, where Annie and Vanessa were still waiting to be served, she slid in snugly between Vanessa and Kieren.

"Push in, why don't you!"

Ignoring her Rae leaned forward and, as if by magic, the barman appeared before her. "I'll have a cranberry juice, please," she said, then leaning forward again she looked past Vanessa. "I'm in the chair, Annie. What are you having?"

"I'll have a white wine. Thanks."

"I'll buy my own!" Vanessa said churlishly.

"I won't hear of it!" Rae smiled, then went on as, unseen by the other two girls, even as she placed the order for Annie's white wine, her left hand had slid downward and sideways and had found Kieren's cock which was already stiff and straining. And still she teased him, rubbing her fingers up and down. The barman placed the wine in front of Annie, and before Vanessa could order her own drink, Rae said, "and Vanessa will have a pint of lager, please."

"I don't usually drink lager."

"Of course you do! Don't be shy….." Rae paused before adding sweetly, "it usually helps you relax."

By the time the barman plonked the lager down heavily in front of Vanessa, Rae was already giving her full attention to Kieren. Giggling prettily at his jokes and licking her glossed lips sexily with the tip of her tongue, she soon had him eating out of her hand.

And all the while, Vanessa seethed. Not content with stealing her Alex and being the root cause of the horrific gangbang, she had ruined Vanessa's life by coming to work in the same office, and now she was setting out to seduce the best looking guy in the whole of Bulliver's.

Vanessa had had quite enough and made up her mind that Rae fucking Carroll would soon be collecting her P45 and be a thing of the past.

However, what happened when they got back to the office that afternoon was something Vanessa would always swear was an accident.

**

She joined Annie, Kieren and Rae as they clustered around the drinks machine for their afternoon fix of coffee. Backing up with her plastic cup in her hand, she seated herself on the edge of someone's desk. Annie came and stood beside her and started up a discussion about the latest celebrity scandal. Smiling as Kieren whispered his chat-up line in her ear, Rae settled herself on the edge of the desk next to Vanessa. Sitting on her right hand side, Rae joined in the conversation.

While the other girls chatted, with Kieren looking puppy-dog eyes at the new love of his life, Vanessa lifted her cup to her lips and then, very casually, flicked her wrist backward, flipping the cup and hot contents over Rae.

Rae jumped up in alarm. "Bitch! You did that on purpose!"

Vanessa rose to her feet. "I did not!"

"Look! My skirt's ruined. You were just the same at school.....
spiteful!"

"It wasn't me who was spiteful."

"You're pathetic!" Rae took the handkerchief which Annie proffered and began to dab at the darkening stain. "Just because you can't hold on to a man! Alex said you're just a lovesick tart who......"

"Alex?" Annie was astounded. "You mean Vanessa's Alex?"

"My Alex now," Rae announced triumphantly.

That was too much for Vanessa. She reached behind her and grabbed a tape dispenser. Then everything happened in a rush as, without thought for the consequences, she swung it madly and without aim. There was a high-pitched squeal of pain as the heavy object made contact with Rae's shoulder.

There was a shriek of female voices, above them all the supervisor's. "Nigel! Do something!"

Out of nowhere, Mr. Pickett appeared.

***

Nigel Pickett's week had got off to a good start. First thing on Monday he had found Vanessa with the oh-so-lovely tits, knocked about and clearly so embarrassed about it that she had let him tit fuck her in his office rather than make any sort of fuss. The memory of his creamy, thick spunk spurting out of his slit and sliding over her satin skin as he pressed the two soft hills of her tits together was one he would treasure for some weeks to come. But then Rae had arrived and all his Christmases seemed to have come at once. A blonde counterpart to Vanessa's darker attractiveness she had wandered into his office about lunchtime and apologised for having opened the wrong door. It had been the work of a moment to shoo Maggie out on a pretext of giving the new girl a 'welcome to the team' type talk. The look of hopeless jealousy that she threw towards the leggy young blonde was another sweet memory. He would make her pay for it in due course. But then, when he had come round to the front of the desk and the girl had sat in front of him, he had been able to see right down into the smooth skinned depths of her cleavage; a dusky hollow between two tanned melons that were easily the equal of Vanessa's. Her long thighs had almost touched the fronts of his trousers as he stood before her and he realised she was looking directly at his groin with an expression of naked hunger.

He had faltered in mid sentence eventually and the blonde vision had risen to her feet, smiling a smile that promised a man heaven. In a dream he had watched her face approach his, felt the softness of her lips on his, smelt the perfumed sweetness of her and heard her whisper how much she admired men of power. Her fingers had lightly stroked his flies and she had asked – actually asked – if he wanted to feel how wet her cunt was. With her tongue still fencing with his and her fingers fluttering at his cock, he had touched the satin smooth skin of her thighs and run his hands up their length, feeling the denim of her skirt bunch as he pushed up into that forbidden area he so delighted in exploring – the world of 'what a pretty girl keeps under her skirt'. In this pretty girl's case there was an exquisite further length of silky thigh and then the hot moistness of her crotch and soft cushions of labial flesh. The little hussy had come into his office commando! He could hardly believe his luck! And what's more at only the slightest pressure from his fingers, her lips parted and allowed him access to the hot little sheath of her seeping vagina. He twirled his fingers inside her and she moaned.

"Please Mr Pickett. I need you so badly!" she whispered, breaking her kiss for a moment.

The fact that he had had her on her back laid on his desk, legs wrapped round his waist, just where Maggie loved him to take her only made it sweeter. She had a cunt in a million though! It was what he had always dreamed that Vanessa would feel like if he had ever been able to fuck her. Her sheath was slick and tight and gripped him ferociously so that it only took him relatively few plunges into her to reach his climax, his hands clawed into her breasts under her raised pullover. He didn't know and didn't care whether or not she had come. But as soon as he had finished ejecting his spunk into her he had staggered clear and wiped himself clean on a tissue – one he would keep for Maggie later – while she sat up cool as a cucumber and reached for her bag to extract her own tissue and wipe herself as if shagging on an office desk in broad daylight was something she did every day. She had flashed him a crafty little smile and left once she had smoothed down her pullover, run a comb through her hair and straightened her skirt.

"I hope we can do this again some time," she had said huskily as she slipped out.

The stupid little tart! Did she really think he had been born yesterday? He always kept tapes when he was on his own with one of the girls. He would let her go on thinking that she had him dangling on a string and when it suited him he would spring his trap and of course Maggie would be only too glad to help nail her if she didn't agree to everything his inventive mind could think up for her.

And now, just a day later he entered the main office to find a full scale catfight going on. It was something he had always dreamed of; two beautiful girls – not overly dressed – going hell for leather at each other. Punching, kicking, screaming, clawing, he wanted to see it all and as he rushed over he got his wish. Rae was on her back on a desk again, long legs waving as she struggled under Vanessa who was raining rather ineffectual but spectacular punches down onto her chest. One of Rae's hands was wedged under Vanessa's chin, making her twist her head away, the other was gripped – his heart flipped as he took it in – deep into one of Vanessa's exquisite tits.

How perfect! One tart too stupid to look after herself and only too glad to let herself be mauled by him for a quiet life. The other tart a manipulative little cow who deserved everything she got.

"Nigel! Do something! Stop them! Stop them!" Maggie was beside him, flapping her arms and blubbing in sheer panic. He gripped her arm so hard it brought her to a dead stop.

"Why? Let the little scrubbers settle their squabble."

He glanced up and saw Kieren – a steady enough lad, gazing in delight up Vanessa's skirt as she got into a kneeling position beside the prone Rae and dug a real punch into her midriff. That seemed to galvanise Rae whose legs scissored into a series of sideways kicks that pushed Vanessa, shrieking off the desk and onto the floor, two chairs and a waste bin crashed and rattled away, Rae threw herself down onto her opponent and in her face Nigel saw that she was completely hysterical – lost totally in the desire to hurt Vanessa however she could and however much she could.

He looked around at the circle of onlookers, horror, disbelief, malicious excitement in the girls' faces. Lecherous fascination on the faces of the boys.

Kieren met his eyes and smiled slowly as the two understood each other. Why risk getting between two such hysterical combatants? It was obviously a deeply held grudge – let them get it out of their systems.

The two men turned to the crowd.

"Stand back a bit there!"

"Give them room!"

With some excited squeaks from the girls in the crowd, a sort of rough ring was described.

"Maggie! Go and lock the door onto the corridor!" Nigel hissed.

"But Nigel," she quavered, her eyes watery with tears of anguish. He grabbed her again.

"Do it you stupid bitch or by God I'll make you wear your cunt chain for a month!"

She gave a little moan and scuttled away.

Meanwhile on the floor Rae was on top and Vanessa's legs were fully exposed right up to the scrap of silk gusset that covered her pussy, Nigel could see the actual outlines of the labia through the flimsy material and made sure he stood where he got a good view of her thrashing limbs. Rae's face was being repeatedly slapped by Vanessa and then Rae stepped things up another gear by reaching down and scratching at Vanessa's face. Her nails left scores down one cheek, the girls screamed and Vanessa went wild. Her body bucked and thrashed, throwing Rae off to crash into the side of a desk, its legs making a hideous scraping noise as it was pushed askew by the impact. For a second Rae was stunned and Vanessa came up like a demented fury. Blood flowed from her cheek, her blouse was torn and her bra had been wrenched apart at the front. As she panted for breath her breasts heaved and shook. Some of the males in the audience, let out soft whistles of appreciation. Vanessa's tits had long been the objects of male speculation in the office and their naked reality was an improvement even on the fantasies.

She reached down and grabbed Rae's shirt, pulling the still-stunned girl half upright and then letting loose a clumsy round house punch that slammed into the side of the girl's breast.

Rae screamed and tried to scramble up but Vanessa was too quick and backed away so fast that Rae's shirt tore as well. The two battered and tousled combatants circled each other, Vanessa wiping her cheek, Rae smiling grimly and shrugging off the ruined shirt quickly.

"Go for it, Rae!" a girl called.

As if in reply, Vanessa shrugged off her ruined blouse and bra too.

"You hiding behind your bra, you fucking cow? Or is it the silicon you're scared of showing?" Vanessa's voice was hoarse with venom.

Rae just grinned and quickly reached behind to unclip her bra, watching Vanessa carefully for tricks.

"Oh yeah!"

"It's tit city boys!" the men gloated as two magnificent pairs of breasts, swung high, prominent and free on naked chests.

"I've got more'n that!" another girl called.

"Why don't you show us then?" a male voice asked to muted sniggers.

"Come round by the stationery cupboard later. It might be your lucky day, Baz!"

There was more laughter but Nigel realised that now there was no danger of anyone questioning his decision to let the fight go on. The air was thick with excitement and arousal.

Simultaneously the two enemies rushed together and there was a meaty slapping sound as the tits came together. The naked legs strained as they grappled for a hold and while Rae got a handful of thick, dark hair and wrenched Vanessa's head back. Vanessa got a knee up.

There was a shocked yelp from Rae as the knee landed squarely between her thighs and she let go, only for Vanessa to get two or three hard slaps in to her face. She staggered back before nails could score her in her turn and toppled over the corner of a desk, her legs splaying wide open and pointing up at the ceiling as she fell back onto the floor again.

Vanessa plainly scented victory and leaped round to follow up her advantage, the crowd surged after her. There was a loud ripping noise and Vanessa triumphantly waved Rae's ruined skirt over her head.

"You never could keep it on!" she jeered to roars of laughter.

But humiliation drove Rae on and without trying to jump up she lunged forwards and gripped Vanessa's legs, then pushed. Vanessa's yell of triumph faded into a shriek of despair as she toppled helplessly backwards, knocking a chair that rolled away and was kicked out of the way by one of the onlookers and then banging her naked back painfully against the edge of a desk. Immediately she yelled and instinctively put one arm behind her as she arched her back and staggered up. But Rae was on her and landed a real punch to her stomach. There were sympathetic 'oof!' noises from the crowd, but both girls were fit and although Vanessa doubled over she stayed up on her feet, which suited Rae. She got her in a bear hug from behind and undid Vanessa's skirt's zip then pulled it to her ankles as she stood back. Hurriedly Vanessa kicked it away and whirled to face her nemesis.

Now the two circled each other warily, wearing only the flimsiest of thongs. Nigel felt his own excitement spiral upwards as he took in the view. Both girls were stunning, long legged and full breasted, the thin straps of the thongs only serving to emphasise the line of the hips and the proud curves of the buttocks.

Vanessa wiped away a little more blood from her scratches, a line of it ran down from Rae's nose.

"Fuckin' Hell! Will you look at that!"

"What the hell's all that?!"

"The bloody perv! I always knew there was something weird about her!"

The voices were low now, there was real tension in the air as the nearly naked fighters circled each other. But what really caused the awed comments was the state of Vanessa's back and buttocks now they could be seen in their entirety and she wasn't moving so fast. Nigel realised his mouth had dropped open and that Maggie's hand was tight on his arm.

Someone had taken a whip to Vanessa, the marks were fading but they were there alright. A belt if he was any judge – and he was.

Maggie was astounded. Who would have thought it! No wonder the girl had been tetchy, she had obviously had quite a going over.

The girls in the audience were aghast and split between sympathy and disdain – maybe she was a perverted disgrace to her sex. The men were thunderstruck and suddenly the crowd's loyalties divided, the men favouring Vanessa, the girls, Rae.

And then the fight resumed.

Rae charged in and Vanessa swayed back, twisted and flung the sweating body past her, using its own momentum. Rae screamed as she hurtled through the air and crashed into the crowd who stampeded back as Vanessa threw herself onto the sprawling Rae and ripped her thong off before parading with it.

"How come I'm the only one in the fucking county who has any trouble getting these off you?" she called as Rae, red faced and trying to cover her groin staggered up. Vanessa adopted a bullfighter sort of pose and waved the knickers at her.

"Come on! Come and get 'em!"

Rae seemed to fall for it but at the last minute she dived for

Vanessa's legs again and this time tipped her – almost flipped her – backwards. She flew clean over a desk, sliding helplessly across its surface, crashed over the chair beyond it and then rolled to a halt at the feet of another one. Rae caught up with her and wrenched her thong down but then landed a hard spank on the buttocks which quivered in the aftershock.

"I'll show you, you cow! You could only ever compete with me by cheating!"

She landed another smack and the males in the audience burst into applause at the sight of the hand prints appearing on the rippling buttock mounds. Vanessa yelped in outrage and squirmed round then surged up and grabbed Rae round the hips, burying her head in her stomach and bearing her backwards. This time both went over another desk and took a keyboard and a printer with them. Vanessa came up first, grabbed the keyboard and began to flail wildly at Rae's face with it.

Nigel and Kieren simultaneously dived in. Enough was enough; these two weren't going to stop until one was really hurt.

Nigel got Vanessa and held her delicious body hard against him as he wrenched the keyboard out of her hand. Kieren held Rae back, arms hooked into hers from behind. The two women looked superb in their nakedness, their breasts shook to the trembling and panting of the fury within them. Their hair looked as though they had been bedded and fucked into oblivion for weeks on end, their nipples were taut and full and their long, powerful legs were parted carelessly. Nigel could feel the delectable curves of Vanessa's bottom against his loins but somehow he wrenched himself back to the main concerns.

"Alright, that's enough!" he called. "Let's get this office tidied up! Girls, have a trawl through your handbags and lockers, see if you can find these two some clothes to go home in!"

Stunned by the intensity of what they had witnessed, the onlookers rather sheepishly started righting desks and chairs or fumbling in their bags for spare pairs of knickers. Slowly the two naked harridans calmed down in the unrelenting strength of the male grips on them.

"Okay, good fight you two," Nigel said as he slowly relaxed his grip. Vanessa moved a hand but only to wipe her face again. Rae sniffed loudly to try and stem her nosebleed. Beside her eye a sizeable swelling was appearing where the keyboard had caught her. The two men eased down slowly and the two women glared at each other, tossing thick manes of hair out of their eyes.

"Annie, take Rae into the Ladies. Vanessa, into my office."

Vanessa naked in his office. How often had he dreamed of that scenario when he had been fucking Maggie in the empty office at nights?

She made no objections and soon some clothes that had probably been rejected by local charity shops had been unearthed from somewhere. Vanessa had squeezed into a pullover three sizes too small and her breasts seemed about to explode it from within. A skirt, left behind at the last Christmas party, just about long enough to hide the ancient knickers someone had found in a cleaner's cupboard, covered her modesty.

"I don't suppose you're going to tell me what that was about, are you?" Nigel asked her as she held a coffee cup in a trembling hand. She shook her head and tears began to shine in her eyes as reaction set in after the fury.

"And you're not going to tell me who whipped you either?"

She glanced up sharply.

"Nigel, not now!" Maggie butted in, coming back into the office from having seen Annie and Rae. Caught between getting Vanessa out of the building as promptly and with as little fuss as possible and a new, totally unexpected admiration for the girl who had given no hint that she was a submissive, Maggie gave her a tight smile and settled on efficiency and a friendly gesture. "Come on, Vanessa. Rae's gone with Annie, Kieren will see you home safely and we'll try and sort it all out in the morning."

Nigel knew there had never been any love lost between the two and looked on with surprise as Maggie hustled the girl out. She had dared to interrupt him! He knew he owed her a thrashing for something or other, but now she could have a real belting for that, just as soon as the office was quiet.

CHAPTER FOUR

The lights from the street outside shone up onto the office ceiling, through the blinds. Only Nigel's desk lamp shed any direct light. At present it was illuminating an array of restraints and implements of discipline that lay neatly on the desktop leather. There was a cane, a crop, two floggers and a tawse. Maggie Huffer had just finished arranging them and now stood patiently awaiting her master's next order. Nigel Pickett however was not in a hurry. He had long ago come to an arrangement with the guys in security and he had two hours yet to torment Maggie without mercy – just the way she liked it.

But tonight he was genuinely angry. She had contradicted him in front of the staff. Now he stalked around her, noting with satisfaction how her fingers twisted and knotted themselves nervously as she awaited his sentence.

Fear tensed her muscles and her tear-bright gaze was frozen to the floor.

"It was only because I'd been so nervous of anyone coming in, Master!" she muttered as he finished asking her for the umpteenth time why she had answered him back. "I just wanted everyone safely off the premises. And the poor girls were……."

"The poor girls nothing!" he hissed venomously into her ear. "The sluts were good entertainment, something you'd better be while I punish you tonight or otherwise you'll be looking for a new master."

He smiled behind her as he heard her whimper. Whips and canes were all fine in their way but words were an under-used weapon in Nigel's opinion. He moved to stand alongside Maggie and watched her chin tremble and her eyes blink away tears. Sweet. He regarded the unrelieved flatness of her chest.

"Tits hurt today?" he asked.

"Oh yes, thank you, Master," came the breathless reply.

"Strip," he ordered and perched on the front of the desk he had shagged Rae on as his devoted slave shrugged off her jacket, unbuttoned her sensible white shirt and bared a torso that was cruelly, tightly bound in black bondage tape. With quivering, hasty fingers she began to unwind it revealing flesh marked as though by tight bandages and slowly her true figure emerged.

Vanessa would have been amazed to see the deep and shapely breasts that were revealed, now freed of their constriction, they swung and rose juicily as Maggie reached up to unbind her sable hair and shake it free, shedding years from her as thick, glossy hair framed a softer face than anyone else at the office had ever seen. She glanced interrogatively at her master who was drinking in the sight of his slave's jealously guarded true identity. He nodded his authorisation and she unzipped her skirt and stepped out of it, revealing remarkably well shaped legs clad in ultra sheer hold up stockings which gave her legs a rather nice sheen. A skimpy thong just covering a shaven delta completed Maggie Huffer's transition from office troll to sensual sex slave. Nigel Pickett reached out and grasped a near-perfect nipple, twisting it with deliberate harshness, relishing his control that was so complete no one even knew what Maggie really looked like. They just saw what he wanted them to see.

"Nipple clamps, the lash and the cane tonight," he announced.

"Yes, Master." Maggie reached out and picked up two screw clamps, handing them to him.

Nigel screwed the clamps slowly up to the maximum pressure she could stand, the tortured nubs bulging out of their constriction and her breath coming in deep, body-quaking sobs as she fought to contain the pain. He bumped her chin against the hard surface as he pressed her face down onto the desk, and took up a flogger with eighteen inch, thick leather tails. After a refreshing workout of some forty lashes, Nigel was feeling a little calmer. Maggie had settled down well with the beating and as he drove his free hand between her spread thighs he encountered a cunt that was responding eagerly to the mistreatment. He decided that it was time for the cane and then a fuck. He considered it her reward, for if she hadn't taken the beating so well, he probably wouldn't have allowed her any cock at all.

If only he could get her to take extreme punishment as well as this every time, he thought as he flicked the cane in the air behind her, he might consider going for an audition at Lewington House. The Masters up there really knew how to make a slave suffer and weren't interested in ones who got noisy and difficult before they had taken their full ration of pleasure from them. They were connoisseurs of slaveflesh and although Maggie was much prettier than he let anyone else see, up at the big house they would want slaves who looked like a screen goddess at the very least!

In front of him Maggie fidgeted anxiously, and he was pretty sure he knew what was going through her mind: she knew the cane was on its way, anticipated its sadistically-sweet, acerbic sting. Why was her Master waiting so long tonight?

Nigel smiled slowly as he surveyed the buttocks in front of him.

Of course!

Brilliant!

The solution of how to break into the Lewington House clique had just presented itself to him. Smiling broadly he returned his attention to the task in hand.

He sliced in the first stroke at full strength. Immediately Maggie reared up, a strangled shriek escaping her and forcing Nigel to bend down and pick up her discarded thong which he jammed into her mouth before resuming the harshest caning he had ever inflicted on her. She deserved it and he needed to think. Nothing made him think better than the sight of female buttocks trembling and rippling under the wicked combination of rigidity and flexibility that a good cane supplied.

He would phone as soon as he got into work the next morning and arrange a meeting with Matthew Bartlett, the mansion's owner and founder of its SM club. If he could dig out a couple of photos from their security folders and tell him about the hatred between the two girls, then maybe a repeat of this afternoon's epic duel could be arranged. And this time the fight could be arranged to go as far as the combatants wanted.

Maggie's muffled wailing brought him out of his reverie of full membership of the inner circle at Lewington House. Her bottom was gyrating madly as she fought to stay down and take the bitterly deep tramlines he was inscribing. He studied the landscape he had created and was mightily impressed with his own skill. Deep angry red trenches and ridges crossed the crowns of both buttocks, where they crossed some purpling was already occurring. He smiled contentedly as he unbuttoned his flies and moved in to take his pleasure to its conclusion, rekindling thoughts of his ambitious plans.

He could warm up the audience by flogging Maggie before

staging his main event; Vanessa and Rae, naked and going head to head until........how far? he wondered as he felt Maggie's well-slicked cunt receive him into it with a submissive combination he could only think of as ravenous docility. To the blood, to a fall or a submission? This would take some thought. After all, he wanted a spectacle not complete annihilation of one or the other, whatever the girls themselves had in mind. It would be his show, not theirs! He gazed down at Maggie's ravaged backside as the coarse weave of his workaday trousers came to rest against it, the broad shaft of his cock stretching the membrane at the back of the cunt as wide as it would go.

Oh well. He still had time to work it out – he would fuck her and then probably resume with the whip until he had resolved the issue. For now though there was only a warm and willing sheath for his cock. Time enough to think again with the whip in his hand.......

CHAPTER FIVE

Rae and Vanessa had exchanged icy glances as they entered the main office within minutes of each other, both of them arriving early the following morning. Nigel, whose view from his office allowed him to monitor the staff exiting the lift as they arrived for work, had been surprised and delighted that the two girls had had the courage to even show their faces at Bulliver's again! Even he recognised that it took real guts for them to face each other again, let alone their friends and colleagues – and let alone him. From the awkward, stiff-legged way they'd made their way past his office into the main, open plan office he'd tried to gauge the discomfort and pain engendered by their respective bruises and probable sprains. He doubted that either had slept much. Not that Nigel had slept much himself!

On the contrary, he had spent a restless night, due in part to memories of Maggie's discipline. Then, as sleep had continued to elude him, he had replayed over and over, like a video clip in his mind, the highly erotic and unexpectedly vicious cat-fight. Until the early hours he'd lain awake tormented, anxious to turn his audacious proposals into vibrant, lucrative but most of all cock-stiffening reality.

Now, around mid morning, that reality was one step closer since he had been contacted by Matthew Bartlett's efficient-sounding secretary returning his call. Just as he had thought they would, the security photographs that he had faxed across to Lewington House, although not overly flattering to either girl, had been sufficient to secure Bartlett's interest and get him an appointment.

Half way through his plethora of e-mail, he looked up from his screen as Maggie slipped into his office to collect a pile of files and slipped quietly out again. Damn the bitch! She should have asked permission seeing as there was no one else present – he would have no choice but to reprimand her later for her lack of respect. It struck him that she had seemed totally demoralised all morning. She had probably developed some guilt complex overnight about having actually enjoyed last evening's unusually severe but totally justified punishment. She had been positively gushing – orgasmically and verbally – with enthusiasm when they had parted. But whatever was eating her now was her problem and he cared little for her concerns! It was about time the woman faced up to the fact that she was his slave and he could do what he liked to her. It warmed his heart to know she carried bruises and livid stripes of her own beneath her bondage tape and workaday clothes.

***

Looking as efficient as always, that morning Maggie's own thoughts were far removed from spreadsheets when she walked into her Master's office to obtain the files. Forgetting her servility as she scooped them up and exited back into the main office, her thoughts were full of the girls she thought of as vile Vanessa and rancid Rae. If she hadn't her authority as supervisor to maintain, she'd have their eyes out! Pretty girls had come and gone through the office before, but never had her Master been so enamoured! Then an unwelcome generosity sidled into Maggie's thoughts that morning. As much as she hated to admit it, she knew she owed them a debt of gratitude, for never in all the time she had been Nigel's slave had his treatment of her been so savage in its lust as it had been the previous night. And never had her own response to his demands been so thrillingly intense, or her own climax so hotly devastating. Yet absorbing as these things were, they were nothing compared to the feeling she had that her Master was planning something......something involving the sluts but not necessarily herself! Fear of being replaced outweighed everything!

***

Nigel tried to concentrate on work, but his attention was completely focussed on the girls at the centre of his scheme. He noticed that whenever they encountered each other on their way to the drinks machine or the photocopier, they held their heads high and tried to ignore each other.

It was the attitudes they adopted around everyone else he found most entertaining. If one of the female staff came in contact with one of them, it was the other girl who lowered her eyes in embarrassment rather than Rae or Vanessa. It was as if all the other girls were the ones wallowing in shame, which Nigel supposed was only fit and proper since none of them had made much of a protest at their unseemly behaviour! There was a distinct chill in the air – an unusual hush over the main office rather than the customary hubbub, banter or girlie gossip. Nigel assumed the other staff, who spoke only to each other in whispers, were sending the two to Coventry. As far as Nigel Pickett was concerned, it was far more acceptable than his expected repercussions of complaints and resignations, mock fights between the other females and perhaps further spats between Rae and Vanessa themselves.

***

Set amid several acres of landscaped gardens and magnificent grounds, Lewington House was one of the finest clubs for discerning and wealthy SM aficionados, located just outside the small, Hertfordshire village of Langley Feldon, where rumour and speculation were rife. The comings and goings of Bentleys, Jaguars and Ferraris, usually with lone male occupants, was watched with interest, discussed over pints of bitter at the local and, with relish and a great deal of scandalous speculation, was a main topic at dinner parties further afield.

Although not members of a secret society in the strictest sense – local gossip had long ago put paid to that – the gentlemen who enjoyed the club's exceptional facilities nevertheless believed themselves members of a clandestine elite whose valued way of life, with its emphasis on male domination and female submission, could only be assured by close vetting of would-be members. Less than half a dozen applicants were accepted each year, and the latest of these up for consideration was Nigel Pickett. Outside the normal terms of membership he might be; given his middle management position – one had to be in line for a directorship at least – but his long standing association with a certain member of parliament who was himself a member gave Nigel a foot in the door.

That afternoon after work, as Nigel drove his silver Mercedes along the slight incline of the long, straight drive through the mansion's landscaped gardens, he was struck as he had been previously by the way the building gleamed white – almost virginal he thought with a smile – in the late sunshine. As required, he drew up outside the imposing entrance which was flanked by huge, marble lions rampant.

A smart, middle-aged commissionaire wearing a Prussian blue and gold uniform descended the white steps with affected regal bearing and opened Nigel's door.

"Mr Pickett," his impeccable, clipped accent was the equal of many of the members'. "Good to see you again, Sir."

"Thank you, Jacobs." Nigel stepped from the car and handed over the keys to have it parked.

"I'll have it attended to right away, Sir."

As expected, once Nigel had stepped clear of his vehicle, Jacobs extracted from his pocket what appeared to be a leather keyfob with three buttons, blue, red and green set in a triangular formation. With eager anticipation Nigel waited as Jacobs made a production of depressing the red button, keeping his thumb on it for longer than was strictly necessary.

There was a squeal of female pain from behind one of the lions. Then the slender figure of a young woman left her concealed station – with head bowed and hands clasped behind her she stepped out from behind the lion. Tall with short, white-blonde hair, her attractive high cheek bones marked her out as Scandinavian. She was dressed in a black, rubber dinner jacket, complete with tails flapping against the backs of her whip-scored thighs. Thanks to the jacket's fastening at the neck with a clip attached to her wide, black collar and at the waist with a heavy metal clasp, her pale, naked, rawly-striped breasts which poked out temptingly – with delightful pink nipples hard and erect – were attractively framed. Her legs were clad in black rubber, platform boots with mile-high spiked heels, bringing her height to almost six feet. Black straps were wound around her waist and along her groins, charmingly held in place by an over-large padlock which thumped heavily against her vulva as she moved. While certainly making intercourse impossible the straps were not simply designed to deter fucking the gorgeously ethereal creature while she was on duty, but to hold in place the devilish electronic devices – sunk into her rectum and vagina – which responded to Jacob's thumb by delivering electric shocks. The blue button sent the pulse zinging through her cunt, the green had the same electrifying effect in her anus. But the red was doubly cruel, sending bolts through both cavities simultaneously with the result that she danced prettily. The poor girl was kept in a near constant state of pain and arousal throughout the hours she was on duty, which made her an unbelievably agreeable fuck when she was auctioned for charity at the end of each day. Needless to say, Lewington House had raised thousands for good causes!

Jacobs fetched repeated shrieks of pain from the girl, he never tired of demonstrating, nor did most of the club membership tire of observing. Nigel was aware of the rigidity of his phallus as he watched the girl hopping, gyrating madly and yelping her agonising way most amusingly toward them. Staggering in her high boots, she sometimes hunched over, hands clenched to her crotch, sometimes she windmilled her fragile arms and flung her head from side to side like a woman possessed as Jacobs varied the tempo and location of the shocks, sometimes short and sharp and at other times long and torturous, using his thumb with the dexterity of a habitual texter.

Nigel smiled at the thought of controlling Maggie with such devices and couldn't help laughing aloud as he imagined her trying to maintain her matronly decorum around the office as she was zapped witless.

Jacobs allowed the girl to stop. With tears dribbling from the corners of her eyes, panting heavily and gasping for breath, once again she bowed her head as Nigel focussed on the rise and fall of her breasts. Jacobs placed Nigel's car keys into her hand then reluctantly returned the keyfob to his pocket.

"Daren't risk the silly bitch crashing a member's car while she parks it," Jacobs explained.

"Very nice, Jacobs," Nigel said as the girl slid into the driver's seat. "Thank you."

"It's a pleasure, Sir," Jacobs replied, smiling villainously.

Within moments, Nigel stood inside the magnificent entrance hall, where a rather beautiful woman behind a desk had him sign his name in the visitor's book. The club rules demanded formal attire in the evenings. And as her never-miss-a-trick eyes took in his appearance Nigel was glad that he had changed from his slightly worn workaday suit into his new, chain store three piece, but wondered if she thought he had overdone it with his self-indulgent, Robert Old black and gold satin bow tie.

With a knowing smile the woman noted the red and silver enamelled badge on his lapel that marked him out as a probationary member and which would, he hoped, soon be exchanged for the black and gold of full membership, giving him access to the dungeons and those other rooms which were at present off limits to him.

He set off down a long, portrait-lined hallway toward the Members' Lounge for his meeting with Matthew Bartlett. On entering the spacious, comfortable but above all relaxing room, he selected a brunette from the host of rubber-clad beauties in attendance to do their Masters' bidding that evening. With varying degrees of earlier discipline in evidence, they wore costumes of red, blue or pink, their breasts exposed and pushed up by the skin-tight bodices with convenient zips up the front. Beneath the short, flared, rubber skirts with zips at the back their delightful quims and delicious bottoms were also exposed, underwear being prohibited in the Members' Lounge. Collars, wrist and ankle restraints were matching rubber with metal rings attached, and stiletto sandals of the same shade completed uniforms that were designed to be highly erotic, practical and, above all, removable.

The girl Nigel selected wore pink.

"What's your name?" he demanded. It didn't matter, of course, he couldn't give a damn.

"Lush, Master."

As her name suggested, everything about her was luscious, from her succulent breasts billowing over the top of the bodice which barely contained them to her hair, rich and flowing as melted dark chocolate, to her cheeky, mouth-watering buttocks and invitingly plump nether regions. In accordance with Lewington House rules, her pussy was shaved and satin-smooth, as Nigel's questing fingers soon discovered.

The weather outside was unseasonably warm, yet inside the imposing mansion fires had been lighted in the huge grates to take off the chill which permeated the old building. And inside the Members' Lounge, where Nigel frigged Lush while gazing out from the floor to ceiling window at the immaculate lawns, a fire was toasting the full-fleshed backside of a naked blonde on all fours before it. The fireplace was flanked by two Versace-suited members who were taking turns to idly torment the voluptuous blonde while they executed a business deal over their glasses of ten year old malt whisky. Using implements which looked to Nigel like tools more properly used in the garden for raking up leaves, they scored deep red furrows from her nape, down her helpfully broad back, and then swerved nastily across her lovely, juicy buttocks. She made no sound – the men would have remained deaf to her cries in any case – she arched her back prettily and tried to pull herself free from the devices which bolted her ankles, knees and wrists to the floor while the men continued their negotiations.

With Lush positioned on his right hand side – conveniently bent double with her elegant hands fastened to her shapely ankles – Nigel glanced over his shoulder at the other members, while at the same time prising Lush's labia apart and embedding his fingers inside her.

"You're wet, you filthy hussy!" he accused. "That pussy's ready to be fucked now, isn't it?"

"Yes, Master," she said mechanically.

"Then it's a shame…." he looked across at the members who sat in a small, conversational group, smoking cigars, chatting amiably and mauling the breasts of the girls who fellated them, "that I'm not ready to do so." The girls' bodices were either half undone or removed altogether, while the men seemed oblivious to the tits they pawed and molested, as well as the lips and throats that serviced them as heads bobbed dutifully.

"It takes more than my fingers up a squelching cunt to get me in the mood," Nigel added, "I need to flay the skin from a bitch before I even consider honouring her with a fuck!" He checked his watch. His meeting with Bartlett was scheduled for five minutes ago – he supposed it was the owner's prerogative to be late if he chose.

On Nigel's left by the next window along, a naked, stunning redhead with milky skin was currently having her nipples clamped by someone Nigel recognised as Pennington, a middle-aged, former stock broker. He went about his cruel business with the demeanour of someone attempting nothing more than tying his shoelaces. The clamps used were much worse – or better depending which way you looked at it – than Maggie's. They had been meticulously demonstrated to Nigel, with the help of the blonde currently being raked by the Versace Suits, on his previous visit. With tiny, skin-puncturing tines along their sturdy jaws, they were joined together by a chain with a fitting in the centre to enable one to fix it to the girl's collar. The only thing they had in common with Maggie's were the screws at the side to tighten the jaws – a girl would have to have pretty tiny nipples in order to tighten them without the tines piercing them!

The redhead whimpered as Pennington tightened them. Bravely she stood her ground, proud and docile with her hands fastened behind her back and her long legs parted. From where Nigel stood he could clearly see weights dangling from chains which were clipped to her labia by similar sharp-toothed clamps, elongating her lips. It was only then that Nigel noticed that instead of the nipple clamps being fixed to her collar they were linked to another chain that lay against her belly and was joined at the other end to the labia clamps.

Nigel smiled and rammed his fingers deeper into Lush's noisily squelching channel. He had pulled up her short skirt and laid it across her recently welted back to give him the desired access. Spurred on by the whimpers and muted cries all around him, he twisted and jabbed his fingers as sadistically as he knew how, almost toppling her over with the force of his brutal usage of her copiously juicing cunt.

He stated the obvious, "Lush by name and lush by nature," as he turned to face into the room, obliging Lush to shuffle around with him.

By an opposite window a naked girl was fitted with a black hood which was moulded to her face. The hoods had also been shown to him previously and he knew there were air holes to fit around the nostrils. The girl was arranged lying back on one of the tables, and thoughts of the delectable Rae in his office flitted into Nigel's mind, followed by the memories of Maggie's indignation when she, in the same place, had been forced to listen to Nigel's account of it. But unlike Rae or Maggie, this girl's hands were secured to the legs by means of her restraints and her legs, though in the air, were spread wide and held open by a man named Byron Franklin who gripped her ankles tightly. The girl, rendered nameless and unrecognisable, must be squawking inside the mask as hot wax was dripped down onto her bare flesh from a height of two feet, by a suave, dark-suited Italian.

Settling into the delights the Members' Lounge had on offer, Nigel continued his violation of Lush's quim. He would dearly love to do more than just frig her – there was a whipping bench standing indecently idle in the far corner with a selection of disciplinary implements laid out nearby – but he was here for a meeting and couldn't afford to be distracted. Well, not until he had put his case at least, no matter how tempting that distraction was.

Without even a glance in Lush's direction, he returned his attention instead to Pennington and the redhead. The linking chain had been removed, though both sets of clamps, as well as the weights, were still in place. Nigel couldn't help but admire her brave acquiescence as she was ordered to her knees and then, with her own trembling hands, pulled a small table toward her and lifted her own, still-clamped orbs, laying them on the table to present them for a thrashing.

Pennington raised the cane......

"Ah, Pickett!"

Nigel turned around to see Matthew Bartlett approaching. He opened his mouth to speak, "Good ev..." but his words were drowned out as the cane struck the tortured breastmeat and the redhead screamed.

"Sorry I'm late," Bartlett smiled amiably enough as he extended his hand, "I was just making preparations in the library."

Barely taking in his apology Nigel was more conscious of the man's aristocratic, authoritarian bearing. Quickly, he withdrew his hand from Lush's vagina, wiped her sap across her backside, then shook hands with the tall, steely-haired owner of the mansion, the man who was ultimately responsible for the cruelty and smooth running of the club. And as he did so, Nigel used the toe of his shoe to coax Lush to move again, this time to make more room for Bartlett and the girl, laden with a silver tray, who accompanied him.

She was a pretty thing who wore red shoes with her skirt, the bodice having been dispensed with. Her hands were bound behind her which made the method of her carrying the tray the main focus of interest rather than the cluster of brandy balloons, decanter of finest brandy and box of cigars placed upon it. It stuck out a couple of feet in front of her, held in place by metal brackets fixed to the sides of the tray which were attached to a pair of nipple clamps biting into her swollen, achingly-hard, cork-like nipples that tipped the breasts lying on its upper surface. Her swan-like neck was encircled by her collar, to which a short, inflexible metal pole was fixed and extended to the centre of the far edge of the tray, obliging her to keep her head upright. Held rigidly in place, the tray had no need of further attachments, except Lewington House would hardly be the finest SM club it claimed to be if life wasn't made as uncomfortable as possible for the lovely submissives, and to this end the corners furthest away from the girl were fitted with additional brackets to which longer poles were attached. Angled downward and inward, they joined at a point level with her vagina, enabling a dildo to be inserted and held in place, ensuring that she would be in a state of continual arousal. In addition, her awkward gait and the obvious reason for it supplied great entertainment value with the minimum of effort, thereby saving the members' energy for other pastimes.

"We'll relax here for a moment," Bartlett told him as he poured them both drinks. He offered Nigel a cigar. "Afterwards, we'll adjourn to the privacy of the library to discuss our business."

Half an hour or so later, having downed his brandy, slipped the cigar in his breast pocket for later and had a few more routine rummages inside Lush's clutching, eager channel, Nigel found himself accompanying Bartlett along the hallway to the library.

It was a much larger room than he had imagined. As in the Members' Lounge, there was a blazing fire in a large grate, on each side of which was placed a worn, leather upholstered, wing chair. In addition to the books themselves, the room also housed a remarkable collection of gentlemen's erotica gathered from around the world. And those of the walls which weren't lined with bookcases had instead elegant cabinets positioned against them. Displayed on the tops of these was a wealth of magnificent porcelain, bronze and ivory statuettes which in former times would have been hidden away, locked away in the vaults of the world's museums. Here they were proudly displayed and the subject matter was very much to Nigel's liking; nudes in various poses, scantily clad dancing maidens and entwined couples jostled for position alongside giant phalluses. And above one collection was another; in place of the paintings one might have expected to find in such a room, the walls were hung with framed sepia photographs along with black and white ones, taken in the early decades of the twentieth century. They were surprisingly and delightfully risqué given their date, mostly studio portraits with a few rare outdoor scenes, all of young women wearing all manner of corsets and other undergarments of a by-gone age. But what made these photographs "must haves" for Lewington House was that they showed the girls either in bondage or receiving a caning.

The room was comfortably furnished with a half a dozen reading tables accompanied by straight-backed chairs, a couple of couches with plush upholstery arranged at angles facing the centre of the room and the main focus of the library; a large, heavy, ornately carved wooden frame in the very centre of the room that was a permanent fixture beneath one of several chandeliers. And charmingly spreadeagled inside the frame on that particular day was a short haired brunette, her image reflected in the many sparkling, geometrically-shaped glazed doors of the bookcases. Also reflected were myriad pin-points of light from the exceptional chandeliers.

"Lovely!" Nigel said as the two men approached the girl, her body so tautly displayed that every fibre and sinew of her young body was clearly and beautifully defined, as if carved from marble. There was a glint of gold at the junction of her spread-apart thighs. A clitoral piercing, Nigel noted with pleasure, just what he had scheduled for Maggie in due course.

"I'm glad you think so." With an upturned palm Bartlett invited, "Please, Pickett, examine her."

Happy to oblige, Nigel circled the vision slowly, assessing her whip-marked body from every delectable angle, slipping a finger into this or that orifice. When he stood behind her with his finger pushing at her anus, he couldn't help his mind wandering and imagining Maggie in her place. The brunette gave little whimpers of discomfort as he pushed his finger past her sphincters and up into her anal passage. And in his imaginings it wasn't her whimpers at all, nor even Maggie's, but those of Rae and Vanessa, his fanciful mind placing them in frames side by side, both wearing the battle scars of one of the fights he was there to promote. If only blasted Bartlett would get on with the discussion!

As if reading his thoughts Bartlett said matter-of-factly, "Well, you've got your meeting, Pickett, so what's this matter you wished to discuss with me so urgently?" His tone was penetratingly frosty when he added, "Something to do with those security shots you faxed across, I understand."

Eager to assert himself as a valuable addition to the Lewington House membership and with his finger still tormenting the girl's rectum......and to prove that Bartlett's acceptance of him into the clique would be justified, Nigel injected a tone of authority into his voice when he answered.

"It's like this, Bartlett. I've come across a couple of girls who may, I think, prove to be valuable additions to the glorious stock of girls you have here."

"You don't think we have enough girls, is that it?"

Refusing to be flustered, Nigel told him as calmly as he was able, "No, it's not that. You see, I've hit upon an idea the other members would find most entertaining, involving the two girls whose photographs I sent you."

"In what way entertaining?" Bartlett asked, ignoring the brunette and taking a seat in one of the leather upholstered chairs beside the fire. Plucking out his finger, Nigel followed him. Settling back in the other chair, he watched the girl trying to stretch her cramped muscles and said simply as he turned to face Bartlett again, "I caught them fighting."

Bartlett's smile was indulgent and, Nigel thought, rather supercilious. "Have you ever heard the cacophony created by a gaggle of girls set on squabbling?"

"No, but I – "

"Then you should hear this herd when they're not on duty! No, Pickett....Nigel...." there was that smile again, "I don't think we could handle any more squabbling girls, thanks all the same."

Determined to remain calm and sell his idea, Nigel pushed away thoughts of his dream slipping away from him. "I don't think you understand. When I say fighting, I mean actually fighting...... scrapping ...... knocking nine bells out of each other, and ripping each other's clothes off into the bargain! I tell you, Bartlett, it was just about the horniest thing I've ever seen."

"You think so?" Bartlett looked thoughtful for a moment and then pulled a thin gold chain from a jacket pocket, stood up and approached the spreadeagled girl in the centre of the room. Nigel watched him crouch down and clip one end to the ring at the girl's clitoris and then stretch it down until he could clip the other end to a ring set in the floor. He had to pull quite sharply to make it stretch and the girl gasped as her nubbin was cruelly jerked.

With that done he went behind her and took down a heavy, leather paddle from a hook on one side of a display cabinet and giving no warning at all brought it down at full force across her delicious backside. The report was loud even in the plushly furnished surroundings of the library. The girl screamed and jerked forwards in her bonds, then made a strange sort of grunt as her clit chain brought her up sharp. Nigel smiled as he watched the logic followed to its conclusion. With a thoughtful expression on his face, Bartlett landed several more heavy swipes from the paddle leaving vivid traces across her buttocks, making them ripple and wobble most appealingly. Each one forced her to torment her own clitoris and when he felt he had done enough to leave her to her own devices, he hung the paddle back on its hook. In the frame however, the girl continued to jerk and cry out. She was too far along the road to orgasm to stop now and could safely be left to torment herself by jerking and stretching her clitoris all on her own.

Nigel appreciated that Bartlett, like himself, thought best when he could free his mind by keeping his hands busy.

"Tell me more about these girls," Bartlett said as he regained his seat.

Nigel raised his voice above the tormented gasps and grunts of effort as the girl wrenched desperately at her own clit.

"They didn't seem in the least concerned about the damage they inflicted upon each other." He waited until the cries reached a crescendo and then finally died away. "I'd go as far as to say they hate each other equally, and it was the intention of both to inflict as much pain as possible. They're good-lookers, too, both of them – the pictures didn't do them justice – one as blonde as the other is dark. They're both big titted, athletic specimens."

The girl in the frame sobbed loudly, racking her body and tossing her head from side to side in the most attractive manner as it dawned on her that one orgasm was not going to be enough, she was going to have to torment herself all over again and the bulge in Nigel's trousers reached monster proportions.

Bartlett stood up and walked round to stand in front of the girl again. Within a moment, Nigel had left his seat and was standing eagerly beside him, watching escaping tears stain her cheeks and listening to her continued gasps.

"Quiet, bitch!" Bartlett commanded. "This is the library and I fear you forget yourself." He gave the tautly stretched beauty a back-handed slap across her appetisingly proportioned tits.

Nigel smiled in admiration at the red patches that flared up.

Bartlett sauntered across to one of the bookcases. He unlocked the door with the key which sat teasingly in the lock, then selected a heavy, leather-bound tome. He beckoned Nigel over and indicated a similar edition which Nigel took hastily from the shelf.

"While the library houses some of the greatest literary work to be found anywhere, as well as many editions of erotic art and photography, on this shelf all the books are fake." Bartlett pointed out the metal fastening across the pages and demonstrated the small catch. At once the book sprang open to reveal its secret which in this case was a box filled with a tangle of fishhooks and chains.

"You were saying, Pickett?" he asked suddenly.

Nigel leapt at what could well be his last chance to persuade the man. As enthusiastically as he knew how he detailed the fight between Rae and Vanessa, all the while wondering at Bartlett's straight, emotionless face throughout his tale.

When he had finished, Bartlett said nothing but an apathetic, "Interesting," and gestured for Nigel to open the book he still held in his hand.

After manipulating the catch, Nigel found inside a selection of adjustable metal bands. Bartlett closed the door and locked it again, and Nigel followed him back across the room toward the frame.

Coming to a standstill in front of the girl once more, Bartlett advised, "Slip one of them over each tit, then tighten them using the screws and watch her udders change colour."

Nigel selected a band that looked to be of the right size, then cupped her firm breast in his hand and fed it through. He repeated the process with the other one, noticing the way her panting stopped and her meaty nipples hardened into juicy peaks.

When he'd fitted both bands in place and tightened them so that her breasts billowed out and were becoming darker coloured, he watched Bartlett select a small fish hook attached to a chain, which he untangled expertly from the others inside the box and eased the fine point through the hard nodule of her erect nipple. Nigel felt the blood pounding through him as he watched the hook being threaded right through the girl's nipple. She cried out again as she looked down at her breast, and her pale eyes widened in fascinated terror.

Bartlett wasn't done yet. But first he raised his eyes to her tear-sparkling ones. "Quiet!" he ordered, adding in a tone meant to chill her blood, "one more peep from you and I'll have your tits hooked by every member on the premises!" Once the hook was in place, he shook out the full length of the small-linked chain and extended it across to the side of the frame, pulling the girl's pierced nub with it, where he fixed the end over one of the hooks embedded into the frame. Then he repeated the process with the other nipple, at last allowing himself to smile as the girl once again began to jerk herself towards climax, this time stretching her tits as well as her clitoris.

"Very pretty, don't you think, Pickett?"

"Yes, indeed!"

Then quite suddenly, Bartlett turned to Nigel.

"I'd have to see them first of course. Arrange it."

CHAPTER SIX

Maggie sat disconsolately at Nigel's desk and watched the gaggle of girls and lads depart, gossiping and laughing, planning their night's activities. Behind them, keeping their distance from them and from each other, went Vanessa and Rae.

Momentarily glassy-eyed, she blinked rapidly to clear away the blurring of her vision. Heaven knew she wasn't a woman given to tears! Never had been. It was just…..she had to get rid of one or both of those wretched girls before she was cast aside by a besotted master. She was perfectly well aware that she could find another one, she knew she was attractive. It was just that being dominated by a man like Nigel Pickett, cruel, selfish and vain, suited her masochistic nature. She didn't want to lose him.

Looking at nothing in particular, she drummed her newly polished, sensibly short-nailed fingers on the desk as she thought. It had been with her bent across that very desk that Nigel had really come of age to her way of thinking. His caning had been harsh and thrillingly laced with real anger and the way he had fucked her afterwards…… impassioned, sizzling, lustily-vital and cunt-bursting…..oh, if only there was some way to make sure it was always like that! At least one of those girls had to go! She could compete with one, it was having the two of them here that was the problem.

Her hand idly swept across the top of the desk; it seemed to her that some of the best times of her life had been when a man had had her bent forwards across a desk. And not only this one, she recalled wistfully. She remembered a time when she had…… suddenly she sat up and smiled, then reached for her "sensible" black handbag, the only one Nigel had allowed her to keep when he had gone through her things, took out a battered notepad and flicked through its feint ruled pages. It gave her a devilish little thrill to think she was dialling that particular number on Nigel's phone.

"Hello?" The voice was the familiar, deep one she remembered so well. It was the voice of the man who had first woken the submissive in her. She had been his P.A. and, though at first she had fought against it, eventually she had fallen under his spell and realised that she was both a masochist and a submissive… a treacherous concoction that could lead a woman into the shadowy realm of her worst, and best, fantasies combined – where high-voltage pleasure and lurid pain were the same thing. The whole affair had become very intense and with him already being married, Maggie had judged it best to move on. But they had parted as good friends.

"Paul?" she asked, shocked to discover that she was scarcely able to control the quaver in her voice.

"Maggie! How lovely to hear your voice again. Don't tell me, you want to come over here and have that divine arse of yours whipped."

"Oh, Paul!" she said, laughing. "You know I'm well catered for in that department nowadays!"

"So, to what do I owe this pleasure?"

"I need a favour." Straight to the point, she congratulated herself.

"Hmm! So might I." His voice deepened and set her heart thumping.

Maggie squirmed on her seat, reviving some sparks of discomfort in her bottom. "I got caned to hell last night. So my arse is definitely off limits!"

"Meet me for a drink and we'll discuss this favour you need. Then we'll discuss the one I need in return."

***

The taxi dropped her off in the car park of an anonymous pub a little way out of town, set back from the road and situated opposite the Langley March cricket ground. As the taxi pulled out into the road once more, Maggie turned slowly and saw a figure step from a sleek, new, black sports car. Her heart gave a little flutter of excitement and she dug her fingers into her palm in an effort to calm herself, for the time being at least. She must get the important business out of the way first, she told herself as he strode toward her. She could not afford the sudden attack of nerves which was threatening to ruin everything and she clutched her handbag tighter, not the sensible one but the glitzy little item that she'd managed to keep hidden away.

Paul Gregory was a tall man with a thick shock of dark hair that refused to stay brushed neatly back off his temples and caused him to sweep his hand through it in an habitual gesture he was no longer conscious of. Looking immaculate in his dark, pinstripe, Armani suit, he wore his elegance as comfortably as other men wore jeans.

To her disappointment those few moments of their first meeting in ages was a little formal, and he remained somewhat distant as they walked toward the door together. But once inside, he gave Maggie a chaste little peck on the cheek before buying her a white wine and taking her to a seat.

Nobody seemed to pay them any undue attention. There were less than half a dozen other couples in the place and just a trio of single men having a pint together and discussing their share options. One of the share club asked the barman to turn the music down. Once he had complied, the place took on a more relaxed mood and the low-toned hubbub and muted music formed the perfect backdrop, Maggie thought. "You're looking as ravishing as ever," Paul told her as they took their places. She knew he picked up on her pained wince as her bottom made contact with the seat and the pain was stirred up again. She didn't like to tell him that just his presence was having a very dramatic effect on her nether regions, though it did confirm the rightness of her decision to risk Nigel's wrath by coming out looking like her real self, and his greater wrath if he were ever to find out about her secret purchases!

The little bag went well with the Prada shoes she had bought off e-bay; an indulgence she had allowed herself from her secret bank account and which she kept hidden in an old trunk of family heirlooms. And her just short of knee-length, classic black dress with the scooped neckline looked pretty good too, once it had been spruced up with a little brooch despite it being a couple of years old. In addition, around her neck she wore the gold chain that Paul himself had given her, and matching earrings.

Her glossy, wavy hair fell thickly around her face, her torso felt liberated and comfortable and her breasts filled her bra to cleavage-sculpting capacity and made her feel more self-confident and relaxed than she had for months – but also more insecure. She couldn't wait to go back to being uncomfortably bound.

But Paul would be much more likely to help her if he fancied her again, and to judge by the gleam in his eye, he did.

They clinked glassed. "To old times," he said.

"To old times," she agreed. It didn't seem right to add "and new beginnings," Maggie thought with a sense of mischief that had been long buried. Instead, she took a deep breath and launched into an abbreviated and censored account of why she wanted Paul to offer Rae a job. She had reckoned that with Rae having so recently

joined the company, her departure would not cause as much fuss as Vanessa's might. And since the fight, Maggie couldn't help but have some fellow feeling towards the girl, who in any case was good at her job and, until the recent set-to, had been a popular member of staff. Besides, from what she had seen of Rae so far, she thought the blonde bimbo might be more easily persuaded than Vanessa.

When she had finished beguiling him with her tale, she produced the ID photo of Rae.

Paul looked hard at it.

"Hmm. I've got a position in Purchases where she might be of use," he said.

"Come on, Paul!" she teased gently, "You're a red blooded male, you can think of any number of positions you could use her in!"

He smiled and ran his hand through his hair, his dark eyes on her red fingernails as she feigned carefree indifference by swivelling the stem of her wine glass between finger and thumb. "Okay. Give me an address and I'll try and poach her." He sat back. "That's business completed, let's attend to pleasure."

After a couple more drinks they went back to his office in his own company's building at the heart of the town. Maggie hadn't wanted a quickie in a hotel room but there was something about being taken by a man of power and prestige in his office that really appealed to her.

As soon as they entered the room, it was the smells of brandy and lavender beeswax as much as the unchanged look of the place that brought the memories flooding back. In the oak panelled luxury of his office he sat in his black, reclining leather chair and smiled at her, and she knew he was remembering also. It had been two years since she had discovered in this very room that a woman could reap rich rewards from her body by letting a dominant man have his way with it. Simply thinking about it was making her want to throw herself at his feet and give herself up completely to his will, for she was already hot and moist in that offering to manhood between her thighs.

"Well let's have a look at this caning then, shall we?" he said, his rich timbre all the more seductive thanks to the terse manner in which he spoke the words.

Maggie turned to face away from him and fumbled her skirt up and then pulled her skimpy black-with-red-lace knickers down. She smiled quietly, she knew perfectly well that her bottom was all shades of purple and red with only odd patches of flesh colour.

"That is not bad!" Paul said at last, and she thought she discerned a note of admiration in his flowing tones. "That's a better tally than you ever took from me!"

She heard his chair creak as he got up and then his hand was on her, feeling cool and rough as he stroked over the welts, his touch soft and fluttering....the calm before the storm, she thought knowingly.

"The only problem is, where am I going to beat you?"

"Oh I think you'll find there's plenty of space left," she said, smiling archly over her shoulder. And once again she became the seductive woman whose existence was so seldom acknowledged, the one that invited trouble. In that way he used to love so much, she lowered her lashes, seeking out his lust through half-closed eyes, and ran the tip of her tongue seductively over her harlot-red lips, the currently prohibited practice coming back to her as if she had never left him.

"Can't see with all those clothes in the way, can I?"

Her heart beat contentedly and steadily as she fought to control her eagerness. It was with an inner smile that she stripped bare and naked as if before the world, and she knew her back was almost clear and quite ready to take more punishment.

"Take off your shoes," he ordered smoothly.

Doing as she was bid, she kicked the Prada shoes aside as carelessly as if they were nothing more than cheap trainers.

Paul slid open a drawer that whispered on its runners and put the leather restraints she remembered so well on her wrists and then raised her arms so that she could just teeter on her tip toes while he clipped them together over a coat hook. It was with almost feline pleasure that she arched her back. Then he used a leather flogger on her. It was a heavier one than she was used to and she found herself jolted forwards, pressing her achingly hard nipples against the wood panelling. The slap and smack of the powerfully wielded whip filled her world as it always did and swathes of vivid pleasure spread across her entire body. She rubbed herself from side to side to stimulate and tease her nipples as the flogging went on and eventually she was responding to every lash with sensual groans of pleasure as she tried to coax more intense pleasure from her nipples while the heat in her back grew to furnace-like proportions.

Paul had clearly seen from the state of her bottom how well she had progressed in her submissiveness and he was throwing the whip with all his force.

Despite already being more heavily bruised and welted than usual Maggie was enjoying herself far more than she had reckoned on. And when the beating did finally stop and she hung panting and gasping in its wake, her red, perspiration-sheened face pressed against the panelling, she felt his hand ease between her spread legs and feel up into her, the finger easily spreading her lips and then sliding upwards. She groaned in relief as at last she felt herself being filled.

Paul chuckled just behind her ear. "Let's get you over the desk and see if you're still as good a fuck as you used to be," he said.

Within a couple of moments he had her writhing on her back, his thrusting making her welts rub against the leather. She wrapped her legs lovingly about him and let her hands flop over the edge of the desk behind her head as she relinquished her will entirely, leaving her body utterly open and available for him. He made a few thrusts, just to ensure he had full and easy penetration and then picked up the nipple clamps he had placed beside her before entering her. Now, as she whimpered and mewed just enough to spur him on, he fed each nipple through the bars and began to tighten the screws, making the hard little tubes of tender flesh bulge through the steel frames. Maggie gasped for real as the pain kicked in properly and she began to move her pelvis urgently on his impaling cock. Paul smiled down at her as he turned each screw one more time and she grimaced and sighed in response. Then he got down to the business of fucking her properly. Holding her hips so tightly that she was sure he would leave finger-shaped bruises behind, he began to pump back and forth and then he reached out one hand and grabbed the chain that connected the clamps and, when he had her full attention, he jerked it hard upwards. Maggie yelped, arched her back and increased the fervour of her motions at his groin, wordlessly urging him on as she herself succumbed to the aphrodisiac of sexual pain and began to spiral upwards towards orgasm.....higher and higher.....any moment now...

Paul fell forwards onto her heaving chest as he pumped the last of his spend into her and she hardly registered the increase in nipple pain as her climax matched his in intensity. For a long moment they lay and recovered, but slowly Maggie let her legs fall away from Paul's hips, he pushed himself upright again and with a sadistic grin began to unscrew the clamps, reviving every bit of the pain that having them put on entailed.

"You're still a bloody wonderful shag, Maggie," he said as he slipped out of her cunt. "If ever you need a whip or a fuck, you know where to come."

"Thanks, Paul. But I'm okay for the moment," she said softly as she smiled prettily, sitting up and reaching for a tissue from her prohibited glitzy bag. "You still know how to show a girl a good time though!" She smiled at him as she stood and wiped herself clean.

They dressed in companionable silence and then Paul took her home.

"Do you fancy a coffee?" she asked as he pulled up outside, feeling ridiculously hopeful that he would say yes.

"No, thanks all the same." He gave her another peck on the cheek.

Slowly and as seductively as possible, she unfolded herself and opened the door. "Don't worry, I'll get that bimbo out of your hair," he told her as she stepped out of the car.

"Thanks."

Maggie smiled as she walked on air to her front door. But it was time to come down to earth now, she told herself sternly. It had been a thoroughly good evening's work, she felt. The only downside was that she would have to try and avoid Nigel seeing her naked from the waist up for a few days, but she could probably persuade him in the direction of a couple of sessions with her on her knees with his cock in her mouth instead of him putting her to the whip.

CHAPTER SEVEN

Vanessa rolled onto her back and loved the feel of the man's weight pressing her down, making his cock spear even deeper into her. His body felt warm and muscular between her thighs as she clasped him to her, letting him pump into her, fill her and satisfy the aching need she had felt earlier down in the bar of the hotel. Beside her ear his breath rasped as he lifted his hips and then plunged down, time after time. Her hands clawed at his back while his curled deeper into her buttocks in response. That was better! Vanessa grimaced in pained pleasure as she raked his back again and he responded with a growl and renewed clawing at her buttocks. She bucked up at him harder and harder, gritting her teeth and loving the feeling of his pelvis slamming into her. The first tendrils of orgasm began to unfurl in her depths and then blossom in her rigid nipples rasping against his chest. Slowly the furnace grew between her legs as his cock rammed in and out, ever faster. Then he arched back as he came to rest at full penetration and spilled himself. Vanessa just managed to rock her hips enough to coax an orgasm from the coupling and then he collapsed onto her.

In the cab home she put her head back against the rest and watched the bars of light from the street lamps flick across the taxi's roof as they drove. Her thoughts were restless, as they had been these past few weeks.

The guy who she had just fucked with had been a pick-up at a bar she had stopped by at on the way home from work. She had been on her own as she increasingly seemed to be these days. Since the fight, work had not been fun. It was as if she was some kind of different species that the others didn't want to mix with. But the guy had picked her up with a light hearted line in chat up patter and he hadn't been bad in bed. So it wasn't his fault that she felt as horny as Old Nick himself just fifteen minutes after he had pulled out of her.

She had changed somehow and, given the effect it was having on her life, it seemed important that she understand what had happened... what was still happening to her. And so, as she savoured the after effects of the hotel fuck, she made a mental list.

She needed more than a simple shag could provide nowadays, she sighed as finally she admitted it to herself. The gangbang in the scrapyard and the fight with Rae had brought something out in her that just wouldn't go away. Her patchy memories of the gangbang included shameless pleasure in being naked in such an exposed place, pleasure at seeing pricks grow rampantly hard and erect at the sight of her nudity. It had made her feel more of a woman somehow and she had delighted in it. She had loved the fierce contact with the men's bodies as they had used her, blatantly and cruelly. And that had aptly demonstrated her vulnerability and made her feel as though she were just a plaything that they could do anything with. And the lashing......she was furious that she couldn't recall how it had felt, but the marks had been scandalously thrilling. Then there had been the fight.

Vanessa closed her eyes; she had no problem at all in recalling the feel of Rae's warm body hard against hers; the way her breasts had felt and her long thighs. But most of all she loved the memory of how vulnerable Rae's female body had felt when she had thrown it or landed a punch on it. Every ripple and wobble played itself behind her eyelids on an endless loop tape and her fingers twitched involuntarily at the memory of her flesh. And then there was the nudity again. At the fight it had been even more thrilling; she had been sober and had felt the effect she was having on both the men and the women. They might be shunning her now but just at that moment when she had been stripped naked, Vanessa knew that her body had enthralled them and it had felt so good, so free; to be naked, to feel cool air on her labia, to feel her breasts swing freely.

She clenched a hand in her skirt at her crotch.

Once in her flat she stripped naked, tossing her clothes anywhere, then she stalked through to her bedroom and went straight to her knicker drawer and pulled out her vibrator before going into her lounge. She threw open the balcony doors and stood in the frame with her legs spread, then she turned the vibrator on and thrust it up into her once-more flooding cunt, groaning with relief as she felt it fill her and then moaning with pleasure at the thought of all the pedestrians hurrying by beneath her. All they had to do was look up......she rammed the vibrator into herself brutally hard; she knew what she would do tomorrow night but for this night she would see how much she could take from her own hand.

After seconds – or minutes – she couldn't tell, of throbbing plunging as her juice aided its gliding in and out, she flicked the button to increase the speed of the vibrations then thought she would go mad as they immediately and randomly shot through her, until the whirring and vibrating became the centre of her entire world. No more, she told herself, even as she held it firmly in position before ramming it once more. Then she eased it out just a little and changed the angle so the upper part of it lay against her clitoris, transmitting its thrilling pulses through her bud with insane ferocity as she flicked it onto to maximum speed. Except she really couldn't stand the torment of it, she knew she couldn't, it was just too much she told herself. All she had to do to save herself from the agonising sensations which threatened to push her over the edge was turn the thing off. And yet she couldn't do it, not yet! Bent on her course she refused to allow herself some respite, adamant to see how much she could stand and how long she could last. And then quite suddenly it was enough and she eased it away from her bud which momentarily seemed to retain the maddening pulses, and thrust it inside again, just as her floodgates opened and she climaxed. She snatched the vibrator from her quim and bit deeper than intended into her lip to stop herself from screaming out – it was one thing to prove her recently discovered exhibitionism by giving the pedestrians a show of her magnificent nudity and outrageous behaviour, and quite another to scream her brains out and thereby draw unwanted attention in the form of neighbours, or worse, the police. As her hand dropped to her side still clutching the vibrator she fumbled for the off switch and, slumping against the doorframe took a minute or two to recover herself enough to return inside.

***

The club was its familiar blend of low lights by the bar, sticky carpets, thudding bass lines from the speakers and the usual mix of couples and singles. Vanessa strode through them like a woman on a mission once more, but this time in complete control of herself. She made straight for the bar and ordered a soft drink. As soon as she could she took a stool and quietly waited, fending off the occasional chat-up attempt with a withering look and an acerbic quip if that failed.

After nearly an hour she found what she was looking for.

Darren had scored with another girl as legless as she had been on that fateful night. She got up off the stool and sauntered along the bar, noting with shame how unsteady on her legs the girl was. God! What a daft little tart she had been then, but not tonight!

She stood behind the girl and smiled at Darren over her head. As soon as he noticed her he stopped talking to his latest mark, but Vanessa had to give him his due, he didn't miss a beat. He bent and said something to the girl who looked around, startled and then tottered away hurriedly.

"I told her you're my wife who's out on parole for GBH," he said. "How are you?"

"Better than I was the morning after you bastards finished with me."

"You were hot stuff. We'd never had one last so long!"

Vanessa smiled at the compliment. "I want a return match." This time she had the pleasure of seeing him discomfited. His jaw dropped for a second before he could gather himself and reach for his mobile phone.

"Oh no!" Vanessa reached out and grabbed his wrist. "Not yet. There's a few things I want to discuss first."

He lifted his eyes to hers and she maintained eye contact in a way she had not done last time. It was in that moment she realised that she really did fancy him, even when sober, and had to remind herself that none of this was about her fancying him. It was about something more important altogether. Even so, not bringing him back to her flat and shagging his lights out was one of the hardest things she had ever done. But it was necessary. She wanted him and the rest of the gang primed and ready.

On Sunday evening they met again at the club and this time Vanessa allowed herself a drink, just to relax her in advance.

"All fixed up?" she asked.

Darren gave her a wide grin and nodded. "Just like you asked for."

They finished their drinks and left; Vanessa's heart thumping so hard she was sure Darren would hear it. Trying to maintain at least a semblance of calm she told herself that such breath-taking surges of anticipation as she felt then were at best unsettling and at worst damaging to the whole enterprise – supposing it didn't live up to such high expectations?

He drove them to an old industrial estate where a warehouse stood waiting for demolition. As Vanessa had suspected when she had reconnoitred, a couple of determined lads could force aside the corrugated tin sheets nailed over the broken windows. Darren helped her climb through and she looked around. It was perfect, better than she had hoped for.

The interior was cavernous and nearly dark except for where a circle of powerful torches illuminated an area of grubby concrete floor which had been covered in gym mats. From somewhere high up in the darkness overhead a chain hung down. In a heart flipping moment of excitement she noted that someone had tied some rope to the hook at the end. Darren moved away from her into the darkness and with her high heels scraping, tapping and echoing on the floor, Vanessa walked forwards. Just outside the circle of light she paused, shrugged off her coat and put it neatly with her sports bag against a wall. Then, dressed only in a short, dark blue skirt and a light blue T shirt with bra and thong beneath them she stepped onto the mats.

"Okay," she said to the dark, "let's get started."

Six men walked forwards, slowly emerging from the shadows until they stood just above the torches which threw the muscles on their powerful, naked torsos into strange patterns of exaggerated relief. They all wore balaclavas and Vanessa couldn't even tell which one was Darren. She felt a rush of excitement pass through her, so powerful she shivered. That was a touch that Darren had added on his own and she loved it. She wouldn't be able to tell who was doing what to her at any point in the evening; and that was fine by her. She wouldn't even know if they were the same men who had enjoyed her in the scrapyard.

Slowly the men advanced into the light and began to circle like wolves, gradually coming nearer and nearer. Vanessa watched them eagerly, waiting for the first move. Nervously she flicked her hair back over one shoulder and adopted a sort of wrestler's crouch – hands held in front of her. Still no one made their move. They just circled her until finally, unable to stand it any more, Vanessa launched herself at a figure she thought might be Darren. She charged forwards, flailing with her arms and fingers. The man swayed to one side and caught her round the waist, lifting her effortlessly off the ground, then spinning her round and throwing her down onto the mats. She landed hard and bounced and skidded for a little way, coming to a stop with her legs splayed and her skirt rucked up to her waist. Immediately another man leaned down and grabbed her T shirt just below her breasts. Lifting her bodily by it he held her for a second until it ripped and she fell again. The next man pushed her onto her face and ripped off her bra. Someone else got her skirt and yanked it so hard he lifted her arse high into the air before it too ripped. Vanessa tried to hit out and scratch, anything to fight back but strong hands held her easily. Then she felt two more hands grab the back of her thong and take a good strong hold. There was a second's silence and then it was ripped also and she felt it tugged and ripped again so it could be flung away and she was left naked.

The men withdrew and she got her arms under her and half pushed herself up to look around her. The last of the men had discarded their trousers and she was surrounded by a ring of naked men with jutting, imperiously erect cocks.

She gave them a fierce smile as she got her breath back. "Come and get it then!" she whispered.

Immediately two men dropped and held her arms, turning her onto her back. She kicked out wildly but two more men got her thighs and spread them, then held them down by kneeling on them. Vanessa cried out in pain and tried to twist and tug at least one limb free, but she was held fast, spreadeagled. The last two men knelt either side of her chest, one took hold of her nipples and began to twist and pull on them, making her cry out again. It wasn't just the twisting, it was because they had hardened the moment they had been grabbed and were being crushed by his fingers, which only made them harden all the more.

Vanessa tossed her head from side to side as she realised she was loving the pain every bit as much as she had thought she might. Then she felt fingers at her labia, they didn't need to probe to find her entrance, she was wide open and they slid into her, rummaged deep inside her for a moment and then withdrew to rub harshly at her clit and make her catch her breath at the sharpness of the pleasure. There was male laughter around her as the two pinning her thighs got up and the man who had been fingering her vagina swung his body rapidly over hers so that she didn't have a chance to try and kick him away. His hooded face was suddenly over hers, his weight on her chest, his hard-muscled thighs between hers and the rigid pole of his cock was barging between her slicked, open lips and spearing up into her before she fully realised it.

Vanessa wasn't going to let him take her so easily though and just as he began to settle into a rhythm, sliding moistly in and out of her, she got her right leg bent back quickly and used it to brace herself as she twisted her torso and lifted her right side off the floor, nearly flinging him off her. She roared with the effort of it and for a moment it was only his length inside her that kept their bodies together. But once the element of surprise was gone, he simply adjusted his position and his weight pushed her back.

There was applause and laughter, Vanessa didn't know whether they were applauding her attempt or his calm recovery. But she didn't care. The combination of his resumed thrusts deep into her and the excitement of trying to fling him off were intoxicating. She tried bracing both legs under her and lifted him right off the ground for a moment but the change in the angle of his penetration was so exquisite she couldn't hold it and collapsed back. He bent his head and began to nip and bite at her nipples. Vanessa felt herself begin to sink into unalloyed pleasure and shook her head furiously, she wasn't giving in without a fight. Summoning up every bit of strength and trying to blot out the insidious delight of the cock sliding freely right up to the neck of her womb, she bucked desperately and twisted, nearly freeing one arm and once more threatening to throw her anonymous lover off. The men cheered as, for one long moment, it looked as though she might break loose, but then her strength failed and she fell back. The man on top of her let out a cowboy yell and began to really fuck her. Vanessa was shocked at his ferocity but loved being so defeated that all she could do was lie underneath him and let him finish inside her. He did so when she was achingly close to her own climax, but his place was taken so fast she couldn't take any advantage of the changeover to struggle and her new lover bit hard on her nipples as he began to stake his claim on her by slamming in to the hilt and staying there while he ravaged her nipples and breasts with his teeth and hands.

She came in a blizzard of splintered lights before he spent and she wrapped her thighs tight around him as he pounded her to the last of his pleasure.

After he had finished the other men let her arms go and as she panted her way back to normality she could hear them talking in low voices and she couldn't deny the thrill it gave her knowing that they were discussing ways of using her.

She sat up eventually and was immediately grabbed by the arms again and hauled to her feet before being slammed back down onto her face. She feared the worst and tried to push herself up again but a heavy body landed full across her back and pinned her down, almost knocking the breath from her. Then strong hands lifted her pelvis and she felt a cold glutinous substance being slapped onto her anus. She kicked like a mule and had the satisfaction of making solid contact and hearing breath expelled in a pained "Oof!" behind her. She kicked again and wriggled harder under the man lying across her.

"Bitch!" A man's voice, slightly breathless came from somewhere above and behind her. It was a familiar gravelly voice and Vanessa suddenly realised her moment of triumph might come at a high price.

Smack!

She yelped as something very hard impacted on her bottom. It stung horribly and she yelled again. This time the ruined bits of her thong were rammed into her mouth to gag her.

Smack!

It had to be a belt! How could she ever have wanted to feel it again! It hurt like a swarm of bees all stinging at once. She gave another muffled yelp as another lash smacked home. Then another. Vanessa tried her best to shift the weight off her back but couldn't, no matter how hard she wriggled.

Smack!

The sight of her desperately struggling bottom obviously entertained the men because she could hear them urging Gravel Voice on.

"Go on! Give her another like that!"

"She felt that one alright!"

"Harder!"

Smack!

It seemed that Gravel Voice was listening to his audience. The belt slammed down harder.

Smack!

Her bottom felt like one single fiery mass of tender flesh.

Smack!

That one cut across the backs of her thighs, just where the buttocks began and Vanessa desperately scissored her legs until she turned sideways the sting was so great.

Smack!

A heavy slap that reached down from her hip towards her delta made her flip onto her face again, like a landed fish.

Strong hands lifted her pelvis again and this time she didn't kick as she absorbed the fierce heat of the beating, whilst knowing that she was in for a buggering. She felt the man who had kept her pressed down, lift himself off her and knew she was about to be taken. It wasn't too bad; strange, uncomfortable at first but when she was allowed to collapse back onto the floor, full length, his cock in her rectum massaged her vagina from the back and countered the horrible feeling of wanting to empty herself.

She was very tight, as Gravel Voice took delight in telling his fellows as he came. And once he had withdrawn, she was entered again, more easily as the sphincter hadn't fully closed. This time, however, she was pulled back up and set on all fours, a hand reached into her mouth and extracted the remains of her thong, allowing a man kneeling in front of her to stroke her face with his fully erect cock, its drop of pre-ejaculate smeared her cheek. She wagged her bottom against the stomach of the man sodomising her as he began to move back and forth as best he could and she licked the side of the shaft in front of her. Then it was bent down and she was able to slide it gently along her tongue and lodge it at the back of her mouth, fighting the gagging reflex.

At her rear end, the action got more forceful as her invader was able to move more freely. The cock in her mouth responded by withdrawing until only the enormous helm was within her lips, then it rammed back in and she felt hands clench themselves in her hair. She began a muffled squeal in panic as she realised she was going to be fucked hard at both ends. She lifted one hand to try and push the man away from her face but it was held by another man. Both cocks plunged into her and she gagged at one end even as she felt her bottom slammed into by the pelvis of the man behind. Deep inside her she felt her vagina ache for filling. Both cocks withdrew and she tensed herself for the next double assault. But had reckoned without the whip.

A wide swathe of her shoulders and back suddenly exploded into hot, stinging pain. She yelped and then gurgled as she was thrust into at both ends.

The whip landed again and suddenly any pretence by the two men fucking her at keeping to a rhythm, vanished. The sight of her being flogged between them drove them to seek their pleasure quickly and Vanessa shook and trembled under the triple onslaught of sensation. She tried to scream around the cock in her mouth and then spluttered helplessly as it spurted thick sperm deep into her throat while in her backside another load was pumped into her and the whip fell remorselessly.

They left her again for a few moments once they had finished with her, the whip thrown down carelessly beside her and she could see it was a heavy suede flogger. Her backside burned, sperm dribbled from her slack lips and her throat burned as well, from having choked on erupting sperm. But she felt utterly content. She knew that at any moment now, the men would be back, hard and erect, excited by her and keen to test her body's limits.

She had hardly framed that thought when a foot pushed under one shoulder and turned her onto her back. Then a man was kneeling between her spread thighs, she could see the thick erect rod of his cock, she didn't know whether it was his first time or whether he was coming back for seconds but she didn't care. Her vagina was desperate.

She arched and writhed in invitation, thrusting her breasts up at him, but he stayed kneeling back on his heels and grabbed her hips, dragging her to him, lifting her up slightly so he could slide into her and then lifting her legs so they rested on his shoulders.

Vanessa gasped in pleasure at the depth of the penetration and then cried out in delight as another man settled himself over her mouth, kneeling like his companion he spread his thighs until his tightly wrinkled scrotum was within reach of her urgently questing tongue. He settled further down after a few moments and she was able to lick at the base of his shaft while in her cunt a hot flood of desire spread through her whole body as the angle of penetration this time began to work at her G spot.

Then the man kneeling over her face leant forward and applied nipple clamps. They were simple ones that opened and shut like clothes pegs. As he exploded pain into her, the man settled lower and Vanessa found herself screaming into his groin as he moved back a little. In her own belly, pleasure blossomed in spite of the lances of pain from her nipples and it overcame them in a storm of conflicting sensations. Above her face the man moved back enough to allow her hands to come up and grasp his rigid manhood. She masturbated it urgently as her own orgasm began to rush towards her and engulf her as her G spot was rubbed mercilessly. She felt the man in her cunt come, just as she herself had to scream her ecstasy and sperm shot out over her breasts. Almost at once the men left her, taking the clamps with them and making her yelp as the blood flooded back into the crushed flesh.

Another man hauled her to her feet and held her until she could just about stand. He spoke and she realised it was Darren.

"We're going to hang you by your wrists and whip you. Unless you stop us of course," he told her. Behind him she saw one of the men flick out a long, thick length of hide. Another man showed her a coil of rope. Vanessa glanced up at the heavy chain, swaying just a little overhead and then back at the lash.

She turned and ran, straight into Gravel Voice.

He grabbed her but she twisted and jabbed her elbow into his midriff. He was ready this time and didn't let go, just threw her back into the centre of the gym mats. She tried again in another direction and this time the man held her face to face. She felt the firmly toned flesh against hers, the way her soft breasts were flattened against him and most of all she felt how helpless she was in his grip of steel. And she was naked.

They got her down and passed loop after loop of rope around her wrists, then lifted her until they could tie them to the rope hanging from the chain. With a sickening jerk on her shoulders she was left hanging, her breasts stretched into taut ovals, her long legs cycling hopelessly in the air.

The whip scorched across her lower back, the tip wrapping around her and biting at her belly. Ignoring the pain in her arms she tried to twist in mid air.

Again, with a scarcely audible hiss the lash ghosted through the air but impacted with an echoing smack, this time across her middle back, the tip making her try and twist in mid air as it bit under her arm, nearly scoring her breast.

The men clearly enjoyed her antics as she heard applause before the next lash which wrapped a little farther around her and did indeed score the side of her breast. She nearly spun herself right around at that and took the next lash half across her stomach and her hip. The one after that wrapped wickedly low, searing across her buttocks and then coming around her hip to snap right at her delta. She gave a sharp cry of panic as much as of pain and lifted her legs as far as she could in an effort to protect herself, but it did no good. Whoever was wielding the whip knew what they were doing and there wasn't one square inch of her body she could protect from the lash.

The ache in her arms and shoulders became a torment all its own as she spun and howled while the whip just went on falling. But then she felt steadying hands at her hips and as she sobbed and panted, her body a mass of fiery pain, another hand slid between her thighs and up inside her with no difficulty at all.

Vanessa could hardly believe it, but the feeling of the hand inside her in the wake of the whipping was stoking her inner fires towards orgasm point. Her cries changed to ones of delirious pleasure as she was lowered to the ground and taken again by three men in quick succession as she lay on her back, legs spread and her arms carelessly thrown over her head.

It took her a long time to sit up and then climb shakily to her feet after that. She was pretty sure that she had never come as intensely as she had done just then. She had to brace her hands on her knees to keep herself up and looked around at the circle of men through a curtain of matted hair. They were all still erect and ready for more.

Vanessa scanned the muscular forms then without warning charged at one, she kept her head low and succeeded in barrelling into his midriff, he staggered back and she broke out of the circle, then turned to face her pursuers – she had no interest in possible escape, just in being naked, subdued and used.

Two of the men came at her from either side and although she kicked and wriggled with all her might she was soon held again by the arms and was taken back into the centre of the mats. They tied her wrists together behind her back this time and had her kneel. One of the men kept a grip on her hair while one by one they wiped their cocks on her face, sometimes just letting her lick them and then bringing themselves off and spurting their jism over her face and breasts. Some came back for seconds and had her suck them until she could milk a few more spurts from them. She lost track of how many she sucked.

She loved every second of it. She loved the way the huge purple helms would spray the thick liquid from the slits in their centres, she loved the feel of the stuff, oozing down her cheeks, dripping from her chin and tightening on her breasts as it dried. She hung her tongue out shamelessly, begging for a taste.

When they had finished she was discarded and pushed down to lie on her front on the mats. However two of the men still hadn't quite finished and she had to take them both from behind, lying deliciously inert under their pounding cocks.

Her breath burned in her lungs as she panted in the wake of the last of the devastating orgasms and by the time she could raise her head, the men had all gone; all apart from Darren. He was fully dressed and when he saw she had recovered he came to stand over her, sneering down at her.

"You're a slut, Vanessa. Nothing but a fuckslut."

She smiled back up at him, enjoying the insults as she lay spread out on her back, naked and helpless beneath him.

"Before I go I'm going to give you what every slut deserves," he said, unmoved.

Vanessa liked the sound of that and wriggled seductively but he bent down, grabbed her hair and yanked her up. She squealed and grabbed his hand but came up as fast as she could. He swung round and dragged her with him until she fell across an old table. The edge caught her in the stomach and almost winded her as he held her face down by his hand still gripping her hair. His other hand came into Vanessa's view and it was holding a long, thin shaft of rattan. Her eyes widened and she squealed again, louder.

The cane disappeared and instead a thin line of agony etched itself across her buttocks just as her ears registered a solid Thwack!

Her abused throat couldn't reach the pitch of her pain and she just croaked her way through five more blistering lashes.

Then he left her to sink down and clasp her blazing buttocks, tears and sperm running down her cheeks. Sperm oozing out of her cunt and backside.

She heard him go, and left alone she could afford another fierce grin in the darkness. It had been everything she wanted. The caning had been unexpected icing on the cake. It had hurt more wonderfully than anything she could have imagined. Her fingers curled inwards a little as she rubbed at her welts. Her body had kept them erect and excited for the whole evening and she had been able to take every single one of their cocks in whatever hole they had wanted. She felt proud of herself and of her body. She had taken on six men and been able to satisfy all their lusts. She could hardly wait to get home and admire the marks they had left on her.

She found her way over to her bag and did what she could to repair her appearance with a towel and some wipes, then stepped into jeans, pulled on a sweater and phoned a cab.

It had been a good evening's work and the men had played their parts perfectly. She wouldn't have a black eye to betray her at work this time!

CHAPTER EIGHT

Through one of the plate glass windows Maggie watched the new girl saunter across the office towards her own office which itself was just outside Nigel's.

He had rung in earlier, something about having arrangements to make for something or other, and asking her to hold the fort for him.

Maggie sat back – still a little sore from the assaults of two men – she had managed to keep Nigel from making her strip by persuading him that what he really wanted was to extend her slut training by making her go down on him in bizarre and public places. Somehow she had contrived to make him think it was all his idea and she smiled at the memory of how well he had taken to it. She had knelt and sucked him off in an alley that ran down the side of a town centre pub. A drunk had ambled by and seen her taking the last of his spunk down so Nigel had bought his silence by offering her services. Maggie licked her lips at the thought of how foul he had tasted and how utterly humiliated she had been. Then there had been the back of that taxi. After that had come the bus shelter and finally, only the previous afternoon after work in fact, there had been his car. A snarl up on the ring road had stopped them and he had had her lean across and take him into her mouth right in the middle of the static traffic. Fortunately the high risk of being seen had turned him on to the extent that hardly had her lips got past his helm than he was pumping lustily into her. It had taken her by surprise and some of his jism had escaped her lips and stained his trousers. She was happily awaiting punishment for that later on.

But for now, Rae was approaching. Maggie had been watching her carefully and was increasingly coming to the conclusion the girl was trouble for the whole office and not just herself. Of course she felt some affinity with Vanessa after seeing the marks on her, but it was more than that. Vanessa had maintained her distance from everyone after the fight, seemingly content to wait and see who –if anyone – would still be her friend. Rae on the other hand, after a couple of days, had begun wheedling and cajoling around the girls, flirting with the boys again; insinuating herself back into their lives. Maggie could spot a stirrer when she saw one.

Rae knocked and came in without waiting.

"Mister Pickett in?" she asked.

"No. He isn't. Can I help?" Outside, the main office began to empty.

Rae shrugged. "Can you give him a message?"

"Of course."

"Can you tell him I've been offered a new job."

Maggie's heart leapt. Thank you, Paul! Whip me again any time!

"And are you going to accept?" she asked, maintaining a perfect air of professional equanimity while her heart was singing.

"Dunno. I might but if Mr Pickett moves me up a pay scale or if he.......well, let's just say if he moves me to a higher paid job that might suddenly become vacant. I'd probably stay." She favoured Maggie with a smile of cold, bright malice. "And tell him I'll be a very, very good girl for him if he does," she purred.

Maggie's delight was swamped in ice cold fury.

"And what exactly does that mean?" she asked. "And I can tell you he won't respond to what sounded very much like blackmail!"

Rae gave her a condescending smile and sashayed blatantly towards her desk. "I don't expect you'd know much about it, Miss Huffer, but let's just say I think he will respond. Yes, I do believe he will!"

Maggie sighed and bit down on her anger, not for her own sensibilities which had nevertheless suffered a blow but because it was Nigel who needed protecting here and she aimed to do just that. There was no need for histrionics, she had dealt with troublesome employees before.

"Are you suggesting that Mr Pickett was guilty of some sort of sexual misconduct with you?"

Rae leaned forward on the desk and gave Maggie a view of her smooth, perfectly rounded breasts in the V of her shirt neck. "If you mean by that he shagged my lights out on his desk, then, yes."

Maggie gave the girl a beatific smile and leaned forwards in her turn. "He always tapes conversations with female juniors, Miss Carroll. So a tribunal will be able to hear every slutty word you uttered, every cheap, crude, seductive trick you tried and

Mr Pickett will deny that anything happened subsequently." She was sure her cool defence had been more penetrating than a fiery display of loyalty. "So if you've been offered another job, I'd take it. I'd take it right now before I tell Mr Pickett about this conversation!"

To Maggie's shock, Rae didn't flinch. She remained practically eyeball to eyeball with her.

"You dried up old biddy! I'll talk to the bloody mechanic not the oily rag! Who the fuck are you to answer for him?"

Maggie was taken aback. She hadn't realised what a brass neck the girl had, she was actually prepared to face Nigel down and demand a better job in return for her silence or more sex. And suddenly it dawned on Maggie which – or rather whose – job was at stake here. Vanessa's.

And despite the history between herself and the dark haired girl she wasn't about to see this nasty little bitch get her own way. She relied on her supervisory role and drew on years of settling work-related tiffs and wrangles. Without raising her voice, in firm, clipped tones Maggie made herself clear.

"That's enough, Rae. You've said your piece, so you may as well go and clear out your desk. Don't bother to hand in your resignation – you're fired!"

"I'm what?" Rae leaned in closer.

It wasn't so much anger in her voice, Maggie thought, it was shock – plain and simple, she had expected Maggie to cave in! And that was something she would never do.

Maggie stood up and walked around her desk. "You're fired!"

Rae used her forefinger to jab Maggie in the chest, between her workday, non-existent breasts to emphasis her words. "You can't do that. You – " she changed tack and gave her a hefty shove instead, "don't have the authority."

Maggie didn't see it coming and staggered, but without losing her footing or her temper. As much as she would dearly love to give the girl a good slapping, she wasn't about to lower herself to gutter level. Besides, she had seen the damage the conceited little tart could do. Only now could she fully appreciate how it must have been for Vanessa.....yes, Vanessa had seen right through the sweet and harmless bimbo image to the bloodsucking she-devil beneath she realised, and from where Maggie stood, the bitch deserved everything she got! She inhaled deeply, determined to remain calm and keep her dignity, promising herself she wouldn't retaliate. "This isn't one of your playground scraps. Don't push me, Rae!"

"Stop me." Rae pushed her harder. "If you can!" Then she changed her target and gave a sharp shove at Maggie's shoulder.

Stoically, Maggie stood her ground, refusing to react to the raw hostility that sucked the air from the room.

"Just give Mr. Pickett my message, you dried up old hag!" Rae swapped her attention to Maggie's other shoulder and it was with greater force that she pushed her, "if you know what's good for you."

Almost toppling, Maggie remained standing and looked at the blonde as if she were a glowering child on the verge of a tantrum. "More threats? You're wasting your time. There's the door," she said, pointing. "Go home, Rae, and don't come back! We don't want you here."

It seemed to Maggie that the blonde's face twisted into an evil mockery of its normal self. It was clear Rae had no intention of going.

"You know what, Miss Huffer? I can't wait to see your face when Mr Pickett tears you off a strip after I've seen him on Monday morning. Who knows, even I might feel sorry for you! After all, you've got enough troubles, being so flat chested and all!"

But it was seeing the unflustered Maggie still standing in the same spot which seemed to nettle the girl most. And when she started pushing her shoulders again, first one then the other with exactly the same non-result, it enraged her even more. Her face took on a pink flush and her eyes glittered with something so unpleasant that Maggie was loath to put a name to it. It was clear that Rae was really losing her temper and that things were about to get a whole lot worse....

"Someone fetch Security!" Maggie called as a precaution, hoping there was somebody left in the office to hear.

"They've all gone home!" The next shove to her shoulder had the impact of a sledgehammer and Maggie was forced to take backward steps to avoid being really hurt. "It's just you and me."

It was too much for Maggie who realised belatedly that if

someone didn't put a stop to it she would be in serious trouble indeed. And as no one came running to help as she was forced into retreat around her own desk. She snatched up her phone with the other hand in passing.

"Security! Security!"

She dropped the phone and, alarmed at the look in Rae's eyes as the blonde continued to push, she knew she had no choice but to defend herself. With a sharp intake of breath which she used as impetus, Maggie put as much force into her retaliation as she could, catching Rae by surprise as she shoved her backwards, making her lose her balance. Seizing her chance and momentarily forgetting her office persona, Maggie followed it up with another shove that turned the tables and had Rae on the retreat, back around the desk the way they had come. Then, with more force than she had intended, Maggie pushed again, except this time it was more of a punch, and pitched Rae back across the room. The girl thrust her hands out behind her to save herself.

As they came in contact with the shelving with its bank of box files, she recovered herself enough to use it as momentum to propel her forward once more.

Two uniformed men arrived just as Rae's hand made contact with Maggie's stomach, sending her sprawling back against her swivel chair. It shot the few feet across the office and came to a bouncing stop against one of the filing cabinets.

The men grabbed Rae and held her back.

Having shown her true colours, as soon as the men's capable hands gripped her slender arms, she reverted instantly to the innocuous girl with the sweet, engaging manner.

Whimpering in a hushed voice overloaded with hurt she told them, "She attacked me!" A couple of sobs for further effect, then she told them, "For no reason. I had to defend myself."

She was nothing if not a good actress and the flutters of her eyelashes and the trembling of her lower lip might have had the men convinced, if they hadn't

known the staid Miss Huffer for years. The accusation was laughable, and they tightened their grip on her. "You okay, Miss Huffer?"

Maggie recovered herself and said primly, "Yes, quite alright, thank you." She made a pretence of pulling out a drawer of the filing cabinet and searching through it. Extracting a file that she didn't want and didn't need she said primly, "Miss Carroll is leaving our employment. Take her to clear out her desk, then escort her from the premises."

Once outside Maggie's office, they relinquished their hold and walked on either side of Rae to her work station. She pulled open the drawer.

Maggie felt a great wave of relief flood over her and allowed herself a few moments to revel in her glory. She had surprised herself. She stood in her doorway and watched the still-play-acting Rae, delicately dabbing at her eyes with a tissue and looking the picture of gentle, feminine vulnerability.

And watching her closely in the otherwise empty office the two security guards knew they would miss seeing the flirty blonde around the place, she had been the source of many fantasises during her weeks at Bulliver's.

Rae transferred from drawer to handbag a hairbrush and comb, then piled up on the top of the desk the other items including her box of tissues, diary and cosmetics while she shook out an old carrier bag to carry them in. Then Maggie watched as the girl, still dabbing at her eyes, walked ahead of the men towards the lifts. She watched until all three had entered a lift and the doors had closed. Only then did she breathe again and turn back to her own office.

She sat back down at her desk and noticed her hands were shaking as she reached for the phone. Her stomach ached with a heavy, acid feel now that the adrenalin rush had faded. She couldn't remember ever having felt such anger before. That bloody girl!

At least Nigel had had the sense to insure himself by recording conversations with young female employees. Of course she knew he fooled around with the pretty girls, it was like watching a little boy in a sweetshop when some of the girls walked by him. His eyes went fixed and she knew exactly what she would find if she felt the front of his trousers. She couldn't resent it, it was just how her master was. And he did have a fabulous length and thickness of cock. Sometimes she fantasised about being allowed to watch him fuck another slave, but it was something she hadn't had the courage to mention to him. She knew his vanity and he might feel that by suggesting it she was suggesting that he didn't fulfil her.

So for the present it remained a fantasy.

Maggie breathed in deeply to try and relax the tension in her stomach. She had protected her master successfully, the girl wouldn't try anything now. She could give him the good news and probably receive her sentence for having spilled his jism the day before.

She knew she ought to ring Paul and warn him about Rae but the last thing she wanted was the girl being bitter and unemployed. Best to let him engage her and then drop a few hints......Paul could handle her. And if she was honest, there was a treacherous part of her that wouldn't mind facing Paul's righteous anger.

Her hand had steadied a little, she noticed as she punched in her master's number in the memory.

"Hello?" Maggie listened intently to his voice, she could usually gauge his mood by the very first word, and today he sounded fairly relaxed.

"Master? Something really important has happened here! But it's okay, I've dealt with it!"

There was an ominous silence for a second or two.

"Tell me!" His voice was terse and tense.

Maggie relayed the whole sorry tale to him; "But it's alright, Jim and Ron watched her empty her desk and she won't try and cause you any more trouble, I'm sure of it.......Master?" Maggie's voice quavered and failed towards the end of her story in the face of Nigel's silence. Then he found his voice.

"Do you have any idea of what you've done? Do you?!" He thundered into the phone. "You stupid bitch! You stupid interfering bitch! I could have handled her! I don't need you twittering round like a bloody fairy godmother........Get yourself over here! Now!"

The phone was slammed down so hard it left a ringing in her ear and her hand shook again as she put the receiver back in its cradle. Her vision was blurred by sharp, pricking tears as she stared at the desk. What had she done? She had only been trying to protect him but for some reason he was so furious that suddenly she was frightened and she sobbed a little as she shrugged her coat on and prepared to go and face him. He could do what he liked but, please Master! Don't leave me! Not for her! She thought as she tottered out of the office still reeling with shock.

CHAPTER NINE

Maggie arrived at Nigel's house an hour and a half later. One of the few remaining detached Victorian dwellings in the area, the kind described as a "villa" by estate agents, it had survived the bulldozer when the majority of them had made way for the larger, executive homes of the new Thornycroft Estate. Located just a stone's throw away from the estate and handy for work, Nigel had lived there since inheriting it from an old, dotty aunt. It was an unremarkable house that had benefited to a questionable extent from replacement windows. With a front garden set to lawn and surrounded by a high privet hedge with a gate it gave the impression that visitors were not welcome. She was not permitted to use the front entrance and so made her way round to the side door and let herself in, something she would never dare do without prior consent, just as she would never turn up unannounced.

The door opened into a small but modernised and well-ordered kitchen where no trace remained of the aunt. Maggie closed the door behind her and almost at once heard Nigel's voice.

"Maggie?"

"Yes, Master."

"Come here."

She found him sitting in the orderly Ikea-furnished lounge, reading and Maggie scanned his face anxiously, looking for signs of the fury he had unleashed on the phone. He seemed perfectly calm now.

She stood in front of him, awaiting some sign, if not of welcome or approval, at least of recognition. The seconds dragged out as she was given every chance to worry about whether she had dressed correctly. She had stopped off at home for a quick bath and a change, her stomach churning with anxiety and puzzlement. How had she failed him? How could getting rid of that poisonous little brat be anything other than a good thing? Surely he wasn't so stupid as to think she was anything other than trouble!

After much heart searching and a few tears at her dressing table, she had chosen to wear her hair in a pony tail rather than the severe style she wore it in for work. It was hard to know what he expected of her these days, whether he preferred her to look fairly matronly in public – until he had her alone – or whether a more flattering style was permitted while travelling to and fro. But seeing as it was evening she had applied a little make-up before setting off rather than waiting until she arrived and applying it in Nigel's bathroom, which was her more normal practice. Instead she had travelled half way across town wearing a tinted foundation and lipstick, a pale pinky tone which she always thought went well with her submissive nature. And mascara, lots of it! Normally she didn't bother with more than one coat but tonight – well, she had somehow contrived to do so much else to upset her Master today, what was one more tiny transgression? Tonight her eyelashes looked as if they were made to flutter!

At least she was wearing the clothes he had chosen for her, not the old maidish ones he favoured for her work style but nice, tidy and reasonably modern. The white skirt a flattering just-above-the-knee length, the blouse a light grey made of crinkled-cotton which she wore open to the third button, with a wide white belt and, over the top, a lightweight darker grey jacket. But the shoes.... ah, the shoes! They were a silvery grey colour, Nigel's choice, of course, not Maggie's taste at all but she accepted that they were killers – in every sense! For although they looked fantastic and would surely make any woman feel like a sex goddess, the way they seemed to lengthen the leg and narrow the calf. They were difficult to walk in and were too narrow to be comfortable and the heels were too high to double as office wear. Not only that but they had a tendency to get caught between the paving slabs. All in all, Maggie thought she looked pretty good given her limited wardrobe. Would it help her at all? She prayed he would look up and appreciate the effort she had made.

"Strip and wait for me upstairs." The order came without her master having ta his eyes off the page.

Inwardly she sighed in resignation. Whatever her crime was, he was going to make her pay for it! She removed her coat in the hall then made her way to the back bedroom overlooking the garden and the fields beyond. But instead of a bed, wardrobes and chest of drawers, there were other kinds of furniture whose uses had nothing to do with sleep. Against one wall was a wooden whipping bench and against another there were shelves that contained rope, chains, clamps and restraints. Hooks were inserted along the front edge of the bottom shelf and from these a number of whips and other instruments of discipline were hanging. But what really caught the eye on entering was the tall contraption.

In the centre of the room was one of Nigel's few DIY projects. Made of heavy wood, it consisted of a crossbeam with two supports at either end, bolted firmly to the floor and his optimism had ensured that it was sturdy enough to take the weight of three women suspended side by side, using the chains which hung down from the crossbeam should the occasion ever arise, though up until then it had only played host to Maggie.

Crossing to the window she closed the Venetian blind. Next she flipped the switch that flooded the room with white light from the four spots, one in each corner, that were directed at the frame. Then following Nigel's command she stripped naked. Usually she regretted the way that all but the most ferocious of welts faded quite quickly but now she was glad that Paul's had completely gone.

The set-to with Rae had left her feeling depleted and she had had a hot, steamy bath to revive herself which had necessitated the removal of the tape which had bound her, safe and secure, all day. She had not replaced it and, as she took her slave collar from the shelf and buckled it around her neck, she knew it was just one more offence for which she would be punished. Add that to her dismissal of Rae and it went without saying that she was in for a rough ride and she couldn't help but wonder if tonight it would be more than she could stand.... he had sounded so angry on the phone.... All she could do was trust that the pain itself and the pleasure that always accompanied it would not fail her in her hour of need and that the kiss of the lash would still.... in that strange way of the submissive, be her reward as well as her punishment.

What really disturbed her however, was the fact that she had failed her Master somehow. As with any submissive, she didn't mind cruelty, it was his anger that she feared. It might result in the ultimate punishment; rejection. Her heart fluttered as she pondered that possibility for the thousandth time that evening with something approaching despair

But then his footsteps alerted her to the fact that he had walked past the playroom towards the front of the house. That was something different, something new.... he never did that and it set her nerves on edge. It was just the way she liked it, making her wait, letting her stew!

By the time Nigel entered the room at last, Maggie was a quivering wreck.

He stood before her and looked her over. Reproach was in his eyes and his posture was taut with suppressed fury. He had stripped to the waist and was wearing the leather trousers she had bought him. It was how Maggie loved to see him and tonight it twisted the knife in her misery. Just as Nigel liked Maggie to project a false image of herself in public, his body was much more toned and trim than most people would have expected.

"The bench!" he said tersely.

"Yes, Master." Maggie went first to the shelf and took down wrist and ankle restraints which she buckled on with swift, agitated fingers and then went to stand beside it.

"Front or back, Master?" she asked, trying for a tone that was both businesslike and deferential.

"On your back." His voice chilled her, it was so dead calm as to be really frightening. Nervously she lay back along the padded beam and put her arms down to have her wrists clipped to the legs. She was about to blurt out a request to know what her crime had been when the effort of keeping it bottled up got too much for her Master.

"She was part of my passport to membership at Lewington House. I'd just got Bartlett to agree to taking a look at her and Vanessa when you decided I needed looking after! Well, by the time I've finished with you, you'll be the one needing looking after!" he said as he squatted to fasten her arms and then clipped her ankles to the other pair of legs, her thighs projected over the end of the bench, her magnificently cushioned bottom just rested on the end. It was one of his favourite ways of fucking her after he had played with her tits for a while. But now his words sent Maggie's heart plummeting even further. She knew that membership of Lewington House was his most cherished dream. To make matters worse, it was one of hers too! It was something they had talked about often.

"B…but how, Master? I don't understand!" Maggie was aware that she was almost wailing, and her stomach tightened with apprehension as the full import of his words crystallised in her mind.

Nigel loomed over her with the suede flogger in his hands, the lashes being trailed through the fingers of one hand.

With no warning he struck down at her exposed breasts. It was so quick, Maggie didn't have time to cry out until the lashes were being drawn back for a second one. Both strokes clubbed at her soft mounds, flattening them and driving hot, delicious stabs of pain through her nipples.

"The fight, you stupid cow! I was going to sell the idea of them cat fighting!" he said as she gasped for breath. Then he set about a thorough thrashing. Through screwed up eyes Maggie watched him really put his weight behind each lash. If his expression hadn't been one of utter fury and disappointment, she would have loved every second. As it was she got the physical high of the smacking and cracking of the leather across her poor tits but couldn't set her mind free to wander in sub space.

He stopped just as Maggie was twisting so much that her shoulders and upper arms were getting almost as much as her tits.

"I'd have flogged you for a warm up and then let the two tarts rip each other up for the main act! I'd have been made a member, no problem!"

Again without warning he switched to her thighs and belly. Again he threw the whip at full force and Maggie adored the new fires that added to the pounding ones in her tits as the lashes smacked home across her engorged labia.

When he stopped that part of the beating, she was panting and crying out at each lash, her head snapping up and tossing from side to side as she tried to absorb so much pleasure and pain delivered so fast. But somehow she had kept a part of her brain still working. There had to be some way she could help him! That's all she had tried to do in the first place, help him. And if he had only shared his ideas, she would have handled Rae differently.

For a long time there was silence in the playroom. Nigel leaned against the wall and got his breath back. Maggie heaved and gasped in the aftermath and gazed in worship at her Master from under her eyelashes. He could really deliver the best when he put his mind to it.

Her mind returned to the problem of how to win back his favour and further his ambitions at the same time. And a plan, albeit a loosely-knitted one, began to take shape.

"Master?" she whispered at last.

"What?"

"How would you make them fight?"

He shrugged. "They hate each other."

"But would they do it from cold? In front of people when they know you'll get the benefit?"

He sprang forwards and roughly buried his hand in her quim, twisting and flexing his fingers hard. Making what should have been a pleasant grope into a torment. Maggie cried out again and writhed.

"That's what I was working on when you had to interfere!" he shouted.

"I know how to make them, Master!" she managed to squeal.

He withdrew his hand and took a large pot of pegs off a shelf, slamming it down hard on her stomach and making her yell again. He took a handful of pegs and with the minimum of foreplay began attaching them to her labia. One straight after the other, with virtually no pause.

Maggie jumped and jerked under each sharp application of pain, struggling to keep her thoughts on track.

"Ow! Vanessa's a sub….Ow! She'd fight for a master! Oh, please no more! Ah!"

"Keep talking slut." Nigel kept adding pegs, jamming them close together, each one biting deep into the soft and engorged flesh.

"And I know who Rae's gone to work for!" Maggie managed. "He's a Master too!"

Nigel stopped and straightened up. She felt his fingers curl around the jaws of the pegs, ready to make them squeeze even more painfully.

She held her breath, partly to endure the pain and partly in expectation.

"Go on. Where's she working and how do you know?"

This was the tricky bit. She simply didn't dare tell him the truth, not now, not that he was looking at her with hope dawning on his face.

"She….she told me…..today! She's going to Gregory's Contract

Hire. Paul Gregory's a Master." Maggie waited to see if he had detected the lie.

"How do you know he's a Master?" Nigel asked at last and Maggie breathed out in relief.

"Because I left him before I met you, Master," she said quickly. "So if we can get Vanessa....."

"And talk to this Gregory guy about Rae........it's a bloody long shot!"

"No, Master! We know Vanessa's taken the whip! And in my office today I saw what Rae's really like. She's a bitch out of control, but Paul can tame her!"

"Hmm," Nigel's brow furrowed in thought. "I thought they'd just scratch each other's eyes out for money. I was working out how much and where I'd get it."

Maggie watched him nervously. "I think it'd take more, Master. Rae wouldn't do anything to help you. Especially not now, and I know that's all my stupid interfering fault," she added quickly. "But I'll do all I can to make it right."

"Too bloody right you will! First things first. How do we get Vanessa to submit to me?"

Maggie felt her heart leap and her quim flood as she contemplated the next few hours.

"Do what you want to with me, Master, and I'll go and get her for you."

Knowing that she felt more smug than a slave had a right to feel, she lay back and waited for sentence to be passed.

She felt the pegs on her labia drawn apart, opening her cunt wide and his broad helm slipped between them followed by the superb width of his shaft that seemed to set exquisite fire to every centimetre of her inner flesh as it ploughed into her. She couldn't help giving a strained grunt as it lodged at her neck and she craned her head up to see her Master standing between her spread thighs, a grim smile on his face.

"It'll be ankle suspension after I've fucked you and then some more tit work."

"Yes, Master," Maggie said and lay back, content in the knowledge that she had bought herself some time and for now her Master was going to take his pleasure with her. She settled herself in deepest contentment as he began to move back and forth inside her.

CHAPTER TEN

There was no time to go home and change first. Instead, Maggie brushed her hair and reapplied her make-up in Nigel's bathroom before she left and slipped quietly out of the back door.

She gave Vanessa's address to the taxi driver. As they drove across town through the darkness she gave no thought to the task ahead, deciding to let instinct be her guide. Nor did she give any thought to how she actually felt about the task she'd been given, didn't give the doubts chance to surface. It was enough that her Master commanded it and she obeyed.

She was aware the taxi driver watched her as she walked toward the tower block and wasn't sure if she was flattered by his attentiveness or nervous because of it, aware only that it wasn't the best neighbourhood for a woman to be alone in at this time of night. Walking straight ahead, she looked neither right nor left and tried not to worry about the group of drunken lads on the corner. She quickened her pace.

There was no entry system, anyone could just walk in off the street!

Inside the building Maggie's sense of unease grew as she waited for the lift. Half-remembered, overheard conversations between Vanessa and the others in the office determined which floor she needed as her fingers hovered over the buttons.

The doors opened and she was faced with a long walkway punctuated by similar-looking doors. She held her head high and was conscious of the way her clicking heels echoed as they struck the bare concrete. And she felt a wave of gratitude for the very different circumstances of the flat in which she herself lived.

At last she came to Vanessa's door. She ran her fingers through her long, loose tresses, depressed the doorbell once and waited.

After a few moments the door opened just a crack, and it was a puzzled sounding Vanessa who spoke.

***

Vanessa heard the doorbell with a sense of irritation. Unfolding herself from the chair she grabbed her short, white, towelling bathrobe and shrugged it on resentfully. Who was calling at this time? Visitors were the last thing she needed. Christ! She was just about to go to bed! Padding barefoot across to the door as she tied the sash, she sighed heavily. If it was that bloke from downstairs complaining her TV was too loud, she'd…. Peering through the peephole she saw it wasn't the man from the flat below but a woman. She opened the door on its chain.

"Yes?"

"Vanessa…"

Vanessa recognised the voice at once, of course, but the woman who stood there looked all wrong, nothing like the owner of the voice at all.

"Yes?" she repeated stupidly, then more hesitantly, "Miss Huffer?"

"Yes, it's me, Maggie. Can I come in?"

The rise in the pitch of Vanessa's voice betrayed her disbelief. "Maggie?"

She blinked, looked again then trusting her gut feeling unhooked the chain, slid back the bolt and opened the door, letting the elegant woman who sounded like Maggie Huffer walk in. It must be the shoes that made her taller. What on earth did she want?

Without waiting to be asked, Maggie stalked through to the small and surprisingly well-ordered sitting room – if one overlooked the heap of clothes that had been discarded in one corner and the magazines – so many magazines! The silver framed, flat screen TV was tuned to some reality show. Vanessa switched it off and gestured toward the bright red sofa against the wall.

"Please, sit down. Can I get you something? Tea, coffee?" she asked, brittle-voiced and anxious. Was she going to take her coat off? If she did, Vanessa thought, it meant that she was settling down for the rest of night and she would never get rid of her! She glanced at the wall clock. It was already five minutes past midnight. Well, if she was late for work they both knew who to blame….the old biddy….except she didn't look like an old biddy anymore, she looked….even mentally the word stuck in Vanessa's throat….stunning. The next thought that infiltrated her overwrought brain was this was Friday night! The office was closed for the weekend. And as the realisation dawned it ejected her only reasonable excuse for throwing her out.

"A coffee would be nice." Maggie sat back and crossed one shapely leg over the other.

But whatever she looked like she was still Miss Huffer, Vanessa reminded herself and was put out by the way she took in her surroundings, viewing them with a look of bemused curiosity.

Vanessa padded off to the kitchen, crossing her fingers that she had two clean mugs. She switched on the kettle and, after a bit of effort located one clean mug at the back of the wrong cupboard, red to match the sofa. She went back to the sitting room and spotted the mug she'd used earlier nestling cosily against the leg of the chair in which she had been curled up. Without thinking she bent over to pick it up and the sudden draft that wafted up to her vulva reminded her of the shortness of the robe and what it was probably revealing. She made a fruitless attempt at tugging it down at the back then straightened up and eyed Maggie cautiously as she made to go back to the kitchen, but was checked when Maggie Huffer actually smiled. The woman never smiled! And that was a shame because, Vanessa noted charitably, she was obviously a pretty woman. For a moment her crabbiness was infringed upon by pure nosiness, a real need to know….what was the whole 'staid old maid' image in aid of? Unless this wasn't Maggie at all, she mused as she stifled a giggle, but her beautiful twin sister. Except she realised now that if she was totally truthful, she had long ago seen the traces of what she had thought was faded beauty lying beneath that cold, hard exterior Maggie Huffer presented to the world.

Was she going to take her bloody coat off or not? Vanessa thought and was only slightly ashamed as her prickly nature returned. She couldn't help it, the Huffer woman had irritated her from day one. And having her here, in her own private space made no difference.

"I'm sorry to bother you," Maggie said in a tone that smoothed the sharp edges of her normal speaking voice, "especially at this time of night, but I felt it was time we put our differences aside. You see, we….you and I…." she smiled again and this time it set her eyes sparkling, "have something in common."

What on earth can she have in common with me? She was still Miss Huffer, she reminded herself.

"Milk and sugar?" she asked, her voice steady and unwavering. She knew it was stupid but she felt as though she were being tested in some way, that it was imperative that she prove she was as efficient at home as she was at work. There was no other reason she could see for a home visit!

"Milk, no sugar."

Vanessa went back to the kitchen just as the kettle boiled and switched itself off. She heaped the coffee into the mugs and added a sweetener to her own. She took the half empty bottle of milk from the fridge, and as was her habit sniffed it to make sure it wasn't off.

Coffee made, she took it to through to her guest then settled herself in her chair again with her legs tucked up beneath her. She wasn't entirely comfortable with having her work supervisor in her own flat. Especially when the bitch was sitting there fully clothed, still with her coat on, while Vanessa herself was stark naked beneath her bathrobe. It made her feel defenceless, wide open to criticism.

"Well?" Vanessa prompted snappily, "what?"

There was that smile again. "I saw the marks, Vanessa, the other day..... I know you'd been belted."

"So?" She hadn't meant to sound like a monosyllabic teenager but the Maggie sitting across from her was a stranger to her. Exactly what was going on in that mind? Who was she dealing with and what the hell would this nice-looking, glossy-haired character think if she could see the state of her now? The Miss Huffer she knew would be horrified!

"It's not an accusation, Vee... may I call you Vee?" Maggie didn't wait for a reply but continued in the same tone as before. "It's not an allegation, far from it. Believe me, I'd be the last one to point the finger! Just tell me, has it happened again?" She watched as Vanessa unconsciously pulled her robe tighter around her, then said, "I'll take that as a yes. Do you want to tell me about it?"

"Why'd I want to do that?"

"Perhaps," Maggie got to her feet and placed her mug on the round coffee table between them, "this would help." She slid off her coat and laid it carefully over the back of the sofa, then removed her pretty grey jacket and placed it on top. Next she unbuckled her belt and laid it on the little pile. When she turned to face Vanessa once more, with nimble fingers she started with the top button and slowly unfastened them all.

The blouse gaped open just enough to reveal a glimpse of her lilac, lacy bra beneath and Vanessa felt pangs of real discomfort. She didn't know where to look, and so kept her eyes on her face.

Maggie paused a moment to retrieve her coffee mug and took a sip. Vanessa felt the first stirrings of panic – the bloody woman was a dyke and about to make a play for her! She knew she was! Why else would she be performing a fucking striptease in her sitting room? Vanessa gripped her coffee mug tightly with both hands and opened her mouth to tell Maggie to leave. But though the words formed perfectly in her head they were not the same ones which left her lips.

"Nice blouse, Maggie."

"Thank you."

"Nice skirt, too." God, she was gabbling!

"Thank you."

Maggie replaced the mug then, as Vanessa held her breath in something approaching terror, Maggie unfastened the cuffs before sliding the blouse back from her shoulders and trapping her own slender arms. It was strange, Vanessa thought, how she could be turned on by men wearing balaclavas who were there only to inflict pain and abuse on her and yet she could be scared witless by a woman whose movements were slow, sinuous and sexy. She inhaled slowly and felt her muscles tense, was aware of a pain in her stomach as it was drawn inward, and watched as Maggie gathered up her shining abundance of sable hair and brought it round to fall over one shoulder. Then with the blouse still about her arms Maggie swivelled round slowly and turned her back on Vanessa.

She heard Vanessa's gasp at the sight of the fresh welts and her whispered "fuck!"

Maggie allowed herself a smile.

"I....I...." Vanessa began, unable to find the words.

"It's okay, Vee," keeping her back toward her she continued. "I understand what a shock it is to discover that there's actually someone besides yourself in the world who appreciates a beating. I remember how I felt when I discovered that I wasn't alone. You see, I've been taking the whip for some time. And I'm frequently subjected to much more besides." Telling herself to go for it while she had Vanessa's rapt attention, Maggie removed the blouse completely. She eased down the side zip of her skirt and slid it down her shapely legs, revealing very fine denier, lacy topped hold-ups and a scrap of lilac lace which disappeared between the cheeks of a nicely proportioned bottom.

Vanessa knew her mouth had dropped open and that her eyes were staring. Maggie's arse was as welted as her shoulders. But there was more to come. As Vanessa lifted her mug to her lips and began to drink, more to steady her nerves than quench her thirst, slowly Maggie turned round and, when she was facing Vanessa once more, she reached behind and unhooked her bra, letting it fall.

This time Vanessa's "Fuck!" was more of a snort than a whisper as she almost choked on her coffee. It wasn't only the sight of the raw welts across her breasts that so shocked her but the breasts themselves; the woman she had long believed to be hopelessly flat chested was actually blessed with very fine tits indeed, and it certainly hadn't been padding that had filled out the cups of her lilac bra. And, as Vanessa eyed the criss-crossing red lines that marked them, conscious of their generous size and the way they stood proudly on her chest without the support of the bra, she noted the multitude of bruises that seemed to be developing, growing darker, all the time. And the nipples which stood out as proudly as soldiers on parade.

They weren't the first boobs she'd seen, of course, she'd seen plenty before at the gym and back in the school changing rooms, in the days when she and Rae were competitors in sports. And suddenly, as her astonished gaze remained fixed on Maggie's despoiled flesh, all she could think of was the day in the office when Rae's tits had pressed warmly against her own flesh, how they had felt soft and yielding as they were crushed against her own, and how erotic that moment of contact had been, tit to tit, hard nipples pressing urgently into her own soft and yielding mounds, while her own equally hard nipples had dug into ...... she shook herself. What was wrong with her? Did she give out signals or something that she didn't know about, signals that said it was fine for women like Maggie come into her flat and start taking her clothes off? Shit! She was taking off her thong!

And there was another surprise. Maggie was shaved, no bush at all, not one single hair! Disturbingly reading Vanessa's thoughts Maggie skimmed her fingers over her entire pubic region, parted her legs slightly and then danced them over her cunt. She twirled slowly so that Vanessa could see that she was welted pretty much all over her body.

When Vanessa was sure she didn't look like a gawping goldfish anymore she said, "The bruises, on your tits?"

"Clothes pegs. Eight on each."

"Why?"

Maggie was facing her once more. Looking her directly in the eye she told her, "Because they hurt, Vee. Because I was punished. Because I like it."

All at once and quite bizarrely, Vanessa's competitive streak came to the fore. She stood up, untied her sash and slipped out of her bathrobe. She was stark naked beneath it and she took pride in her own sensational figure. With an upsurge of pleasure at her own exhibitionism she took a couple of small steps toward the other woman and slowly twirled so that Maggie could see her own marks. It was her turn to smile at the other's shocked intake of breath. Now she had Maggie's full attention and emboldened by her reaction, Vanessa confided in a clear voice.

"You asked if it had happened again. Yes, Maggie, it has. But you see I…. well, I wanted it to because…." She hesitated, trying for a casual effect while her heart's thumping told a very different story, "the first time I was too wrecked to take it all in but the second time….the second time, Maggie, I stayed sober because I wanted to experience it all. Not only that but I set the whole thing up."

"Don't be ashamed of it."

"I'm not…..well, not really….a bit guilty maybe but – "

"Don't feel guilty, either. I don't. I revel in it. I know what you all think of me at work. And that's okay because that's the way my Master likes it. I get my reward later. You see, I have needs, too."

"Master? I don't understand."

"Relax, Vanessa." Maggie reached out her hand. "Let me have a better look at you."

She skittered her fingers over Vanessa's bruises and other marks, making her flinch as little blasts of pain were activated.

"Sorry," she said, but continued anyway. "I see you got a good going over, as I did tonight." She gave a little giggle, "and I bet you can't guess why."

Vanessa told herself she didn't care why, but her curiosity had always been her downfall. "Why?"

"Sit down, Vee, make yourself comfortable and I'll explain everything."

Vanessa felt resentment bubbling at being invited to sit down in her own flat. Nevertheless, she returned to her chair and sat, her legs curled beneath her as before. To her surprise Maggie settled herself kneeling on the floor, facing her. And she didn't object when, very gently, Maggie took hold of Vanessa's legs and pulled them from beneath her, arranging them so that her feet were flat on the floor.

"That's better," she said, running the back of her hand soothingly up and down Vanessa's thigh while she talked. "I was punished tonight by Mr Pickett because ...."

"Pervy Pickett?"

"Ssshhh. Not so loud. Yes, Mr Pickett. He's not pervy, Vanessa, no more than you or I. He's the dominant to my submissive. He's my Master, I'm his slave."

Vanessa opened her mouth to interrupt but there was something about the way Maggie's fingers were skimming along the upper reaches of her inner thigh that stopped her.

With her free hand, Maggie nudged Vanessa's legs apart and she began to skim her fingers up the other thigh in the same way. Her voice took on a mesmerising quality as she continued.

"I sacked Rae. Mr Pickett was angry and so he punished me. He had that right because, as I said….."

Welcome as the news was and surprising as her words were, it wasn't the words themselves that held Vanessa's attention but the soft tone of her voice and the gentle eroticism of her butterfly touch. She felt as though she were taking part in someone else's bizarre dream. And her own right hand sought out her pussy while of its own volition her left hand rose and then came to rest on Maggie's head. How soft her hair was! So soft…. her fingers idled with the strands… was every other woman's hair this soft? Did her own feel like this? And then, while Vanessa's own fingers were occupied, Maggie's alighted on her vulva and, gently plucking Vanessa's fingers from the folds, she replaced them with her own. Vanessa closed her eyes and leaned back and, while one of Maggie's forefingers stroked her already glistening pussy lips the corresponding finger of the other hand sought out Vanessa's bud which obliged them both by poking out from beneath its protective hood. Vanessa shivered as Maggie applied gentle pressure and then began to rub it briskly, while the other finger slipped right inside her.

Ohhhh….. Goddddd! She had a woman's finger up her cunt! She was squelching….. the noise…..the finger, stirring…..all the time, stirring….. a woman's finger…..this wasn't right, not what she was….she wasn't a lesbo…..Vanessa wanted to die of shame. Except she couldn't because this was someone's dream and she had no control over it. And besides that, the other feelings, feelings so erotic – like nothing she had ever known before – were just too strong. Ohhhhhh! It was wonderful, different from when a man did it and yet nothing on earth could have helped her explain why it was different, it just was. Vanessa's left hand joined the one still fiddling with Maggie's hair. Then suddenly and without prior thought or consent she was drawing Maggie's head closer, feeling warm breath on her cunt…. she almost melted to nothing as Maggie's tongue replaced her fingers, first licking up and down her glistening crack…..licking at her folds…… then flicking her hard, tingling clitoris from side to side before suddenly plunging her wicked, knowing tongue inside the hole that was feverishly eager to accommodate it. And Maggie's hands were on her thighs, easing them further apart so that her access was improved. Her tongue lapped, then plunged deeper….how long was it? It lapped, it plunged, it wiggled and Vanessa squirmed.

She heard far-off moans of delight as she neared orgasm and could only assume they came from her as Maggie continued to lick her out. And the thought intruded into her sweet delirium and with a bolt of shock she remembered who she was, where she was and who was doing the licking. Shit! She couldn't come in her supervisor's mouth! Except she couldn't stop it, it was too late for that! Her muscles went into spasm and with a cry of humiliation-tinged ecstasy she climaxed, her fingers curling and gripping at Maggie's hair. "Shhhhiiiiiiit!"

At last it was over. The tongue was removed. Her fingers relaxed. And Maggie raised her head.

"Okay, Vee?" she smiled, her lips and surrounding skin coated with shiny, female juice.

"Yeah, s'pose so."

Maggie eased herself upward and within a heartbeat she was half sitting, half lying across Vanessa's lap. She brought her face closer and breathed, "Taste yourself," before covering Vanessa's mouth with her own and entwining her tongue with Vanessa's.

Vanessa's arms reached around her and, for the next few minutes, the two kissed as passionately as lovers.

It was Maggie who broke the kiss first.

"Thank you, Vee."

"Thank you, Maggie." Vanessa's voice was weirdly matter-of-fact, even in her own ears.

Maggie stood up. Her face was a surprisingly deep shade of pink since it had been she who had initiated the whole thing. Vanessa simply kept her eyes lowered to the ground, grabbed her bathrobe and offered her guest another coffee. Maggie accepted and, by the time Vanessa returned with the two mugs, Maggie was sitting fully clothed on the sofa once more with her legs crossed, looking as if the past few minutes had been wiped from her memory.

"So how does this thing with you and Pickett work?" Vanessa asked as she went back to her chair, clutching her coffee mug as if it were her life support.

"Basically, I obey him and if I don't, he punishes me. One thing he's very strict about is how I present myself at the office." Before Vanessa could ask the obvious question, Maggie reached down to her handbag and withdrew the reel of black, glossy bondage tape which she tossed across to Vanessa. "He makes me wear it to flatten my tits," she explained. "He says they're his tits and no one else must ever see them or know they exist."

"So what would he do if he knew you'd been flaunting them here?"

"I wasn't flaunting them!" Maggie defended herself then amazed Vanessa all over again by giggling. " Well not much and besides, tonight's different because it was my Master who sent me here."

"To seduce me?"

"You didn't object."

"That's not the point! Is that why you're here?"

"Sort of."

"I told you he's a perv!"

"Not at all. The thing is, a man like Mr Pickett has needs."

"Don't we all!"

"Yes, Vee, that's exactly what I meant. From what I've seen and from what you've said, I think I can safely say you're a good candidate for discipline. Obviously, Mr Pickett saw the state of you before, when you and Rae were fighting. He mentioned to me that he may have an opening…."

"An opening?" Vanessa's voice rose alarmingly. "Shit! What is this?"

"Exactly what it seems, Vee." In time, the girl would understand what an honour it was to even be considered but right now Maggie's thoughts were of her own loss if she didn't accept. "Mr Pickett thought you might be interested in taking up the position alongside me."

"Me and Pickett? Oh come on! Pleeeeze! Have a heart!"

"Think it over. I'm sure you've discovered for yourself that there's nothing like a beating to make a girl horny. And once you're horny, you need something to relieve it, something inside. Okay, if you're like me, and it seems that you are, you'll have at least one vibrator! But it never really takes the place of a cock, does it? It's okay for a short-term fix but, in the end, there's nothing like the real thing. And Mr Pickett is extremely well endowed in that department."

Vanessa laughed. "I know that! It's not hard to miss when he's got you up against the wall in his office, or when he's got the thing out and is showering spunk over your tits! Why else d'you think I haven't reported him for sexual harassment? I've wanted to, but….hey, how can you do that to a guy with a dick that big?"

The two women laughed and the atmosphere eased immediately.

"And he knows how to use it! You should feel it inside you, Vee. I'm not talking about a quick bunk up in the office – don't get me wrong, I love that as much as the next girl…." her voice trailed away as she realised that she often had been the next girl, after Nigel had had his fun with one of the other office girls. Pushing the thoughts and the accompanying emotions aside to deal with later, she continued, her mind set on the all-important recruitment.

"What I'm talking about is having a cock like that pounding into you when you're tied in position with your body stretched to its limits, unable to escape and utterly, utterly helpless. Or after you've gone through the agony of pegs on your cunt lips then been whipped there while they're still on fire….or worse, while you're still wearing them! Imagine all that, being whipped to orgasm… and all the submission that entails, and then as the icing on the cake getting a pounding to die for from a cock made in hell because, believe me, Vee, a weapon that size was never designed by God! Only a devil would come up with such an evil, dastardly, wonderful creation as Nigel Pickett's fuck-wand!"

Once again they giggled, not a polite little titter nor an embarrassed chuckle to break the silence but a long, helpless bout of girlie giggling that cemented their relationship and moved them on to the next stage.

As they regained their sensibilities and without a word passing between them, Vanessa stood up and for the second time slipped off her bathrobe, leaving it where it fell at her feet. At the same moment Maggie stood up also and once again began to unbutton her blouse.

But this time Vanessa crossed the short distance between them and it was she who eased the sleeves down Maggie's arms and removed the garment, flinging it aside as Maggie removed her skirt once more. As they stood in the small sitting room, Maggie in her underwear, stockings and shoes and Vanessa stark naked, they brought their faces closer together, fanning each other with warm, trembling breath. Giving no thought to where….or to who…. it was all leading, Vanessa's wide, generous lips homed in on Maggie's soft pink ones. They kissed a couple of times, soft and exploratory, then once again they were locked in an embrace. As they stood with their arms about each other, their fingers skimming gently over welts and bruises with their long hair sensuously tickling each other's shoulders, Vanessa felt a quiver of delight pass through her as Maggie's big, soft, lace-supported mounds pressed against her own, the delicate fabric deliciously scratchy against her skin, teasing her turgid nipples into even harder peaks. She reached behind Maggie's back and unhooked the bra, drawing the straps along her arms but leaving it in place while their tongues entwined and they became lost in each other's embrace.

If asked later, neither woman would have been able to say

exactly how or when Maggie became stripped of panties, shoes and stockings, nor which one of them led the way through to Vanessa's bedroom. Whose idea it was that Maggie should stay overnight was never discussed, each girl accepting it as a natural progression.

Beneath the duvet of Vanessa's double bed they caressed each other way into the early hours, gentle yet insistent fingers exploring each other's bodies in a relaxed, lust-induced felicity. As all kinds of new and wonderful sensations encompassed them, they tantalised each other with tingles of arousal and bolts of intense pleasure that were like nothing Vanessa had known before. If any thoughts at all flittered through their brains they were floaty and fragile notions, Maggie's of her Master's pleasure when he heard of her success while Vanessa's were of how it would feel to have pegs biting into her breasts.

Neither kept score of how many orgasms they had nor whose turn it was to agitate the other's cunt. And when sleep overcame them at last, it was Vanessa who was snuggled into the crook of Maggie's arm, her fingers splayed across the soft cushion of Maggie's left breast.

***

Somewhere around dawn, Vanessa pushed back the duvet. With all kinds of extraordinary yearnings nibbling away at her early morning awareness, she knelt astride Maggie's legs. Gazing down at her, she was able to note for the very first time how beautiful a woman could look in the mornings before she had had chance to make herself decent for public regard. And it came as something of a shock to realise that Maggie's dishevelled hair and the little black smudges beneath her closed eyes, caused by not removing her mascara the night before, rather than making her look plain unattractive made her seem somehow more..... used instead! Used....it seemed an odd word but somehow appropriate, for if everything she had said was true, Maggie was indeed used! Once the notion had formed she couldn't budge it, and she considered that she also had used Maggie, and that Maggie had most definitely used her! And she remembered also how used she herself had felt – and looked – when she had returned home after the gangbang in the warehouse. And she wondered if that look alone turned a man on..... the way it was turning her on as she looked down at

Maggie.

She looked so peaceful with her eyes closed and her breathing steady.....was she asleep or just pretending? It was something Vanessa herself had done many times with lovers to enable her to just lie back and enjoy without putting any effort in. Was that what Maggie had meant about being submissive? Or was it just laziness? Did it matter which? She slipped two fingers between Maggie's nether lips and then ploughed deep into her squelching furnace for the thousandth time, and she was rewarded yet again by having them squeezed by strong muscles, a feeling she was fast becoming addicted to. Amazing.... she'd never even touched a woman before tonight....except for Rae, of course, but that had been different.

Gratified by Maggie's soft moans of pure enjoyment, Vanessa experimented with another finger and then another. And then, brazenly and with no other thought than to double the pleasure of two women who were sharing new experiences, she pushed hard and watched in amazement as her whole hand was sucked in and disappeared up to the wrist. Even as she marvelled at the feel of those exquisite cunt lips encircling her wrist she began a thrusting movement, building up a slow but persistent pounding until Maggie was stirring. She increased the speed. Her hand and wrist began to tire, then actually hurt with the unaccustomed act. And she couldn't help wondering if it hurt men too, when they fisted a girl. Fisting a girl.....Christ! That's what she was doing, actually fisting a girl, and in her own bed! Still she continued and as Maggie's sleepy moans transmuted into discomfort-loaded groans it dawned on her that she was causing pain to another human being... not in the same way she had Rae but in a sexual.... and, she hoped, pleasurable way. It wasn't that she was trying to be dominant exactly nor that she wanted to hurt Maggie, not the way she wanted to hurt Rae but more a case of wanting to understand what it meant to be a submissive, to accept the hurt willingly. For if she could understand Maggie's acceptance then perhaps she could understand herself!

Her mouth fell open in awe as Maggie's head thrashed about on the pillow, her eyes still closed and her hands....ah, her hands.....they were clutching the bars of the white metal and brass headboard. She wasn't moaning now, she was panting and squealing, sweating and screwing up her eyes as she gripped the bars tighter. And she looked so beautiful as her head tossed and her body bucked that Vanessa knew she herself wanted to look just like that, to be so lost in the moment that nothing mattered except the sensation of it.

And then with a scream the like of which Vanessa hadn't heard before, except from her own lips, Maggie tensed in orgasm.

She opened her eyes and smiled.

Slowly, Vanessa withdrew her hand. "Good morning."

"That's some alarm call!" Maggie said.

Suddenly overcome with nerves as daylight filtered through the thin curtains hanging at the balcony doors Vanessa uprooted herself and moved back to her own side of the bed.

"I'm going to have a shower," she announced, "then I'll get breakfast. What do you want?"

"What have you got?"

"Dunno. I don't do shopping much."

Maggie smiled. Somehow the fact had come as no surprise. "Why don't I have a look around, see what I can find and make us breakfast while you have your shower?" she offered. "Then we can talk."

It was Vanessa's nervousness and sudden discomfort at the unusual situation that made her snap.

"Talk? What about?"

"How much you're going to enjoy being a slave to Mr Pickett. And how we're going to arrange it all. You'll have to call him 'Master,' of course."

CHAPTER ELEVEN

The new girl had been everything that Maggie had promised in terms of looks, but in terms of personality she had proved to be a whole lot more. Paul had heard nothing but good reports about her during her first week and then, just an hour or so previously, he had met her for the first time.

The day after his memorable encounter with Maggie, he had given his manager strict instructions to contact her via e mail, offer her a post and interview her but he made it clear he expected Ms Carroll to be appointed, should she respond to his invitation. She had responded and, according to the man, turned up promptly on the due date, given a good account of herself and had started work on the following Monday morning.

Then, towards the end of today there had been a knock on his office door and once he had asked whoever it was to enter, Rae Carroll had appeared.

He had been taken aback by her physical presence at first. Her blonde and blue-eyed good looks were almost pure nineteen fifties pin-up gorgeous, and her figure also had that ripeness about its curves. However, it was plain from the way the girl moved that it was not due to any corsetry but to fitness and nature's bounty. Her mouth was classic cupid's bow and she had used a pale lipstick which understated them to just the right degree in Paul's opinion, her nose was straight and thin, and just a little too prominent for the fifties pin-up but it gave her a more modern type of beauty. Also, he noted, her eyes were a shade darker blue than the classic dumb blonde stereotype. She wore a simple but striking, aquamarine shirt tucked neatly into a light grey, pencil skirt that ended a couple of inches above her knees. Her legs were shapely, long and strong without being overly muscular.

She was stunning.

She looked around her nervously, her shoulder length hair glimmering and swinging, and then gave him a brief but brilliant smile.

"Oh dear! I think I'm in the wrong place!" she said with a self-deprecating chuckle. "I was looking for personnel......I've only just started here ....and someone told me it was on this floor. I'm terribly sorry."

"You must be Miss Carroll?" Paul asked.

"Yes!" she said with another bright smile. "I just started in Purchasing." She looked around again at the panelling and the leather inset desk, the wing armchairs and the board table and her expression changed to one of acute anxiety, her eyes opening wide in dismay.

"You're not…..? Oh goodness! You are…you're Mr Gregory! I'm so sorry!" She clutched the envelope she was carrying close to her chest and began to back away towards the door.

"I am, but it's alright," Paul replied, standing up and coming round from behind the desk. "You came highly recommended you know. Are you settling in alright?"

He came forward until he was standing directly in front of her and admitted to himself that Maggie had not deceived him, she was something! Immediately he found himself envisaging her twisting and quivering under the whip, groaning and sighing as her master took his pleasure with her fabulous body.

"Thank you. Yes, I'm fine," she said, her voice just a little husky. She tidied a stray lock of golden hair back behind one ear and smiled back. "It seems a very friendly company to work for."

"Thank you. I've always tried to make it so. If you have any problems, don't be afraid to bring them to me."

"You're very kind. And I'd like you to know that I am quite willing to work overtime or at weekends…….anything that will help the company." The envelope she was holding had moved back down to her stomach and Paul could see the start of a lovely smooth valley of cleavage. She looked up to engage his eyes and licked her lips, a pink little tip just appearing and disappearing.

It was a blatant 'come on' and Paul was a little disconcerted, he had been aware that his invitation could lead on to other things, it was how he had first seduced Maggie. But normally it took a few weeks of happy, highly sensual pursuit. This one seemed to want to offer herself straightaway.

Alarm bells began to ring in his mind.

"I'll bear that in mind Ms Carroll, and now if you'll excuse me…….?"

She flashed him one more brilliant smile and turned to walk out of the door, her hips swaying and her buttocks pulling the skirt tight across her delectable bottom.

Paul shook his head as he drove. A girl who was that blatant could be real trouble, but what a prospect for domination! He needed to talk to Eve, and had texted ahead to her.

She opened the door of her apartment already fully corseted and in black hold up stockings with black four inch-heeled court shoes. Her short, highlighted hair framed her face. She wore a thick leather collar at her neck and from it a chain lead dangled between the inviting mounds of ripe, corseted breastflesh.

As soon as Paul was inside the door, she dropped to all fours and he picked up the lead. Looking down at her from this angle he was struck by the difference between Eve and Rae. Eve was a mature woman in her late thirties and her custom-made, heavily boned, red satin corset made the most of her breadth of hip, her reasonably trim waist and her broad shoulders. All shapely and desirable and promising what he knew she could deliver, endurance under whatever he cared to do to her. She would make a perfect counterfoil to Rae Carroll.

Eve came to heel and crawled along beside him as he took her into the lounge. His whisky was poured and waiting for him. He settled in his chair and she waited patiently on all fours in front of him. He reached forwards and stroked her buttocks, pale and inviting above the dark band of the stockings, swelling out from the corset's constrictions. He smacked them hard.

His palm stung pleasantly and a shock wave rippled through Eve's bottom. He smacked her again, and then again. His hand warmed up and left pleasing prints on her. He let her have two more hard ones and then settled himself, putting his feet up on her back as she continued to kneel in front of him.

Eve was a gently spoken teacher of English Literature at the local college. He had met her at a development agency forum and gradually, over the course of several dates, they had realised their needs mirrored each other's. He had helped with the purchase of this apartment that overlooked the canal and the fields and hills beyond the town. She lived her life quite independently of him there, but when he called or texted she cancelled any social engagement and made herself available.

She knew he was always on the lookout for new slaves and she had a couple of vanilla lovers herself, it was an arrangement that suited them both.

Paul told his footstool about Rae.

"......She's an ideal candidate for a good thrashing, she thinks she's the bees knees! But I reckon she could be a real bitch and that's why Maggie got shot of her. I'll thrash her too in due course!" he finished.

For a moment Eve was silent. She shifted her hands a bit for more comfort.

"Stay still, damn you!" Paul barked. "I'll crop the arse off you if you move again!"

"Yes, Sir. Thank you Sir," Eve replied meekly, quite unperturbed. "If this girl is as spectacular as Sir says, I expect she's quite used to manipulating every man she comes across. And Sir is quite a target for a girl on the make. I would suggest that Sir does nothing at all."

Paul took his feet off her back and sat forward, reaching down to free a warm, heavy handful of breast from the corset and squeezie it, watching the soft flesh bulge out between his fingers. Eve sighed in pleasure.

"Explain."

"Well," Eve started, then caught her breath as Paul took her nipple in a vice-like grip and twisted, smiling at her sadistically as she struggled to continue. "She....she is used to......men falling at her feet......Ah! Oh, Sir!" Paul twisted harder and with his other hand spanked her again.

"Spit it out!" he urged her.

"Yes, Sir! If Sir makes her do all the work, she'll be angry and challenged to try harder. Then when Sir is ready, and she is desperate for him to respond, she'll be easy pickings."

Paul had let her finish without further molestation and she had kept her gaze respectfully fixed on the carpet. He smiled again and stood up, tightening her leash.

"I think that's good advice, you slut!" he said. "Heel!"

Eve turned until she was facing the same way as her master and was poised beside his right leg. Paul bent down and slipped his fingers between her buttocks. He didn't need to grope for her entrance, she was open and wet for him immediately. Her vagina a warm, tight channel for the relief of lust.

It would only get wetter and more welcoming for a beating. He straightened up and led her to the bedroom where, he had no doubt, in accordance with his instructions she would have laid out his favourite flogger, the cane, her restraints and the lengths of chain to fasten her wrists to the hook he had carefully embedded in the ceiling.

Rae had left him with a pounding erection but it would be quite a long time before Eve got anywhere near it. She hadn't been beaten for a few weeks and would need harsh treatment before she fucked at her best.

CHAPTER TWELVE

"I am not prepared to wait any longer!" With his elbows resting on the desk behind which he was seated Nigel rolled a pencil that he held between thumb and fingertips of both hands. "I've fobbed Bartlett off all I can. Deliver her to me in the next two days or find yourself another Master!" The pencil snapped in two.

It was the ultimatum that Maggie had initially dreaded but after her first night with Vanessa, she was fairly confident now that she could do it – if only her Master weren't in such a hurry! Didn't he realise how many changes the girl was being asked to cope with? To rush it could prove counter productive. Still it should be possible…

They were in Nigel's office at the end of the second week since Maggie had been sent to ensnare Vanessa. At first she had been fearful that Vanessa would blurt it all out to the rest of the staff, adding a spiteful twist to the tale that would make Maggie out to be some kind of pathetic, old lesbian hag whose tacky come-on she'd had to physically fight off. But to Maggie's relief Vanessa had been discreet although there had been no hint that she was keen to develop their relationship. Even so, Maggie was pretty sure that once the offer was made and the time set, Vanessa would be eager to take it up. It was just a matter of finding that time, the right moment. Her greatest wish was to share that sensually obliging, well-toned female body with her Master.

It was as Nigel returned his attention to the letters awaiting his signature that the solution came to her.

"Master, I think that that's exactly what I will be able to do. You're going away this weekend, aren't you?"

Without looking up, Nigel gave a grudging nod.

"Well I'm sure you were planning on disciplining me thoroughly before you go."

"Of course." He added his signature to another letter.

"Then please do and leave the rest to me. I think there's a fair chance you'll have Vanessa bent over your desk next week!"

He raised his head and Maggie watched the delighted expression spread across her Master's face as he absorbed the prospect of having Vanessa's potentially explosive and long-awaited body as his plaything. And having played with it herself, she could sympathise.

***

Vanessa was almost on the point of believing that her encounter with Maggie had been nothing more than a horny, alcohol-fuelled dream. For a fortnight now the office had gone on absolutely as normal. Neither Miss Huffer/Maggie nor Nigel Pickett had treated her in any way differently, obliging her to carry on as normal also. At first she had been relieved that no further advances were made toward her and found the unchanged circumstances comforting, then gradually she had felt a bit insulted, and over this week hurt and puzzled. The memories of making love with Maggie were still deliciously vivid and she had found that on reappraising Nigel Pickett, now he seemed content to keep his wandering hands to himself, he was someone she could...maybe ....perhaps.... be interested in..... if he was all that Maggie cracked him up to be!

But neither one of them had made a move and she was fed up. It had taken her a while to get used to the idea but now that she had, she wanted to play with another woman's body again; and she wanted a man to use her..... really use her... to beat her and fuck her as if she were nothing more than a whore he had found in the street, to make her do all sorts of filthy things she had never even dreamed of.

The previous weekend she had been so desperate and horny she had nearly phoned Darren but she was still too excited at her encounter with another woman. The shock that she was turning into a lesbian, for God's sake, had been hard to come to terms with but increasingly she wanted a session with Maggie and Nigel Pickett together and that made another word hover in her consciousness....if only she could call it to mind.... well, whatever they called it, the thought of that particular threesome seemed the only scenario that would satisfy all her new desires and she often grew moist between the legs just thinking about it.

What was worse was that with Rae gone, all Vanessa could think about was sex, lesbianism, pain and Nigel Pickett. Over the last few days, it had seemed as if she was thinking about them all, and all at the same time as well.

So when Maggie stopped by Vanessa's desk late on that Friday afternoon and asked her to come to her office, Vanessa responded with a smile and followed her with her heart singing and a hot,

~ 122 ~

warm feeling in her belly. From behind she noted how Miss Huffer even walked differently to Maggie – short steps, slightly hunched shoulders. Maggie moved easily and gracefully and Vanessa longed to see her again. So, lesbian it was, then!

"Got anything planned for the weekend?" Maggie asked as soon as the office door had closed.

Vanessa shook her head and grinned broadly at her.

Maggie glanced quickly out at the main office to make sure no one was watching and returned the grin, adding a salacious wink for good measure.

"How about my place for dinner tomorrow night, and stay over?"

"Yes, sure! But how about Mr Pickett? Won't he want you?"

"He's busy this weekend. So it'll be just us girls again. But next week I think you'll be ready for him."

Vanessa giggled. "But is he ready for me?"

"Champing at the bit! I just wanted you to have a bit of room to sort your feelings out."

**

Unlike Vanessa's flat, Maggie's third floor apartment was located in an altogether pleasanter part of town. Bargee's Wharf was part of the Feldon Lock and Marina development built on the old Jamieson's Paper Mill site. Also unlike Vanessa's, there was a security entrance phone. Vanessa depressed the button alongside Maggie's name and waited patiently for permission to enter the building and then took the lift to the third floor. As anxious as a teenager on a first date, she was suddenly afraid of what was expected of her. That first time it had been so unexpected and had seemed so natural but this time – what if she made a fool of herself by doing it all wrong?

She waited outside Maggie's white panelled front door decorously dressed in a dark claret, near knee length skirt teamed with a plain dusky-pink sweater with her unbuttoned coat worn over the top, clutching a bottle of wine in her hand. Maggie on the other hand opened the door to her dressed only in a long, cream coloured, silk wrap with only a scrap of scarlet lace as a thong and black high-heeled shoes.

With her heart racketing in her ribcage, Vanessa stepped wordlessly into the small, laminate floored entrance hall. Saying nothing, Maggie smiled a greeting as she closed the door then took Vanessa's coat and let the wrap fall open. Vanessa's mouth went dry with hot arousal as she surveyed the unmarked, smooth orbs.

"Do you want a drink first?" Maggie asked, her voice husky with suppressed lust and excitement.

Unable to utter anything other than a nervously trembling, "Ummm…" Vanessa shook her head slowly. She had been dreaming of this moment for two long weeks and now that it was finally here she was so very afraid of messing it all up. It's now or never! she told herself sternly. Summoning up every ounce of resolve and as gracefully as she knew how, she moved forwards to embrace Maggie's soft warmth once more, her lips and tongue seeking her new lover's. And her lover's tongue seemed as eager as her own as they tangled.

It was Maggie who drew back first but only to suggest breathlessly that they adjourn to the sofa in the living room. Vanessa kicked off her shoes before entering, the only thought in her head a wish that Maggie would remove the wrap altogether. A few minutes later, she did.

Much later they snacked on pieces of the Chinese takeaway Maggie had bought, then momentarily sated and with glass in hand they wandered through her spacious, two bedroom apartment, gloriously naked and relaxed in the wake of their orgasms. Maggie opened the vertical blinds and they stood side by side with their arms about each other and looked out over the marina where brightly painted narrowboats were moored, before giving in to the lure of the food once more. Returning to the living room they licked the sauce from spare ribs off each other, Maggie paying particular attention to Vanessa's navel and the decorative jewelled bar which pierced it before moving on to her nether regions, declaring that Vanessa's pussy had been specifically designed as an accompaniment to that dish.

For her part, Vanessa fell in love with crispy duck nibbled from Maggie's breasts and sweet and sour sauce sucked off her nipples. Between bouts of giggles, kissing and fondling, they demolished three bottles of wine and through a haze of wine-induced, blissful harmony they made love on a bath towel spread on the deep lounge carpet. Vanessa's heart was full with all kinds of warm, tender emotions and she found herself aching for all the new experiences Maggie promised. And with such longing uppermost in her mind Vanessa proclaimed Maggie's bottom the star of the show. It exhibited fresh and enticingly livid traces of a harsh caning that sent her mind soaring with all kinds of new and exciting possibilities, and announced that she could hardly wait to see her own arse decorated so finely.

Vanessa had Maggie lie face down and knelt over her thighs, gently kissing each and every tramline scored into the smooth skin. She followed them with her tongue and loved the way her trail of saliva made the marks glisten in the lamplight. She even delved passionately between her buttocks, fetching moans of delight from Maggie that engendered powerful tremors of excitement in her own loins. She took mouthfuls of wine and dribbled the liquid slowly as she licked, and once her mouth was empty she licked every trace of the wine up again.

Inevitably the slow build of pleasure led to complete abandon and Vanessa flipped Maggie onto her back and lay on top of her, with her own cunt over Maggie's face, meanwhile she buried her face in Maggie's fragrant crotch. She wondered at her own audacity as she held the soft lips of her cunt apart and rummaged furiously with her tongue, rasping it across the hard little nub of the clitoris, plunging it into the pungent warmth of that sweet and musky vagina. Maggie groaned into Vanessa's cunt as she responded and as Vanessa finally reached the crisis of her pleasure, she was aware that she was clawing her fingernails into the tramlines so that Maggie bucked under her making penetration even easier.

"How many did he give you?" Vanessa asked eventually as they lay breathless beside each other, naked and uncaring on the lounge floor.

"Twenty good hard strokes," Maggie said proudly.

"Any reason?"

"He knew you'd get to see them and he wants me to tell him what you think."

"I think.......I think he's a cruel bastard." Her full lips broke into a slow, playful grin. "And I want him to be that cruel to me too."

"I don't think you need worry on that score! Now lie on your back, I want to try Egg Fried Rice out of your navel, with chop sticks dipped in your pussy juice."

Vanessa tutted and then laughed. "Damn! I hate it when this happens to me on dinner dates!"

CHAPTER THIRTEEN

Paul Gregory ran the keeper of his riding crop across the deep, rounded mounds of Eve's breasts, letting the leather flap tease her nipples. He had already worked her hard with a thick leather paddle and some nice bruises were already blossoming. Eve was looking down at them with an expression of rapt interest. Since Paul had taken her advice regarding Rae, she had experienced an intense schedule of sessions as her Master worked off his frustrations on her. She had had to cancel several assignations with lovers due to sporting fine arrays of welts and bruises on various parts of her body. Currently it was looking as though her breasts would be slowing down her vanilla life for a couple of weeks.

She was tied to one of the posts at the foot of her four poster bed, with her arms behind it, thrusting her large breasts forwards to invite Paul to entertain himself with them.

He flicked the crop quickly and watched it smack across her left one, sending a pretty ripple through it and making Eve sigh with pleasure.

"The girl actually had the nerve to turn up in a bum scarf and with half her stomach on show to ask if I needed any help with anything while Pam is off ill! And topped that by telling me I needed a younger PA! She was practically crawling over my desk to get at me!" he told her.

Smack! Another flick of the crop, across the right tit this time.

Eve smiled as she watched her breast swing and ripple under the harder swipe.

"Sounds to me as though she's ready to admit defeat, Master," she said.

Paul thought for a second and shook his head. "I'll see if she'll try one more time."

"Don't forget to keep the CCTV running," Eve reminded him.

"As if! Now then, let's finish you off,"

He stood back slightly and Eve straightened up, pulling her shoulders back to offer herself better to the whip.

Paul lifted the crop back and set about a proper beating, forehand and backhand, making Eve jig up onto tiptoes after ten lashes or so. By twenty her breasts were reddened, pulsing mounds of pleasure pain and he considered she was properly prepared. He swore he could hear her heart thumping! He untied her and took her from behind on the bed so that he could grip his hands in the tenderised flesh as he fucked her.

As he would soon fuck Rae Carroll.

***

Paul's PA was still absent the following day so he was ready for the knock on his office door in mid afternoon, and sure enough Rae Carroll entered. In her own way she had impressed him. Her come-ons were almost comically unsubtle, but she just wouldn't give up! Obviously he was the first male who had ever stood between her and anything she wanted and with an inward smile he took pride in the achievement. He sat forwards behind his desk and looked at her seriously but with a carefully maintained neutral expression. No mockery, no lust, no encouragement. Just a blank for her to throw herself against.

Today she had chosen a white T shirt which clung tightly across the magnificent swell of her breasts, the scoop neck allowing the first inch or two of cleavage to be prominently on display. And what a cleavage it was, like a deep and mysterious crevice between two uncharted mountains. But it would be him who mapped them out with bold red contour lines.

Her skirt was tight too, a short denim one that tautened across her mid thighs as she walked, emphasising their smooth, tanned length. White, strappy sandals completed her ensemble with their heels adding their emphasis to her legs.

"I couldn't help noticing that Pam's still away, Mr Gregory, and as I've finished all I need to do for the day, I wondered if I could help you at all?" She had reached the front of the desk and as Paul had known she would she leaned on it, giving him an eyeful down the front of her T shirt.

Game on again! He didn't sit back, he just let her see that he had seen what was on offer and ignored it, then in a cool but courteous tone he thanked her for her offer and told her he had made other arrangements.

For once she didn't give him her customary smile and at last Paul saw a flicker of anger in her eyes and her lips compressed for just a second. She seemed to think for a moment and then, turning sideways a little, she cocked her right thigh up onto the front of his desk and perched her bottom on it, showing him nearly the entire length of her upper leg.

"Have I told you I don't mind working late? Or weekends?" She leaned on her right arm to bring her closer to him and crossed her left leg over her right, both satin smooth thighs almost fully on view.

"You have, Miss Carroll." Paul kept his tone as neutral as he had on all her previous visits.

"I need the overtime and......"

Paul watched her carefully, for the first time there seemed to be a hint of something genuine in her voice.

"....you see Mr Gregory, I find men of power very attractive. And I'm really quite prepared to do anything you want me to." Her blue eyes met his and he saw for the first time that there was honesty there. It was time for him to make his move.

He stood up abruptly, making her jump up off the desk.

"You do not have the slightest idea what my requirements are when it comes to women! And I do not think you would want to know. Now go away Miss Carroll, I am tired of your games!"

Not giving her any time to react he strode to the door and opened it. She looked pale and shocked as she walked across after him, he could have sworn there was a sparkle of tears in those big blue eyes. Two doses of honesty in one day were obviously unusual for Rae Carroll – not to mention a man rejecting her most blatant advances.

By mid morning the following day she was back. But this was a very different Rae Carroll. She had reverted to sensible and well cut clothes and when she entered his office, she stood well back from the desk, her hands at her sides, fingers clasping and unclasping nervously.

"Well? What is it this time?" Paul was deliberately hostile now, it was time to flush her out.

"Mr Gregory....Sir. I really am very attracted to you, I'm sorry if I've made a fool of myself, playing silly games."

There was a huskiness to her voice that he felt came more from her effort to keep from crying than any attempt at seduction. He let her go on.

"But if you will give me a second chance, then I really would like to do whatever you want me to."

Her tone was contrite and Paul could not detect the childish pretence that had characterised her earlier attempts to ensnare him.

"Crawl to me!" he growled.

"What?"

"Hands and knees! Now!"

He sat back and waited to see how the immediate future would pan out. Conflicting expressions flicked across her face, disbelief, anger and then determination and perhaps just a hint of excitement. She hitched her skirt up and dropped onto her knees and then her hands and began to crawl to the desk.

Gratified at the speed with which she had obeyed, Paul came round to stand at the front and she came to a halt at his feet, her hands just inches away from his polished designer shoes. He stared down at the back of her head. She made no move to look up.

"Do you really want to know what I require of my women?"

"Yes, Sir."

Paul smiled. "Then meet me at the front doors; eleven thirty Sunday morning. Don't be late! Now go, and I do not expect to see you before then."

"May I stand up now?" she asked. Paul was taken by surprise somewhat, he had been concentrating on her submission rather than planning ahead in detail.

"Yes. You may," he told her gruffly.

When she had stood up, he was amazed at the fire in her eyes and the determination he saw in the set of her jaw. She might not know what she was letting herself in for, but if the previous weeks had told him anything about her, it was that she was a determined girl. He watched the roll and sway of her buttocks as she walked out – this time with an unconscious, natural grace rather than an imitation catwalk sway - and he could feel his fingers itching in anticipation.

He owed Eve a real seeing-to that evening, he rang and told her so.

CHAPTER FOURTEEN

Vanessa made her way to the Ladies as the rest of the office emptied at the end of the day. Her heart was hammering as she redid her make up. The summons had come at last just two days after Nigel had returned and Vanessa had torn herself away from Maggie's arms on Sunday afternoon.

As she leaned across the washbasin toward the mirror to re-apply lipstick, she realised

that more than ever she was feeling estranged from those she had previously thought of as friends in the office. Not only had they ostracised her after the fight but all those who had toadied up to Rae were saying quite openly how much they had disliked her, now she had disappeared overnight. Some had even tried to befriend Vanessa again but she had made it clear she wasn't interested.

"Let them all go fuck themselves!" she muttered as she swept the mascara wand over lashes already heavily mascara-laden.

She was far more interested in the new people in her life and the new experiences they could give her. And she was about to undergo another whole slew of new experiences in the next few hours. And it was then that the word that had eluded her for so many days finally sprang to mind.... bisexual....yes, that sort of sounded right. She was no expert but was pretty sure that the word meant liking men and women! Was that what she was, then? Bisexual or lesbian? She let out an exasperated laugh. What was wrong with her? What they called it didn't matter anyway, it was what they were all going to do together that was important!

Nigel himself had stopped by her desk and had asked her to report to him at the end of work.

And it was such a different Nigel Pickett!

Now they both knew the people they really were, gone was his smarmy manner and obvious intention to grope whatever he could get away with. He was self confident and assured. He was Maggie's Master. And not that bad looking either! How was it she had never noticed those cool, grey eyes beneath the heavy black brows! And dark hair without a grey one in sight!

Vanessa entered Maggie's office in time to find her putting on a bit of lipstick. She had already shaken her hair loose from its workaday style and the Maggie she knew and loved was slowly emerging from the dowdy Miss Huffer. She smiled over at Vanessa as she snapped her bag shut, left it on her desktop and stood up.

"The Master is waiting. Shall we go?"

Together they went into his office. He was standing by the window, gazing out thoughtfully with his straight back toward them, and already laid out on his desk were the items that made Vanessa's heart pound. She caught glimpses of buckles and leather lashes, ropes, clothes pegs, and her heart skipped a beat, nipple clamps.

He turned as they entered and Vanessa again saw the change in him. He was certainly more relaxed....she'd swear he'd unfastened the top button of his shirt and loosened the knot of his tie... and yet he was somehow more....well, masterful. It wasn't anything she could put her finger on, it was just there in his bearing. As she fastened her gaze upon him she reflected on how the prospect of having her naked and compliant in his office would previously have had him almost salivating with obscene glee. Now he was coldly authoritative and calmly in control.

"Strip please, ladies. Vanessa, help Maggie with her binding and Maggie, help Vanessa with her restraints."

With Maggie beside her, Vanessa had no compunction in obeying. She knew how nudity and vulnerability would excite her. And, trying to keep her eagerness in check, she stripped off and for once in her life folded her clothes and piled them neatly, placing them on a chair while Maggie did the same. Wearing nothing but her belly bar and pride, Vanessa turned and began to tear away the bondage tape that so cruelly imprisoned Maggie's glorious tits! She wondered how Maggie could stand it all day and couldn't really get her head round her explanation that it made her feel safe and secure.

Once Maggie was naked, it was Vanessa who received attention. The thick leather bands that Maggie buckled onto her wrists felt wonderful and she had the first inkling of what Maggie had meant. Without lessening the thrill of being naked they made her feel controlled and constrained.

"I will whip Vanessa first to assess her and mark her arrival. Arrange it please."

Maggie carefully moved the assorted whips to one side and

helped Vanessa, which set Vanessa's pulses racing. The very thought of being prepared by a woman for a man to use her was a turn-on and, as Maggie positioned her in front of Nigel's desk and had her bend forward, she felt so overwhelmed that for a moment.....less than a heartbeat.....she considered calling the whole thing off. But she didn't and when Maggie gently eased her legs apart she let out a ragged breath and fought to control her excitement. Maggie roped each ankle to a deskleg, next she came round to Vanessa's head and pulled her wrists down to anchor them to the front legs. Vanessa watched her breasts sway as she worked.

Nigel came to stand over her and she felt his cool hand stroke down her back and begin to explore her buttocks, caressing their firmness and roundness. She caught her breath as she felt his fingers begin to slide down towards her quim, not softly as Alex had done – it was the first time she'd thought of Alex in ages – but firm and knowing he slid them slowly down and then parted them so that he stroked on either side of her lips, tickling the sensitive flesh of her upper thighs and leaving her fluttering desperately in his wake. This was not the Nigel Pickett she had known. This was Nigel Pickett in control; making her squirm with impatience while he calmly took his time.

"She is exquisite, isn't she?" he said.

"Oh yes, Master," Maggie agreed.

Vanessa's heart swelled with pride and then at long last she felt the leather lashes of a whip trail across her back, and guessed it was some sort of flogger with heavy, broad blades. It was a soft, sensual feeling and for a moment she was disappointed – it wasn't what she had expected at all! She heard Nigel shuffle his feet slightly to brace himself and then the lashes were lifted away. Was that it, then?

They landed with a deceptively soft slapping noise but drew a tight band of pain across her middle back that made her gasp in surprise. The pain was sharper and deeper than she had experienced before and after two more had scored her, she felt the blades of sensation begin to burn in her core, firing her cunt into a hot, liquid response. This was more like it! Three more equally heavy and unforgiving lashes made her heave and twist slightly as the heat grew and the pain drove her pleasure onwards. She bit her lip in an effort to keep from voicing either for she was afraid that to do so would see her cast aside as useless. She had to prove she could take the pain, but as the beating continued she was unable to keep from whimpering. And she heard the sound of her own voice blending with the Slap! Slap! of the lashes and became even more turned on than ever.

Nigel kept the lash working on her with relentless regularity, making no allowance for her to deal with the pain from one lash before another was blitzing her all over again. Vanessa couldn't help crying out and twisting more and more as the flogging went on. She couldn't tell what was pleasure and what was pain any more. Nigel was slower and more relaxed with a whip than any man had been with her previously. By this stage the other men would have been driving themselves into whatever hole they wanted and pumping their stuff into her. But Nigel – who had always been so keen to use what he could of her – now that he had all of her was being slow and cool. When he stopped, she found, as the fires continued to surge within her, that she was desperate for him. Instead she got Maggie.

"Feel her and report," Nigel said.

Vanessa moaned with pleasure as she felt Maggie's familiar and cherished fingers slide into her and swirl around expertly.

"She's extremely wet, Master," she told him, so matter-of-factly that Vanessa felt like an anonymous plaything and not her lover at all!

"Clamps," he ordered. "Lift her."

Maggie's hands took hold of her at her shoulders and lifted her, at the same time Nigel reached under her and Vanessa let out a strained hiss of pain as she felt toothed jaws close on her nipples, which had hardened treacherously under the beating and made Nigel's undertaking that much easier. When he had done, and on his command, Maggie let her go and she yelled as her body crushed her breasts against the hard wood and the clamps bit at her nipples, engendering pain that eclipsed everything that had gone before and reverberating throughout the breasts themselves. Her fingers, curling and uncurling, scrabbled against the wood of the desk leg.

Then Nigel beat her again, this time working the whip across her buttocks. The feel of the leathers so close to her engorged labia was an exquisite torment and the occasional slap directly on them was a new sensation that she lapped up, even as she cried out. The various points of deliberately and coolly apportioned pain – nipples, breasts, buttocks and pussy – melded into one hot and raw sensation that she couldn't have put a name to even if she had tried. It was like nothing she had ever experienced before and she felt as if the sensation was everything, nothing else existed.

She only realised how much she was sweating and panting when he stopped, and then the cock she had longed for was inside her with virtually no warning, she must have been so open he just glided straight in to full penetration. The slow, deliberate build up of the beating produced far more intense feelings inside her tight tunnel than any man had produced before. But it seemed she wasn't suffering enough for his liking and he dispensed even more pain, this time digging his fingers hard into her welted hips and began to surge back and forth inside her and within seconds she was growling and moaning with growing excitement, unable to still her fervid trembling, the force of his thrusting making her jerk against her bonds which held fast, setting up a whole new sensation. And the biting jaws of the clamps that were repeatedly battered against the desk top with her weight crushing them into her heated flesh made it feel as if her nipples were in danger of being pierced right through. She heard herself groaning loud and breathless, like some wild, demented creature. It was all too much! Maggie came to crouch down in front of her and stroke her face and kiss her as she orgasmed more loudly than she ever had. But Nigel was still not finished and Vanessa groaned vehemently as she realised he was still pleasuring himself in her stinging cunt. Maggie left her and went to stand by her Master. She heard her cry out and assumed that Nigel was twisting her gorgeous nipples as he neared his own climax. And suddenly she found she was soaring away again and sensation was all that there was as someone's hand pressed down on her back, intensifying the fires in her breasts and she exploded into a second orgasm that went rippling on and on as Nigel spurted his load into her and Maggie joined her cries to Vanessa's.

Even when Maggie had untied her it was some time before Vanessa could summon up the energy to stand and unclamp her nipples in response to a terse command. When she did it was to see Nigel caning Maggie as she knelt in his chair with her bottom in the air. Her wrists restraints were clipped together behind her back. Summoning Vanessa with no more than a crook of his finger Nigel showed her how, if she hauled them up, Maggie could be made to present her bottom even higher. It was strange to be naked beside Nigel in the peace of a post orgasmic trance. He was still fully clothed and that seemed perfectly right to her. He should be clothed and in control, it was hers and Maggie's place to be naked and vulnerable. She tugged hard on Maggie's wrists and enjoyed her squeal of discomfort as she was forced to straighten her legs to lessen the strain on her arms, and thus to present her bottom at an ideal height for Nigel to strike it. She got a real thrill from being obedient but, more than that, her complicity in another's discipline sent fiery tingles of arousal directly to her quim and she wondered if that was how Maggie had felt when restraining her.

She found she was thoroughly enjoying watching another girl undergo what she herself enjoyed so much. The noise the cane made was even more exciting now that she could see how a female bottom rippled and swayed under its assault, and Maggie's was turning some interesting colours as well since her Friday beating was still working its way out.

Nigel stopped for a second and directed his steely gaze at Vanessa.

"She'll be out of service as far as the cane is concerned for a couple of weeks. So I'll have to use you."

His choice of the word 'use' went straight to the heart of Vanessa's excitement and invigorated her fantasies so vividly that she felt her cunt release a fresh surge of juice and she moaned softly and clenched her thighs together, partly to disguise the outpourings of sap and partly to milk a little more pleasure.

"You can expect to be heavily caned as I am used to an experienced slave," Nigel added, and Vanessa knew she had to respond. And when she did, she would have to call him 'Master'. She looked at him. He was examining Maggie's welted hindquarters with an intense expression on his face, ignoring her entirely and flexing the cane between his hands; hands which Vanessa now knew were much stronger and more capable than she had dreamed.

"Yes, Master. Of course." Naked and proud, she uttered the word and she felt she had truly passed a milestone on whatever journey she was on.

"Come here," Nigel's voice broke in on her thoughts and she dropped Maggie's wrists and went to stand beside her Master.

"Open her. I need to fuck her." The terse expletive and the matter of fact manner only served to heighten Vanessa's excitement. She eagerly reached between the crimson blotched and bruised cheeks to part Maggie's thickly engorged lips. Her eyes feasted on the glistening pink flesh as she pulled the lips apart. Behind her Nigel pulled out his cock and moved forward.

Suddenly and for the first time since she had entered the office, she had a real sense of where she was and she was struck by an altogether different sense of excitement as she imagined what Security would think, or the office cleaners, if they should happen upon them. Her heart responded by pounding madly.

"Put it in her," he ordered. Vanessa looked down and saw the magnificent cock that had so recently fucked her to the stars and she took hold of it with all due reverence, relishing the steel hard feel of it beneath the smooth skin. As he moved further towards Maggie, Vanessa gently bent it down and steered it between the spread fingers of her other hand and into Maggie's waiting vagina.

It was the first time she had ever actually seen a woman fucked and she loved the way the broad helm and the shaft of the cock spread the lips apart and how neatly it was accepted.

As he had with her, Nigel clawed his fingers into Maggie's welts and Vanessa loved the sound of her muffled yell of pain.

"Stroke my balls while I fuck her," Nigel commanded.

Vanessa needed no further encouragement. The huge ball sac was tight and crinkled as she gently rolled and cupped the balls. The position that Maggie was in made it hard for her to move very much and so Nigel was free to dictate the speed of the fuck, he began by making short, jerky thrusts and then slowly built into a rhythm of long and deep thrusts that in turn developed into a faster and faster rhythm that had Maggie jerking about helplessly under his onslaught. At last he held steady and sighed with pleasure as he spent inside her and then he stepped back.

"You may get up," he told Maggie. "Then sit against my desk while Vanessa cleans you out."

Maggie slowly straightened up, looking red faced and tousled, and more beautiful than Vanessa had ever seen her, then she climbed off the chair and wincing slightly she positioned herself against Nigel's desk, the edge cutting hard into the crown of her flogged buttocks. She spread her legs and, with newly-discovered obedience Vanessa knelt in front of her, smelling the animal musk emanating from her vagina. Already glistening rivulets were streaking her thighs and, as Vanessa reached out her tongue, hardly believing what she had been ordered to do and relishing the humiliation of it she began to lick, slowly. The mingled liquors tasted strong and tangy and no longer held any warmth but had cooled alarmingly. Not that that stopped her! Quite apart from the mental high she was getting from being so close to Maggie's cunt and being naked in front of Nigel, she derived a lot of pleasure from the taste as well as the lewdness of the moment, of the use her Master was putting her to. She was a filthy slut, she knew she was, and she loved it! And then, in a moment of real daring she plunged her tongue right inside Maggie's cunt and hooked out the liquor that still lingered there. Then realising she hadn't been told to go that far, she withdrew her tongue and resumed her licking.

She took her time about lapping between the lips and foraging at Maggie's clitoris and Nigel pronounced himself well pleased with her once he was satisfied that Maggie was clean.

"We'll stop off for a meal on the way home and then I think Vanessa should join us overnight. You may dress, ladies, but no underwear."

CHAPTER FIFTEEN

Paul was slightly surprised to find that Rae had turned up in tight jeans, T shirt and leather bomber jacket. His surprise must have shown as he climbed the steps to the glass front doors.

"I couldn't decide what was best to wear, so I just came as I was......I hope I won't be wearing it for long anyway," she said with a shrug and a rueful grin.

Paul didn't favour her with an answer but just motioned her to follow him.

Once in his opulent office and still without speaking, he opened the doors of the cocktail cabinet that stood at one end of the board table. She opened her mouth to state her preference but before she could speak he activated a small catch at one end of the shelves and swung out the entire assembly of shelves – bottles and all. Behind it were rows of hooks screwed into the back of the cabinet and from them hung the implements of his pleasure.

For a long moment Rae stood stock still with her eyes open wide in shocked horror and her perfect mouth open in an O shape.

"That, Miss Carroll," he turned slowly to face her, "is what I require from my women. Submission to my discipline. Giving me pleasure through their pain."

"I...I..." she stammered and then licked her lips and cleared her throat. "After Friday morning I sort of had an idea.......but when you actually see it!"

"Are you frightened?"

Rae nodded. "Yeah! But not scared.....if you know what I mean," she added with a nervous smile.

Paul decided he liked this Rae Carroll much better than the manipulative little tart she had been over the previous weeks. At least this one was honest.

"Still find me attractive?" he asked.

She nodded again. "Yeah! Very! But if you.....hurt me......will you...?" she let the question hang in the air.

"Will I fuck you afterwards? In all probability," Paul supplied the words she had baulked at saying. It was a stone cold certainty he would fuck her lights out, not a mere probability, he had to admit to himself. She was a dominant's dream, beautiful, nervous, excited and brave.

"Strip down to your knickers and then come here, I want to feel your cunt before I whip you," he said briskly.

It was to her credit, he conceded, that she didn't bat an eyelid and he watched in awe as her body was revealed. The thighs he had already seen and knew they were a delight, but the thin straps of her thong, arching over her hips made them seem even longer, her buttocks were tight, high and prominent. Her stomach was flat and her enjoyably heaving breasts stood proudly on her chest, crowned by nipples that were lighter than on some girls but darker than on some blondes, the areolas were smooth and a beguiling shade of dark pink. He noted that the nipples were hard and standing out nearly a clear inch. In a nutshell, she was ravishing! When she had smoothed her thick, blonde mane of hair down after pulling her T shirt off, she obediently came to him, wearing just a triangle of pale grey lace at her crotch. As if she had been born to submission, she kept her eyes averted downwards as he reached down and slipped his hand inside the top of the thong. He felt a short fuzz of silky hair and then his fingers slipped easily between her lips and into the hot wetness of her entrance. Cupping his hand he felt up inside her surprisingly capacious but very moist sheath and flexed his fingers. He heard her give a soft moan of pleasure and immediately withdrew his hand. He had found out all he needed to know, the next few minutes were for his pleasure and not hers.

"Hands on head, spread your legs," he told her. To his amusement and delight she obeyed at once, so he left her in that position while he selected collar, wrist restraints, his favourite flogger with the exceptionally long lashes and a riding crop. He glanced at the cane – that could wait until she was broken in.

He buckled the thick leather restraints around her wrists, tightening them until they were a snug fit. He encircled her lovely, graceful neck with the usual collar which was equally thick and heavy with a large buckle at the back of the neck and a thick steel ring at the front. Now she at least looked like a slave! He briefly considered putting her on a lead but decided against it.

"Firstly, the collar," he informed her tersely, "is not your property. It belongs to me, and I will use it on whoever I please. However, whenever you are required to wear it, you will consider it binding – in other words, when you have it on you should consider yourself my property and subject to my will. Obedience is everything, Rae, you will obey every command I give even if it seems improper, painful or absurd. To disobey me is to court punishment, over and above the normal discipline you will submit to. Let's try it out." He paused just a moment while he considered what to do next. "Rae, kneel."

Rae knelt. Thinking she was to crawl as before, she dropped to all fours.

"Did I say 'all fours?' No, I did not! Kneel, hands on head!"

When she had adjusted her position to his requirements, she gave a nervous little smile. "Sorry, Mister Gregory."

"Master! You will call me Master. Now, apologise properly!"

She flicked her tongue over her dry lips. "Sorry, Master."

He took up his desk tray and scattered drawing pins on the floor before returning the tray. "Your first test of pain, Rae. It's a mild one. Kneel on the pins."

He knew from having Maggie do the same and Eve on occasions, that the deep carpet meant that only a mild pricking resulted, but Rae wasn't to know that yet. He watched her with amused curiosity as, with a sweet docility, she did as he bid, wincing at the pinpricks but gaining in confidence as it turned out not to be as bad as she had feared. Still wearing her thong, kneeling on the pins and with her hands on her head, she kept her eyes downcast. He walked over to her and standing behind her, with one hand he massaged the back of her neck before closing his fingers and gripping it tightly. She gave a satisfying little mewl of protest.

"Quiet!"

With his other hand he yanked her hands downward and releasing his grip on her neck he clipped the wrist restraints together. Next, he walked across to the shelves and returned with a metal spreader bar with chains dangling from each end.

"Open your legs!"

When she'd complied, he put the bar between her feet and dealt with the right chain first, drawing out its length and wrapping the end around her right ankle, taking it up to her wrist and clipping it back on itself to hold her secure. Repeating the operation he joined her left wrist to the corresponding ankle. She was held fast, unable to free herself by any kind of manoeuvring. He circled her a couple of times while his eyes did a quick inventory of the tantalising charms awaiting his pleasure and he concluded she was merely discomforted, not in pain. Well, he'd soon change that!

He stood in front of her once more and took a turgid nipple between finger and thumb of each hand. Wasting no time on gentle fondling he went right to the heart of the matter, twisting her nubs so sharply that she let out a shriek. Now that was more like it and he repeated the process, twisting them the other way. Again she shrieked. It seemed a shame to stop her but he did anyway.

"Quiet! If I have to tell you again I'll gag you." Again he twisted, and again, then told her, "Do something useful and open my flies."

"B....but M...Master.....my hands....."

"You've got teeth, haven't you!"

It wasn't a question and at once she craned her head toward him and began the arduous, near impossible task of opening his flies. First there was the little hook at the waistband to contend with, and all the while he kept up his spiteful manipulation of her long hard nipples, fine specimens that were surely made for clamps, pegs, needles and all manner of other torments. But alas, those delights would have to wait also. At last she had the end of the zipper between her teeth and with admirable determination she eased it down.

"Time to prove you're not all talk," he spoke with such contempt that she must surely be feeling like a worthless slut by now rather than the refined sex goddess she thought she was, but just to be sure he put extra emphasis on the next word, as if he were addressing the dirtiest whore on the planet, "lady!" He watched with amusement as her face turned a deep shade of pink. And then at once his steely cock was buried up to the hilt in her sweet mouth, almost choking her with its girth as its length sought out her throat. Forsaking one deliciously-hard nipple he gripped the back of her head and drove her face hard against his crotch, enjoying every moment of her spluttering, gagging attempt to suck him off. God she was good! But he wasn't about to build her up again.

"You call this a blow job? Listen, you scheming little bitch, I could get better fellatio on any street corner." She spluttered in the most delightful way and she did things with her throat that were positively obscene! The girl was a natural and he looked forward to many happy times ahead as he said mockingly, "Do you know what you are, Rae? You're a fake!" He alternated the twisting of her nipple with harsh pinching. "I'm a hard man to please. Do it properly or it ends here, now, with you being thrown out on the street as a waste of space!" He loved the look in her eyes – he hadn't seen that much distress and pleading all in one go since he had first disciplined Maggie! And then he was coming, shooting vast amounts of hot spunk down her throat with explosive energy. And when he pulled out of her, leaving her all aquiver with jism dripping sluttishly down her chin, he was forced to admit that there was real potential there! He released her nipple. "I suppose you want a fuck now?"

"Y....yes....pl....please, Master."

He refastened his trousers and snatched up the flogger from where it lay, deciding to leave the crop for another day. "Not yet, Rae, you haven't earned it. I told you right at the beginning that what I require from my women is submission to my discipline, although discipline, as yet, you have not tasted. I also told you that I find my pleasure through their pain which, as yet, you have not experienced to the required degree." He side-stepped to provide easy access to her luscious tits and backed up a bit to give himself room. "These are both matters we can rectify now. Brace yourself."

He shook out the tails of the whip then swung it hard in a horizontal arc so that her chest took the full impact of the whole whip. Her breasts flattened and then rebounded to their usual shape in an instant and her strong body adjusted just as fast, only a slight backward swaying and a gasp of shock betraying her first experience of the whip.

Paul continued the beating by landing three more solid, thumping blows across the meat of both breasts. She remained steady and no more than slight whimpers escaped her lips. He flicked the whip downwards a few times, making her prominent nipples wobble pleasantly. He tried taking her by surprise and slicing in a few blows across her lower stomach with no warning, the lashes thudding home across her pubic fuzz and then slightly above. She let out soft grunts of surprise and her stomach tensed but otherwise she stayed the course with a docility that claimed Paul's reluctant admiration. He had lost count of the lashes at about eighteen and by the time he paused to catch his breath he reckoned she had taken about thirty solid lashes.

She not only had great potential, she was fit and strong too.

He was aware that his trousers felt extremely tight once again as he bent down to play with her thick, rubbery nipples that still insisted on standing out proudly, begging for punishment. He pinched and twisted them cruelly, looking for a reaction but getting only an impassioned gasp and a backward tilt of the head as she relished the pain with a maturity that was at stark odds with her experience.

Suddenly Paul felt an urgent need to release the build up of excitement in him that Rae's toughness and docility under the lash had caused in him. Roughly he pushed her backwards and with supreme ease she allowed herself to collapse onto her back, effortlessly allowing her legs to splay to her sides to allow her back onto the carpet. Her stomach muscles were obviously in extremely good condition as it was a movement accomplished with grace and control. It also left her thighs wide apart in front of Paul, inviting him to take what was on offer. Eagerly he knelt between them, snapped the fragile straps of her thong and tore the scrap away from her cunt. He could feel its wetness even as he did so and the revealed vagina was open for him, the hole clearly visible between the plump, engorged lips, the clitoral hood drawn back and a sizeable clitoris exposed. He reached forward and rubbed it hard with his thumb and made her gasp in pleasure.

His fingers fumbling in his haste he freed his rampant cock from his trousers and then let himself down onto her, she squirmed a little as his weight pressed her wrists into her back and he knew they would cause her discomfort all the time he enjoyed her. It would be fun to see how she coped. He slid forward a little more, causing her to moan softly as his full weight bore down on her, but all he could think of was the soft, wet sexflesh, nuzzling against his helm. He bucked his hips and felt himself slide easily into her, he slid up her a little more until he was in her to the hilt and then he began a hard, unforgiving, rhythm. Slamming himself into her time after time, not caring for the softness of her vagina, just going all out to plunder her deepest depths. Even in her strained position, she attempted to thrust back at him while she gave moans of mingled pain and pleasure.

For a moment he propped himself up on his elbows and stared down at her. She gazed back through heavy lidded eyes. He ducked his head and gave each nipple a hard bite. She cried out at last when he told her how he would, in the future, pierce those nipples with needles and thread more needles through pinches of skin on the breasts themselves. And as he began to thrust in earnest, seeking only his own pleasure, she responded with cries of growing ecstasy and as he achieved a climax that felt as though half his innards were being dragged out through his cock, beneath him Rae gave three almighty bucks that almost threw him off her. And then they both collapsed.

About half an hour later Rae went onto tip toe and kissed him timidly on the steps of the office building.

"Thank you," she whispered.

"You have some talent, Rae. As we discussed, I'll train you for the moment," Paul told her. "Report to my office on Wednesday afternoon straight after five o'clock and I'll introduce your delightful arse to the riding crop or the cane."

"Yes, Master." She gave him a genuine and brilliant smile and then walked off. Paul watched her go – a relaxed, self confident sway to her hips. She had proved herself submissive, fit and strong. Not that he was going to tell Maggie that! He wanted to know what her ulterior motive had been, the cover story wasn't all that had been going on. He suspected that she would be in touch.

CHAPTER SIXTEEN

Vanessa took a sip of her Pino and looked across the table at Nigel who was ordering dinner for the three of them. It was a pleasant, fairly intimate sort of place – positively swanky compared to Vanessa's usual eateries! She didn't know what she was having to eat because Nigel said it was up to him as their Master to choose. Vanessa wasn't entirely sure why but she suspected that it was just another way that he exerted his dominance over them. As far as she was concerned his reasons didn't matter anyway. What was important was that it was the second time he had taken both his girls out to dinner and she hoped that like the last time, the evening would end with the three of them in his bed.

The memories of the first time were still vivid. It had stripped her mind of any doubts about how she should define her new-found sexual orientation. She simply didn't care what the label was. She loved it.

He had allowed her and Maggie to go to bed ahead of him while he finished a nightcap of ten year old malt whisky and by the time he came up, they were deeply entwined, so Vanessa hadn't really registered Nigel's naked body climbing into the bed on the other side of Maggie. A male hand had suddenly been fumbling for her breast while she was suckling at Maggie's nipples. Maggie's groans of pleasure grew louder as she felt her master's firm and smooth body press against her back and from then on the night had been one sensual explosion after another.

Some moments even now stood out clear and intense so that to recall them, which she did often, replaying them nightly when alone in her own bed or when she was idling at work in front of the computer, and they always left her hot and wet; there was the moment when she had been lying head to toe with the other two so that she could kiss and lick Nigel's superb length of cock as well as lap at Maggie's fragrant cunt, still leaking Nigel's sperm. At her own groin, from behind, Maggie's tongue roved into places she never would have believed a woman would put her tongue but the feeling was exquisite! Even more so since every time she arched her back, she thrust her vulva onto Nigel's gloriously abrasive and undeniably skilful tongue. There was the time when Nigel had lain on her, his shaft spearing her to her cervix while Maggie had kissed her face… soft, angel-kisses from forehead to chin. Perhaps that had been the most erotic moment of all, when her cunt was under siege while Maggie had mischievously wooed and soothed her into the very sweetest submission, only to tighten the mental screw that little bit more.

"Fuck her hard, Master! Make her scream, I love hearing her scream and then let me lick her out." Maggie had looked down into Vanessa's wide eyes and smiled archly, adding an ardent, "Please, Master!"

She had duly screamed and he had duly allowed Maggie to lick her clean. Nigel's stamina had been awesome and Vanessa didn't care a hoot about the fact that there had been giggling at work about the way her eyes never left him now when he was in the office. If they only knew what she knew…. Fuck! Nigel was such a skilled performer he could drive her insane with just the tip of his tongue – if she had only known that the man she had thought of as Pervy Pickett had a tongue that could wriggle its way into even the tiniest crevice of her cunt and give her an orgasm that could send her half way to the moon she would have encouraged his advances long ago. Not to mention his awesome fucking…..

But just now he was speaking and she wrenched her attention back to his words.

"…….So if we can arrange it, would you like another crack at Rae Carroll? This time for money. Big money!"

"Sorry?" she spluttered at the sudden shock, and found her amazement greater than her embarrassment at her unladylike conduct. But Rae Carroll had been the very last person on earth she had been thinking about. Money? What had that to do with anything?

She felt Maggie's reassuring hand on her knee beneath the table.

"Our Master wants to join a very wealthy SM club, the sort of place that the country's high flyers go to, to unwind. It's not far from here and the entertainment….you'll like this bit, Vee…. is centred around the submission of women to their masters. And our Master thinks that if he could stage a fight between you and Rae, as good as the one you had in the office, for the members, then we could all join. And from what I hear it's heaven for girls like us. We're not the only ones, there are others like us – think what it would be like to be amongst our own kind, girls who serve their Masters the way we do."

Even then much of it went over Vanessa's head for such was her joy at being with the two people who had come to mean so much to her that she could not see beyond that evening. She looked across at Maggie's warmly smiling face, her eyes sparkling with delight at the prospect of another night in Nigel's bed. Then she looked at Nigel. He was regarding her with deep intensity, his eyes boring into her in a way she was becoming familiar with; a way that turned her knees to water and had her fingers fluttering in their haste to undress for him. Never in a million years would she have thought that her boss at work had such a well-toned body beneath his workaday suit.

"Whatever you want," she said, and she meant it. There was one condition though and she flashed a saucy grin from one to the other as heated anticipation flooded her veins. "Can I stay over with you after dinner, please?"

Nigel and Maggie smiled.

"Of course," Nigel said. "And I'll do some needle play on Maggie's tits for you. How's that sound?"

It sounded perfect to Vanessa.

***

"Paul, it's Maggie."

Paul smiled grimly and put the phone on speaker so he could sit back at ease. "So, what have you got to say for yourself?"

"That depends rather on how things are going," Maggie's voice was a little tremulous and he picked up on it and did his best to inject a touch of displeasure into his voice.

"The girl was a total bitch. A scheming, manipulative tart. Do you have any idea how much trouble she caused me?"

She was clearly uncertain how to proceed and her voice was coloured with contrition.

"Oh dear! Paul, may I ask…..is she…..is she still…..with you?"

Paul looked to his right at the naked figure with the heavy leather hood over its head, blocking out all sound and sight. It was stretched out on the board table, buttocks pushed up into delicious prominence by the hard surface, its wrists and ankles strapped securely to either end. The thighs and buttocks were heavily striated with thick red lines caused by the heavy strap that he had left lying across its back.

"Yes. She's still here," he said.

"May I......may I come and see you?"

His answer was swift and conveyed, he hoped, grave displeasure. After all, even a slave as experienced as Maggie must be kept on her toes!

"On one condition. Your new master doesn't touch you between now and then. I want you in prime condition for punishment. Be here on Friday evening."

He hung up and then went back over to Rae, who jumped when she felt his hand on her back. In the week or so that had passed since he had broken her, she had surpassed all his expectations. She was immensely fit and seemed to love having her body tested to the very limits. But so far he hadn't been able to find any limits! But then he still had a lot of things to try. In his experience, the hood usually had one of two effects on the wearer – they either felt safe and warm in their cosy cocoon, or totally lost and notable only as a body to exploit....or ignore! Apart from smell and touch, all that was left to her was thought and sensation, both of which would be crystalline and sharp without the hindrance of the other senses. With slow delicacy he took up the thick strap and pulled it away so she would have no idea where the next lash was going to fall.

So what did Maggie want? He ran the leather tongue through his fingers, admiring the depth of Rae's chest and the way her breast squeezed out to the side on the polished mahogany. Her breathing continued deep and even, although she must be expecting the scorch of the lash at any second.

Why had Maggie been so desperate to get rid of such a splendid specimen as this? Oh, he knew she could have been troublesome – but it just didn't seem to add up. The story she had told him about her making eyes at her master.......he would have thought that Maggie was capable of coping with that kind of inconvenience – there was more to it than that.

Suddenly he lifted the strap right back over his shoulder and let fly. The Crack! of the impact shocked even him, but Rae's breathing hardly did more than check for a second and her head lifted. He watched the red flare bloom on her pale skin across her shoulders and then lashed her again across the buttocks this time. Then without a pause he let fly three, four, five rapid lashes with no pauses between them. Two bit deeply across her shoulders, one smacked her quivering buttocks, the next bit at her thighs and the final one he pulled back to deliver so that the end of the strap snapped down on her left thigh and bit deep into her groin. Her head flew up at that last one and a strained cry came from under the hood, where a stopple blocked her perfect, delectably soft mouth with great efficiency.

Paul undid the ties at her wrists and ankles and helped her to her feet, then he unbuckled the hood and pulled it off Rae's head. She emerged blinking, tousled and flushed but with admirable submission dropped straight to her knees.

This time he allowed her to use her fingers to undo his flies but still the clever working of her throat on his helm prompted a quick ejaculation but this time she swallowed every drop.

Maggie knocked on Paul's office door in a state of deep unease. She knew just how awful Rae Carroll could be and Paul had sounded so angry!

If Rae had irritated him that badly then her plan was hopelessly derailed and she might even lose Nigel to Vanessa, forever. Much as she adored watching Vanessa develop as an adventurous sub, she could see that Nigel was entranced by her as well and the fear of being displaced fleetingly caught in her throat. But the saving grace of the situation was that for the moment he was even more entranced by having two compliant and submissive women at his beck and call. Whether that would be enough to compensate him for losing his chance of membership of Lewington House, of waving goodbye to his long-held and valued goal, was something that remained to be seen. There had to be something she could do.

She had come straight from her own office and was wearing her usual Miss Huffer clothes and with her hair pulled back unflatteringly.

"Yes?" Paul said when she entered, looking up blankly from his work.

Her heart sank. Not a good start. This was not going to plan at all.

"It's me……Maggie," she stammered.

"What the hell are you looking like that for?" he asked after a moment's silent astonishment.

"It's how my Master wants me to look."

"Why?"

"He says that only he should know what I really look like." Without being told to she removed the pins from her hair and shook her shining, sable tresses free. A single hair caught across her lips and she raised a trailing finger to pull it away.

"I see. You know I get the feeling there's an awful lot you haven't been telling me and I'm going to thrash every last ounce of truth out of you. You know where the equipment is, get the cane out and strip down!"

Maggie obeyed, still not knowing whether anything could be salvaged of her plan but well aware that Vanessa was going to be on the receiving end of another fabulously painful caning, even while she was suffering under Paul's hands. Looked at like that, she thought as she swung the drinks shelves aside and took out the familiar thin, whippy scourge of female backsides, she might as well enjoy what she could and hope for the best.

Paul was fascinated by the state of her breasts and watched in silence as she unwrapped them and released their glory. He marvelled at the way such magnificent specimens could be flattened so completely, then spent some time playing with them before clamping the nipples cruelly hard and having her bend forwards over one of the long sides of the board table. She heard him swish the cane in the air a few times and then retreat a couple of paces. Her insides trembled in a most alarming way for she felt as if her whole future would be decided over the next hour or so. Nervously she craned her head around.

"Look to the front!" Paul snapped. "I will be asking questions about this wretched Rae Carroll and each question will be preceded by a stroke of the cane delivered as hard as I can. The more of the truth you tell me, and the quicker, then the sooner your pain will stop…….and I don't intend this to be a pleasure for you, Maggie, not in any sense of the word. Now get down!"

Her knees were trembling as she obeyed his terse command and feeling very vulnerable and naked, in a delightful but scary sort of way she had not felt since the early days of her slavery, Maggie pressed her clamped breasts down and screwed her eyes tight shut as she heard Paul begin to stride towards her.

Crack!

She couldn't help crying out instantly as fire blazed through the fleshy cushions of her arse cheeks. It was the hardest stroke she had ever taken and she was momentarily blinded by the pyrotechnics behind her eyes.

"Tell me the real reason you wanted me to employ Rae Carroll," Paul ordered. But before she could catch her breath and reply he strode forward and another numbing slash ripped across her bottom. The echo of the fireworks blended with the new explosion and once again there was a frightful heat across her flesh.

"She was a bitch and she was going to try and blackmail my Master!" she howled as soon as she had breath enough to spare for speech.

"She fought with another girl, Vanessa! I knew he fancied her as well and I was scared I'd lose him!"

Her voice rose to a shriek as she heard him stride forward again.

Crack!

"A real fight, not an argument!" Once again the footfalls. But there was no time to brace herself.

Crack!

"Master was furious with me when he found out what I did! He wanted her to fight Vanessa again but for money and so we could join a club!"

Crack!

This time it was quite a few moments before she could stop sobbing and her whole body shook. She hoped like hell that one day Nigel would find out how hard she had been beaten for him. Just as Paul had promised, this went way beyond pleasure, into the realms of .....of what? With her arse ablaze and her thoughts in disarray, she had no time to work it out and her tears puddled on the polished wood as she tried to form words to beg for mercy.

"Please don't hit me again! Please I'm telling you the truth! I admit I didn't care if she caused you trouble, I just wanted her out of my life – and Master's! No!!"

She heard the footfalls and another scalding hurt speared deep into her abused buttocks.

"Please! I'm telling you the truth! Give me a chance!" She sobbed brokenly for a few moments more but mercifully there were no footsteps from behind her. She sniffed and snuffled and began a detailed account of what had really gone on, the truth flowing out of her as if a dam had been burst. Instead of the glossed over story about petty rivalries she had originally used to get him to take Rae on she opened her heart. And she finished with Nigel's plan to have the girls fight for money and membership of Lewington House.

"I hoped you might tame her and then you could make her fight for you," she said finally, exhausted.

"You're a scheming minx, Maggie!" And to a despairing scream from her he marched forward one more time and inscribed more bitterly deep and bruising tramlines across her raging backside.

He stood back and examined his handiwork critically.

It was definitely one of his better efforts he decided. The tramlines were deep and long, testament to how hard he had laid the strokes on, marking the depth to which the buttocks had flattened under the strike. Already there was some bruising around the deep red that in turn surrounded the lines. Her body was shaking as she sobbed in pain and despair and that was making the devastated hinds quiver most pleasingly. Her Master should be proud of her, he thought. One had to admire her capacity to stand it! And once he had given Maggie the good news about Rae, it was clear that he ought to meet him. But first, should he put an end to her suffering? No, she was far too pretty.

"Hold fast, Maggie. I've not finished with you yet!"

He strode in again before she could respond and cracked home another lash that flattened the delicious curves of her arse and sent an exciting shock wave through the meat of the buttocks. Maggie's scream was a throat rasping one that only briefly interrupted the not-quite-heart-rending sobbing.

He stepped back and considered again. Really if it hadn't been for the blatantly open and bedewed cunt between the agonised buttocks, he would have stopped there. But as it was she threw her head up in the most attractive manner and she howled as the shaft of the cane curled back as he swung it forwards yet again and then it impacted, devilishly harsh – and ball-boilingly satisfying

– with the tip leaving a deep crater on her hip as he mis-aimed just slightly.

Her fingers were no longer clenched on the table's edges, they were fluttering and waving back by her bottom, her palms submissively out begging for mercy.

"Move your hands if you don't want them thrashed too!" he told her, implicitly rejecting her plea. She was going to be so grateful to him when he broke the good news.

He watched the hands move hesitantly back to gripping the table and then strode forwards, putting all his strength into the stroke. Then he did it again. And one more time. The fact that she just groaned in the wake of her bottom flexing, rippling and swaying in the aftermath of the strikes alerted him to the fact that she had probably taken all that would be any fun to inflict. He put the cane down, unzipped his flies and with some trouble pulled his throbbingly hard cock free, then he approached her once more and with some reserve of strength she reared up in surprise as she felt him nudge her entrance and then push into her. He kept pushing till he was lodged right up to the hilt and he was pressed against her rear end.

She groaned once more and as he leaned over his gaze took in her tear-streaked face and the mess on the table where she had snuffled and cried her way through what he admitted was a diabolically harsh beating. He could feel the way her body was trembling as each sob was wrenched from down in her very depths and he decided that if he was going to have any fun with this fuck, it was time he broke the good news.

He took a fistful of her hair and pulled her head back so he could whisper in her ear as he began to move inside her.

"You were right, Maggie. I could tame Rae Carroll quite easily………and I did! I broke her to the whip a couple of weeks ago. Tell your master I'll meet him and we'll discuss terms."

He felt the tension drain out of her like water through a handful of sand. Her voice, huskily low-toned from her sobs and screams, oozed more gratitude than he had ever reaped from her before.

"Oh, Paul! Oh, thank you! Thank you! Please fuck me as hard as you beat me! Let me suck you dry! Bugger me! Do everything you want to me!"

He laughed as he set to work fucking her. Later on he would do everything she asked and send her home to her Master in a state that would delight him no end.

**

Vanessa opened the back door of Nigel's house later that night and couldn't help giving a squeak of dismay as Maggie limped into the light of the kitchen. Her hair was a fright, her cheeks and chin had crusted sperm on them but she was grinning from ear to ear.

"Fuck! What happened to you?" Vanessa asked as Nigel came through from the lounge.

"Paul Gregory happened to me!" she said with a laugh, and then turned to Nigel. "Great news, Master! It worked! It all worked out fine. He's got her under his thumb and he's sure she'll do whatever he says."

"That's excellent news, and just as well for you," Nigel replied. "But I take it he was not amused by your dumping the bitch on him under false pretences."

"Not at first, but I think he was feeling better by the time he'd finished with me!"

"What did he do to you?" Vanessa asked a little too eagerly as she took her coat.

Bright-eyed, Maggie laughed again. "It'd be quicker if I told you what he didn't do to me!"

"Just make a proper report!" Nigel snapped and instantly Maggie quietened down and gathered her wits as best she could given her present state.

"He wants to meet you, Master," she said simply.

"When and where?"

Maggie risked another impish grin and began to unbutton her blouse. "He said he'd give me a message for you that I couldn't forget."

She shrugged off the blouse to reveal she was braless and Vanessa gasped at the thick rope-like welts that covered her entire torso, breasts as well. And even Nigel gave a snort of amazement when he saw the note. It had been drawing pinned to the inside curve of her left tit and now she proudly pushed out her chest to offer it to her Master who, without praise or compliment prised out the pins. He handed them to Vanessa and read the note. He smiled.

"That'll be fine. And I expect he asked me to confirm if I could make it?"

Maggie nodded, biting her lip.

Nigel went to a drawer, took out a notepad and scribbled quickly, then he returned to Vanessa who anticipated his command and held out the pins. He stuck his note to her right tit, told her to dress and gave her the cab fare.

He and Vanessa were in bed when she returned for the second time and fell in beside Vanessa once she had undressed. Nigel told her to go to sleep but Vanessa gently kissed her breasts in the dark while both girls explored each other's welts with their fingers until Nigel sleepily threatened to thrash them both where they lay if one of them didn't give him a blow job immediately. Vanessa scrambled to obey and Maggie relaxed, almost delirious with pride and relief, as her Master dug his fingers into her tits while he came into Vanessa's increasingly accommodating mouth.

CHAPTER SEVENTEEN

The phone rang. Matthew Bartlett was alerted to it not by the bell, because that didn't ring, but by his phone secretary. She was on all fours by the side of his desk with the cradle's incoming call alarm wired to the rings in her labia. She gave a muffled squeal as the current was fed directly into her cunt. He reached over and took the handset from the cunt of another girl who was acting as his keyboard cushion. She was lying on her back on top of his desk with her hands restrained behind her back and her legs spread, her ankles tied down to the desk legs at one end and her head hanging off the other end with her long hair hovering just above the waste bin. A heavy leather hood rendered her completely anonymous and only the gentle rise and fall of her breasts betrayed any life. His computer keyboard lay on her stomach. He sat back with the handset. It was a specially designed instrument for Lewington, it had a phallus shaped handle below the actual handset so that it could safely be stored in a cunt without transferring any sticky secretions to the hand of the user.

"Bartlett here," he said. "Pickett! Where the hell have you been? I was expecting to eyeball those girls weeks ago." He sat still and listened for several minutes.

"So we're definitely back on track are we? Good! I'll wait to hear next week then."

He sat forward again and rammed the handle back into the desk girl's cunt, then idly twirled and tugged at her right nipple.

With his other hand he opened a drawer and pulled out a folder, he placed it on her lower stomach and from it he pulled the security photos that Nigel had originally shown him. He studied them for a little longer and smiled slowly, his assault on the nipple becoming fiercer. Eventually he put the photos down and went to look out of the window, where just outside, sparrows and starlings gathered around the bird table and splashed around in the bird bath. The bath was a shallow stone basin standing on a stone table. A girl had been tied down onto it on her back with her legs spread around the bath. Her body had been liberally sprinkled with bird seed so the sparrows and – Bartlett smiled to himself – the blue tits, swarmed over the naked form, pecking at her breasts and stomach. The girl was hooded and tied down so tightly that no movement beyond breathing was possible, making her an erotic sight as well as a practical asset to the gardens.

As he watched he brought his thoughts back to the photos of Pickett's girls. They were clearly good looking and he had to admit it, Pickett's idea had merit. Good looking girls who obviously hated each other and who would gladly do to each other what the onlookers would love to do to them – that could be a very lucrative proposition. And of course if they could be persuaded to keep their enmity going, there were other clubs as well.

Matthew Bartlett could feel the twin passions of his life; money and SM, coming together once again.

He turned around and approached the hooded head of the desk girl, whose mouth was held open with a ring gag, he reached into his trousers and freed his cock, then sank it between her anonymous lips, pushing in until he felt her practised throat stroke his helm. From above her he could see her throat work as well as feel it. Her breasts pushed her hard little nipples up at him and he braced himself by grabbing them then bucking his hips urgently at the girl's mouth. He had a meeting in a few minutes and just needed to release a load of spunk to be able to relax and handle it easily. The girl didn't fail him and he looked down to enjoy the sight of her throat working hard to swallow down every drop of his precious spend. He knew that being on the receiving end of a mouthful from him was considered an honour among the Lewington girls.

He pulled free once he had finished and bent down to take a towel from the phone girl's mouth, wipe himself and replace it. Then he left for his meeting.

**

"Twenty, Sir!"

Rae Carroll's voice was breathless and excited and she looked down at herself with nothing but pride, Paul noted with pleasure. Each of her spectacular tits was adorned with ten pegs and a nipple clamp. He wasn't finished yet though. He wanted each tit to sport three 'zippers', close together lines of pegs terminating at the areola. She had another ten to take on already whipped tit meat that he thought was probably quite tender by that time. Her wrists were raised and clipped to her collar which he had turned backwards so that the ring was at her nape. Her legs were spread and once he had finished with the tits he was going to start with the whip between her lovely, soft thighs. It was only six o'clock and her session had barely lasted an hour, she could take plenty more yet.

She really was coming along a treat and when she wasn't hooded she watched everything he did to her with the most expressive eyes that he had ever come across – and currently it was a look that revealed fascination and concern that tangled with an eagerness bordering on naked hunger. And she obeyed his orders with an engaging willingness that suggested she had been waiting all her life to be bossed around. And maybe she had, he mused as he let the jaws of yet another peg close on her flesh.

"Twenty-five!" she whispered.

Paul moved to work on her other tit and glanced up at her face; nothing but rapt attention and an excited smile.

He began to let the jaws of the peg close and then with them hovering over her succulent breast said, "You know a girl called Vanessa."

Her reaction was all he could have hoped for. As the peg's jaws closed, she jumped.

"What? How d'you know the bitch!?"

"Count the peg!" he told her sternly.

"Er.....twenty-seven! Where is the cow?"

"Wrong! And you do not ask me questions!"

Instantly her expressive blue eyes fastened on his, wide and anxious. For a moment there it had been the old Rae, brassy and demanding, but now the submissive was back – he was fairly sure.

"Brace yourself for punishment," he told her and went behind her. Between her legs the tails of a whip dangled, the handle lodged firmly in her cunt. He tugged it down and shook out the tails. She let out a grunt as it was wrenched from her body but settled her feet more firmly in anticipation of the lash.

He gave her ten with no warning and with no relaxation in his rhythm, he just blasted ten, fast, hard lashes and then stood back to assess her. Her ribs were heaving under her skin as she panted in the wake of the thrashing.

"That was for counting wrongly. Now for the indiscipline."

He gave her twenty in the same remorseless fashion. It was pure discipline and, just like with Maggie, not intended for her pleasure and when he went back to stand in front of her, her eyes were sparkling with tears.

"I'm sorry, Master!"

He was willing to bet she was, and that she was pretty furious with Vanessa too! Just the mention of her name had caused her to take thirty very hard lashes and from the look in those startling eyes, he was pretty sure she would want to get even. He was meeting Nigel Pickett the following afternoon and this reaction boded very well for future business.

He squatted down and re-inserted the whip into her oozing cunt then stood up and went back to the pegs.

"It was twenty-six. This is twenty-seven!"

Her breath hissed between her teeth as another pair of finely-sprung jaws snapped closed on her tit.

"Twenty-seven," she counted.

CHAPTER EIGHTEEN

The meeting between Nigel and Paul was arranged for Thursday afternoon. An agreement had been made by phone to keep Rae and Vanessa apart for the time being but Maggie was to be present at the meeting.

Eve had been told to make herself scarce and her apartment suited their purposes exactly.

Maggie arrived with Nigel at the appointed time to find Paul already there.

Nigel wasn't at all sure how he felt about sharing her – in all her natural splendour – with another man, especially when that man was her ex-master. But Paul had insisted and, for the sake of his plan, Nigel reluctantly agreed. After all, he'd have to share her at Lewington House if.....or rather when he became a member! He'd had her dress in stockings – with lacy suspenders – beneath her cream, knee-length dress with a scoop neck and pearly buttons from neck to hem. No underwear beyond that was permitted.

In the lounge there was a frosty moment when Paul forgot he no longer owned Maggie and gave her the order to pour drinks. Maggie's submissiveness landed her in trouble because she obeyed, unthinkingly. Nigel went icy calm until she stammered an apology and Paul too apologised with such a disarming grin that peace broke out at once.

For a few moments the men made small talk and the ice continued to thaw. Then quite suddenly, Paul changed the subject.

"Well, we both know what we're here for," he said, "so I suggest we get on with it." He unfolded himself and stood up. "This way."

Once inside Eve's delightfully feminine, rose-and-oyster coloured bedroom with little pink porcelain vases of flowers everywhere, Paul was minded to suggest to Nigel that Maggie be suspended and he opened his mouth to speak but noticed Nigel's attention was focussed on the sturdy, antique four-poster bed that Paul had picked up at auction.

"It goes so well with the apartment, don't you think?" he said.

Nigel nodded his agreement and as his gaze wandered around the room he wondered what a place like this would cost. He could certainly appreciate its suitability – the ceilings were certainly high enough to suspend a girl from! And then he noticed the two chains hanging down and smiled.

Paul took the smile as a green light on his unspoken suggestion. He directed Maggie to where he wanted her to stand a couple of feet away from the end of the bed and positioned her between the posts once she had stripped.

Standing exactly where he indicated, Maggie stood facing into the room. In the full-length mirror she could she herself standing with her legs open wide with the oyster coloured quilted duvet on the bed behind and cushions galore in rose, oyster and pink propped up against the pillows.

"So, these two girls – Vanessa and Rae. What is it between them?" Paul asked as he stretched Maggie's arm upward and fixed her restraint to the chain which hung from the ceiling.

"Hatred," Nigel said offhandedly as he twisted the wrist restraint on her arm to site the ring more conveniently then attached the other chain.

"Has to be a man at the heart of it," Paul said with casual arrogance. Crossing toward the bed he bent down to pull a chain from underneath the bed that was looped around the bottom of the bedpost and then he fixed her ankle restraint to the other end.

"I'm not so sure," Nigel secured her other ankle to the corresponding chain. "It seems to go way back." He waved his hand in a dismissive gesture toward his slave and willing to concur with the other man's preference he asked, "Gag?"

"No need. The place is pretty isolated and the walls thick. Besides, I'm rather partial to Maggie's screams. Blindfold?"

Still not completely at ease with the man who knew his slave so well and not sure what his preference was – and not sure if he wanted to concede to all his preferences anyway – Nigel's answer was an equivocal, "No."

Paul picked up on Nigel's unease and understanding that whether he meant to or not he – Paul – was adding to the dilemma, he pointed to one of the tall, antique pine wardrobes.

"I'll leave the choice to you. Help yourself."

Nigel opened the wardrobe to find an impressive collection of whips, floggers and paddles hanging neatly. Also, stacked on four shelves were several different hoods and blindfolds, an assortment of gags, ropes of varying lengths and thickness and chains, needles, candles, clamps. The temptation to be greedy and choose a bucket-load was almost overwhelming but Nigel was determined to play it cool so he selected a device for crushing breasts – Maggie would like that – and a flogger with long, flat leather blades for himself and a braided leather flogger for Paul. That would do for starters, he told himself as he re-crossed the room.

Believing that verbal abuse and ridicule were much overlooked joys Nigel told her sneeringly, "Pay attention, slut. You're going to be in so much pain when we've crushed your tits that it'll be pure agony when they're bound for work tomorrow. And it'll give me a real hard-on to think of your suffering all day. In fact, I'm so looking forward to it that I might bind them before we even leave here and keep you bound all night!" By way of explanation he told her former master, "I find the bitch more governable when those fucking melons of hers are kept under control. And she's a better shag too."

Paul concurred happily as he helped Nigel to fit the metal breast bars in place.

Made from two adjustable horizontal bars, one above the other and an inch wide, the fit could be adjusted by moving the top one up and down the vertical rods at each end, to which wing nuts were fixed. There was also a central rod to separate the breasts. Working together the masters fed Maggie's lovely mounds through the twin openings, pushing the device bruisingly back against her ribs. When they were satisfied that it was a snug fit, with a nod of agreement they began to tighten the nuts so that the two horizontals were drawn closer and closer together, squashing her breasts between them. Ignoring her whimpers, Paul returned to the real reason for their meeting.

"So these girls," he began as they tightened the nuts further to inflict even more discomfort, "you're sure there's enough interest in the idea?"

Maggie groaned as her breasts were agonisingly crushed almost flat at their roots. She'd grown used to having them flattened against her chest by the tape but this was something completely new. And the fact that she was to some extent enjoying it, in that strange way that many submissives have of extracting pleasure from even the cruellest torment, wasn't of interest to the two dominants. They had far more important things to discuss than a slave's pleasure!

"I've spoken to Bartlett and he agrees with me that there's considerable mileage in the idea. But only if we allow them – encourage them – to take it as far as they'd really like to go."

He paid no attention to his slave's groans of pain as they fixed the nuts in their final position and neither man noticed her sly smile at being the plaything of two dominants who were running together at last.

"Yes, I imagine it's got to be more than just slapping each other around a bit," Paul said.

Maggie's breasts blossomed in a most attractive way from the device and the men watched as they began to change hue, first an attractive pink which turned red before their eyes. Not only that but her rubbery nuggets hardened into praiseworthy tumescence though neither man deigned to comment.

"When they fight again, it's got to be like when they were in the office – I assume my slut's told you – and then beyond."

Maggie's tits were taking on a slight blue tinge and the nipples were growing ever darker.

Paul took up the braided leather flogger. Nigel followed suit and reached for the bladed one.

"Tits or cunt?" Nigel asked generously.

"Cunt."

Hardly had the word left his lips before Paul dealt a devastating blow between her legs. It had the thud of a sledgehammer and Maggie sucked in her breath.

Less than a heartbeat later Nigel's leather struck her fully across the ballooned meat of her imprisoned breasts, producing a scream such as he had never heard pass her lips before; even the needles hadn't engendered such a pain-soaked sound. It was most gratifying. Appreciative too of the wet-and-wide-eyed look on her face he struck again, this time with Paul's thudding lashes landing a split second after his.

"I take my hat off to you if you've really tamed that blonde bit," Nigel congratulated, then struck again.

Maggie cried out as the strike detonated across the taut skin of her breasts and shuddered through to her insides. She glanced down at her breasts and welcomed their sweet suffering as a token of her Master's affection, for he did so love to torment her tits to anguish. Only one thing would have made her happier – to see Vanessa suffering in the same way alongside her.

Nigel squeezed in another strike before Paul, who delivered a thunderous whack to her cunt straight afterward.

Maggie's yell faded abruptly as the impact was so fierce it drove the breath from her.

"I'm confident Rae's under control, yes," Paul said at last. "What about this Vanessa character? Will she co-operate?"

"She'll do what I say."

And so they continued, first one then the other laying down the hellish strikes. Until finally they were unable to carry on a conversation for the shrieks and yells emanating from Maggie's throat, they decided they would have to gag her after all. Once again Nigel made the choice and he came back with a very decent ball gag.

"Good choice. Blue to match her breasts," Paul laughed.

This time they synchronised their blows so that she received a demolishing thud to her honey-drizzling nether regions at the same time as a breast-exploding strike. And as her eyes widened and muffled groans added to their sense of well being they exchanged ideas about their proposed venture.

After a while, Nigel queried if they should change implements and was delighted when Paul suggested a single tail. Not only that but he suggested they have another shot of malt first.

"We could do with a breather," he said. "It really takes it out of a man."

Nigel was happy to accept and before he followed Paul back into the lounge, he slipped a heavy leather hood over her head and zipped it firmly up at the back. Left in silent darkness that brought the world suddenly to an end, Maggie sobbed as her breasts pounded and ached, her crotch stung and burned furnace-hot and fierce. And, quite irrationally considering her cruel bondage, her heart soared.

Her two dominants had clearly settled down and were getting along just fine. Even better, it was clear that the cause of their increased good humour was her body and that boosted her sense of femininity no end. They both enjoyed playing with it and it was very unlikely that they were going to stop now. And somehow just knowing that brought about a deep sense of self-worth. They had tried to make her anonymous with the hood and, though she always found the idea of being just an object was horny, it also had an opposite effect – she knew exactly who she was! She was happy, whole and perfect….well, almost. Her mind was at peace anyway, it was only her agitated, pain-racked and pain-seeking body that refused to co-operate! She had to tell herself over and over that this was just a pause in the proceedings. She tried as best she could to be patient but it really would have helped if they had freed her poor breasts.

She had no concept of time and unable to see her surroundings, her mind set off on a switch-back of emotions. Minutes became hours and it felt as if her breasts had been crushed forever. She fidgeted as much as her bonds would allow and eventually, as the pain became too great and blotted out her peaceful euphoria of moments earlier she whimpered. Then her heart nearly jumped into her throat as she felt a hand on one inflamed nipple. It was insanely sensitive after the abuse it had suffered and the merest touch sent daggers of pain stabbing into her breast. And with the touch came the knowledge that the two men had probably been standing right in front of her, enjoying her distress. That was sweet!

Then she felt hands unscrewing the brutal wing nuts and the pressure began to ease, however the pounding only increased as blood flowed back. She let out a gag-muffled moan and heard both men chuckle in a way that had her melting all over again. She knew that when dominant men enjoyed a submissive's suffering like that, that sub was in for a hellishly good time. She felt hands at her ankles, unclipping her restraints and then she was turned around to face the bed and re-fastened. Coils of arousal started up again, beginning in her twitching cunt and ending in the warmth of her belly. She always enjoyed a good leathering to her back and inwardly she smiled. Once more her heart soared, but this time with the stark recognition that she was an object after all – a beautiful, vulnerable and willing object to be used for their pleasure.

Then the hood was unzipped and pulled off. She blinked in the bright light and in that same way as when Nigel removed her tapes she recoiled at the relative freedom as she shook her hair out.

"I was very impressed with the office look you impose on her," she heard Paul tell Nigel. "It took me a while to recognise her."

"Thanks." There was such a note of pride in her Master's voice as he went on that that made Maggie's heart flutter too. "They're good tits and I like the thought that she has to keep them just for me. Do you want to start?"

"I'd be delighted."

From nowhere a heavy impact almost knocked her off her feet and it was only the chains that kept her upright. A stinging pain scorched into her skin from her left shoulder to the side of her pain-soaked right breast. She jerked and twisted instinctively, even though there was nowhere she could hide, even had she wanted to. Another lash scythed across her back and she wrenched at her chains again.

"I suppose we ought to see this man Bartlett then?" Paul asked as a third lash sent lightning-pain across her flesh. "She's got terrific tits for whipping hasn't she? Here, you take it for a bit."

"Thanks."

In an instant her eyes were screwed up in pain and she nearly scoured her throat by trying to scream at the next lash. It was one of the hardest Nigel had ever delivered and its venomous tip curled right around her ribs and snapped at her stomach.

"Nice shot, Nigel!"

While Nigel was bolstered by Paul's praise, he watched as instinct had a woozy, air-brained Maggie trying to stamp her feet and hunch over while the chains inhibited her success. He merely accepted Paul's compliment without a word and acknowledged Maggie's futile struggling with a smile as he prepared for the next strike. Then the nerve-shattering lash caught Maggie's left breast and set her to trying to twist sideways in a most amusing way.

"How much were you thinking of paying the girls?" Paul asked thoughtfully, his hungry gaze eating her up as he took in the erupting, fiery lines across Maggie's flesh.

"I hadn't really arrived at a figure," Nigel said and then fired in a lash that bit round her hips and smacked right into the tenderness of her groin. Maggie groaned and tried to close her legs.

"Hah! Good shot! Why not just pay them prize money?" Paul suggested.

Maggie heard the whip changing hands again and braced

herself for an assault from her left. But instead of feeling frail after such a beating as she had so far endured, at that moment she felt empowered….it was as if she were the one with the real power because it was her ripe and yielding body that turned them into nothing more than lustful partners in pleasure. And their casual use of her as they discussed matters which, on the face of it, seemed of more importance only heightened her sense of worth rather than decreasing it. After all, this afternoon they were incapable of discussing business without her there.

"I've never been much of a betting man I'm afraid," Nigel said as Maggie recovered shudderingly from Paul's thudding lash across her buttocks and another dig into her groin.

"It's simple," Paul said. Another lash that wrapped her sensitised breast made the chains jingle as Maggie reared onto her toes and twisted all over again. "You just sell tickets and set aside some for prize money."

This time Maggie rattled her chains noisily as yet another lash made her jerk madly.

"That would get rid of any need to pay them up front, certainly."

Maggie tried to suck in as much air as possible to calm herself in the respite as the whip was handed over once more.

Nigel set about making her buttocks radiant with welts and gave her hardly any time between lashes.

"Indeed. And of course, we could build in incentives to fight till they dropped," Paul explained.

"I hadn't thought of it like that," Nigel said, taking a brief rest. He joined Paul in taking in the streaks emblazoned across Maggie's perspiration-beaded flesh. "It seems I'm not much of an entrepreneur either!"

He returned to the attack and made Maggie jump and twitch time after time, her gag-impeded screams once again making conversation difficult. Giving up for the time being he concentrated his efforts instead on his slave, laying several blinders down over a matter of minutes.

When at last she hung sweating and limp without as much as a whimper, with her eyelids fluttering the men resumed their conversation as if there had been no break.

"Never mind, Nigel. You're a good man with a whip and that's all that matters," Paul said. "Bartlett will want a cut, but we can negotiate that. Now, I don't know about you but I reckon this piece is just right for taking us both for a richly deserved ride."

They took Maggie down and with her arms draped around their shoulders helped her stumble over to the bed. When they released their hold she buckled at the knees and fell forward. They let her sprawl face down on the bed for a moment to prepare herself for them and Nigel coiled the whip carefully.

"I think I'm very glad you came on board, Paul. You can provide the business sense for this project, so please feel free to choose your hole."

Paul looked down at the slack-limbed form on the bed. Between the shapely and deliciously whipped thighs, a slight damp patch was already visible on the satin quilted duvet.

"For old time's sake, I'll take her twat," he laughed. "She was always a great shag after a beating. But I insist you come round one night and let me watch you cut loose on Eve, I reckon I've been too soft on her now I've seen you in action."

Nigel was delighted at the compliment and was only too pleased to cede Maggie's cunt to Paul in return. He helped him drag Maggie further across the bed with her arse closest to Paul who had his back to Eve's dressing table beside the window while she was facing the three little white shelves of girlie-type knick-knacks. She just had time to spot Eve's incongruous, pink cuddly bunny before Nigel blocked her view entirely as he moved to take his place at her mouth. Leaning inward with his knees pressing hard against the mattress, he cupped her head in his hands and just looked down at her and their eyes met in a moment of stark understanding. Then he released her and stroked her hair before running his fingers through his own, stalling she thought, as he waited to see if Paul stripped naked or just plunged straight in.

When she felt hands lifting her hips as Paul arranged her more satisfactorily she tried her hardest to help by shuffling her knees under her just a little, while with concentrated effort she watched Nigel unzip his trousers, she knew it would be willpower alone that kept her going. She was anxious to repay the men by giving them the best fuck she could and didn't want to let either of them down. For as much as she had once loved Paul she realised now that she was more deeply in love with Nigel than ever and would always remind him of how gloriously he had beaten her tonight. As she watched Nigel unbuttoning his shirt, she told herself she would always be grateful to Paul – he had rescued her plan as well as inspiring Nigel's whipping. She was going to be such a good girl for them tonight!

She craned her head round to watch as Paul stood behind her – gloriously naked with a tanned and sculpted chest – she noted his strong fingers holding his thick cock when he took aim. Then her gaze watched his concentrated, passion-infused face as she felt him slide into her, spreading her and stimulating her sheath exquisitely. She closed her eyes and savoured the feel of it. Hands unbuckled the gag as she began to move in response to the thrusts behind her and she felt that life couldn't get much better – this was gilt-edged living – and she opened her eyes again as she turned her head eagerly to the front to embrace her master's divinely proportioned, rock-hard cock with her lips and do him the service he deserved. She was pleasantly surprised that he had also stripped naked and although not as tanned as Paul he was just as hard-chested and toned. Both men dug their hard and ardent fingers into her welts as they fucked her and Nigel's were exceptionally keen as he mauled her tits. So painful were their joint ministrations that even around the thick and lengthy cock that filled her mouth and throat she was able to gurgle her appreciation.

It was amazing how they worked together, she thought, timing their thrusts so that they went into her moist, warm holes at the same time, she was delirious with pride at how hard she was being tested. And she knew without a sliver of a doubt that she was equal to the challenge! She'd show them what a real slave could do! She gripped hard with her internal muscles, and then with the extraordinary control that hours of practice had resulted in, she did a series of rapid clenches of her pelvic floor muscles that drew moans of pleasure from her former master as he spurted a pleasingly heavy load of warm spunk deep into her. And as her present master began to spurt into her throat she swallowed with practised ease at the same time. There was just a little at first, but true to form it was followed by an enviable amount as if he had been saving it up for a week, which he most certainly hadn't. The fact that she herself didn't come – she had been close several times but was just too exhausted – was a minor detail that she hoped Vanessa would be allowed to attend to later.

CHAPTER NINETEEN

Two days afterwards, in his playroom with the Venetian blind drawn for privacy and the light on, Nigel set the digital camera carefully and used the whipping bench in lieu of a tripod. He took a moment to direct the beam of the free-standing light toward his subjects. Then he hurried around to pick up the suede flogger – the new one with the easy-grip handle – and began to belabour Maggie and Vanessa's backs. They were both suspended, side by side by their wrists in his frame and their welted nakedness repaid his trouble in building it a thousand times over. Their screams as the lash fell blended into a duet of pain that set his heart beating faster. What the hell he had done to deserve two such bloody wonderful sluts he couldn't imagine, he was just thankful he had done it! Even so, there were limits to how much a man could take.

"Quiet!" He didn't want to gag them, not today, not for the camera. They both had beautiful mouths, especially Vanessa whose wide mouth was blessed with exceptionally full, fleshy lips that promised a man the suck of a lifetime.

He gave them a quick score or so of lashes and then went back to the camera to check that it had captured the sequence properly. They looked lovely together, side by side, like sisters with their sleek, dark hair parted at their napes and swept over their shoulders to present him with easily assessable canvases to work on. He took another sequence and then another of him whipping the girls with different whips. Then he zoomed in on Vanessa, who had delighted him by turning up today with her gaudy belly-bar removed and, in its place, a plain ring, just like the ones he had seen piercing the tits and cunt lips of the Lewington girls.

He freed Maggie and then had her film while he took a stock whip to Vanessa's back. Then he had her track around Vanessa's erotically athletic, naked body – a body which would soon be making him a good deal of money – hung by its wrists and panting in the wake of a sound thrashing, her magnificent breasts scored and tracked with narrow, pulsing welts. She looked superb.

Job completed, he took the camera from Maggie and reviewing the films he congratulated himself on the excellent results. The explicit images not only captured the aesthetics of a well-toned sub's hard-earned stripes but also hinted at the sizzling sensuality that was at the very core of the girl. With the camera still in his hand, as he approached her and thrust two violently-driven fingers of the other hand into her shamelessly wet and fuck-ready tunnel, he couldn't help wondering how Paul was getting on with the other slut, whether he would capture the essence of her sexuality the way he – and Maggie – had with Vanessa.

Across the town at that very moment, things were shaping up very nicely. Paul had the delightfully co-operative and naked Rae hung by her bound ankles from a hook that hung from the small chandelier nearest the door of his office, her fluttering fingers were just unable to touch the carpet as she swung to and fro and twisted under the driving whip, the cord hissing and slicing at her at the end of the long, whippy pole.

Like Vanessa she wasn't gagged. Although Paul had warned her to keep quiet, it didn't really matter how much she screamed for apart from Security - who knew better than to interrupt him - the building was empty. And while Paul set about the task with steely determination to get the very best from her, Eve filmed it.

An hour or so later Paul reviewed the pictures and announced himself thoroughly delighted, he packed Eve off to her apartment with a promise he would be by later. When she had gone he released Rae and, after she had tidied herself up, for the first time he took her to dinner where he explained the nuances of his relationship with Eve.

What he didn't discuss was the reason for the films and photographs. For the time being it was best to let Rae think he just wanted them as a reminder of her!

***

"I would have liked to see the girls in the flesh!" Bartlett said as he finished viewing the DVD. The way he lingered over the word 'flesh' left Nigel in no doubt that the filmed images had done their work.

"Couldn't do it," he explained. "Put them in the same room and there's fireworks."

"But they're worth the admission price if you just hung 'em up and flogged 'em," Paul put in.

Enjoying a private viewing, they were seated in the Lewington

House cinema which had been temporarily closed to the members. A small affair with around twenty-four seats arranged in four rows of six, there was virtually round-the-clock viewing of the very best BDSM material available, plus the delights of the members' own efforts. There was also a pocket-sized bar at the back.

"But how do I know they're going to do the business?" Bartlett insisted.

"That's our problem, surely," Nigel said. "If they don't perform, we refund the money and you can have them for whatever you want to do to them all night for free."

"That's fair, you've got to admit," Paul said.

Bartlett considered for a while.

"Okay. Let's decide on the rules and hope they play ball!"

When at last they had thrashed out specifics with which all three agreed, Bartlett invited them, as his personal guests, to dine with the members, after which they were free to enjoy the hospitality of the Member's Lounge where the rubber-clad girls were only too pleased to entertain them.

And as Nigel enjoyed fellatio from a nipple-clamped brunette while a blonde impaled herself on his presented fingers, he watched Paul with a hot little number in blue. The place was a paradise for men like them. He realised that now he had been in three different rooms that had until then been barred to him, and couldn't help but wonder when he was actually going to get into all of the rest of them.

It all hung on those two girls!

***

On Sunday morning, Paul met Rae on the steps of his building as usual and ushered her upstairs to his office again. Since her ankle suspension, she seemed even more keen to see where her submissiveness could lead her to – perhaps even replacing Eve – and she positively skipped over to the cabinet and opened it for him to decide what he was going to use on her. Paul, however, was tense. Vanessa had agreed to the fight with complete ease. If it was what Nigel and Maggie wanted, that was fine with her.

He had established that Rae still hated Vanessa, but would she go the last few yards?

He watched her eyeing all the equipment.

"Don't just stand there! I want you naked with anklets and wrist restraints buckled in place in thirty seconds. Do it!"

While she rushed to comply he selected a couple of long, sturdy-linked chains. Then turning to see her standing obediently with head bowed and hands on head, he looked her over and mentally compared the perfectly formed and erotically-charged super-bitch of a few weeks ago with the obedient, yieldingly-sensual, softer Rae that stood before him. She was still as hot for it as ever, of course, but he couldn't help but wonder if the new Rae would be aggressive enough for their requirements. She had certainly been a charming dinner companion and had, to his surprise, taken the news about Eve quite calmly.

He was unable to resist the temptation of her expensively fragranced body a moment longer and reached for her breasts. Then, with the chains dangling from one hand and hanging down between their bodies, he tweaked the nipples mercilessly, squeezing and wringing them as he covered her glossed-lipped mouth with his own. And as his tongue probed every corner of her lovely, wet, yielding mouth, flicking over her teeth and tangling with her own equally ardent tongue, like a good submissive she kept her hands on her head.

Forsaking her tits he pressed himself against her, crushing the chains into her body as he wrapped her in his strong arms. He ran his fingers down her welts, eliciting little tongue-muffled moans. Then still without breaking the kiss he reached for her linked hands and deftly joined the restraints together. And as he kissed her deeply, enjoying her as a lover might and revelling in her melting response, he tried to actually visualise her going hell for leather at her equally horny opponent.

That was enough to snap him out of it and bring the reason for her being there sharply into focus.

"Lie on the floor!"

As she settled herself on her back with her arms above her head, he shook the chains to separate them. Then once again using the hook disguised as part of the chandelier, plus a similar hook in an identical chandelier some feet away, he raised and spread her legs, then fastened the anklets to the two dangling chains. These he then shortened until only her shoulders touched the carpet and her superb body formed a long curve up towards the ceiling. Then he strode toward the cabinet again and selected his implement from the impressive array.

He positioned himself, with the vicious-looking cat in his hand, so that she'd see him framed by her own legs. He saw the horror in her eyes as his intentions became clear to her. Enjoying her distress immensely, smirking down at her he added to it by slowly running the nine, long, weighted tails through his fingers, and watched the changing expressions on her face as the layers of her terrified, wanton desire were peeled away until there was nothing left but the naked submission of her acceptance. "You'll like this one," he told her before adjusting his stance for the best delivery. Knowing it would hurt like hell, he waited until the faint jingling that accompanied her trembling had died away and then set to, whipping her between the legs, laying the lashes down long and hard, each strike precisely placed along the very seat of her womanhood. He noted the contortions of her beautiful, flushed face as she fought the urge to scream. And still he kept going, every devastating blow underlining the fact that she was more alive then than she had ever been. She was sobbing as her body jerked under each strike, and just when he thought she would never give in to the un-released screams that were choking her, she emitted a cry far superior to anything he had wrung from her before. Satisfied, he tossed the cat aside and within moments had stripped off and was knelt over her head.

Her face was streaked with tears but her eyes were bright and she sighed happily as he took rough handfuls of breast and kneaded them harshly. He had seen that look before with slaves and recognised it now as the look of a soaring heart – it was the moment when a slave would do anything for her master.

"I want you to fight Vanessa again. And this time I want you to win," he told her.

Her tongue had been flicking at his scrotum teasingly and now it stopped.

"How did you know about that?" she asked, her voice hoarse from her screams and arousal.

As briefly as possible, he told her that he had met Nigel and he had told him how Vanessa had seen her off in a spectacular scrap.

Beneath him, Rae suddenly struggled and set the chains

jingling again.

"Bollocks! She never beat me!" Her voice was harsh as her sudden anger made the words tumble over each other. "She never has! Only by cheating. I'll massacre the lying bitch…….."

That was a yes, then! Paul grinned to himself and took her down before silencing her continuing protests by the simple expedient of stuffing her mouth full of his cock.

CHAPTER TWENTY

A narrow gravel path led off from the car park and into the meadows that surrounded the gleaming, white mansion of Lewington House. The gravel gave way to an older path, beaten by many pairs of feet over the years. Rarely used these days, it tapered off into an overgrown "right of way" as it wound past a copse of trees and through a field that had been left to return to the wild and then the narrow pathway suddenly became a concrete and gravel path that ended up in a spacious, three sided yard with a large barn running across one end and semi-derelict stables enclosing the two other sides. The farm house it had once belonged to had been demolished as part of an abortive plan to build a swimming pool there. But that had all been before the big house had been purchased and turned into the depraved playground it now was. Even the club members were unaware of its existence – why should they be? Up until the day of the fight, it had not offered any female delights.

But that had all changed in the couple of weeks since Nigel and Paul had signalled to Bartlett that both girls were raring to go. It had been decided that things should proceed as fast as possible to keep the girls hot and Bartlett had had to have the old barn cleared out as best he could manage. The fight was set for the first Sunday afternoon of the following month, and in the end that had meant that sacks of feed, heaps of old agricultural tools, a rusting pre-war motorbike, a hardly less ancient tractor and other assorted debris had only been pushed to the sides. By the time the day came around, apart from the lingering musty smell and earthy odours that mingled with petrol fumes that could not be eradicated, everything was ready. A makeshift, square ring formed by three ropes attached to four fence posts driven into the earth floor, scantily padded with foam packed into sacks and tied onto them, had been set up in the middle. Around it folding chairs had been loosely arranged into ranks. At the back some old bales of straw had been laid down as crude terracing. A generator thumped and grumbled out at the back providing what light was necessary to complement what came in from the holes in the roof.

Some of the lads who normally ensured that members' behaviour in the dungeons stayed within bounds were playing hoses over a pile of rich red clay that had been dumped in the slightly dished centre of the yard and a perfect setting for mud wrestling was well on the way to completion.

Matthew Bartlett looked about him happily as the members made their way, excitedly chatting and laughing in small groups down from the house. He was glad to note that none of them seemed to mind the long walk. Pictures of the two girls had been posted in the house and on its website and tickets had simply flown out, despite the hefty asking price. He was delighted to see that one or two quite well known figures in SM circles were present. There was the young man whose own club had recently opened up in Squire's Langley and who had gone from despised gypsy to aristocrat in one huge bound, he was talking and joking with John Carpenter – owner of The Lodge itself, the club all others aspired to imitate – Bartlett had invited Carlo Suarez the legendary slave trainer for the modern arenas and John Carpenter's partner but it looked as though he would have to settle for Carpenter on his own.

As people stopped off at the bar – champagne bottles in buckets of ice with glasses ranged on the tops of trestle tables, served by some of Lewington's best looking girls wearing nothing but weighted nipple and labial clamps, and a welcoming smile – then disappeared into the barn itself, Bartlett roused himself. Raising his hand to acknowledge one of the longer-standing members, he gave himself a mental shake. He just hoped the two stars' alleged hatred of each other really was strong enough to propel them into a public display. This would be very different indeed to their office brawl and either one might yet get cold feet. They had both been promised big bonuses for staying the course of all ten rounds that had been planned for them. But would it be enough?

From inside the barn the MC began to welcome the guests and explain how the competition would be arranged.

".......The first round is simple, Gentlemen!" he called. "We thought it best to keep it that way so the contestants can understand it!" He paused for condescending laughs which duly materialised, and then went on. "The winner of Round One is the girl who strips the other one naked first! Both contestants will start fully dressed of course and Mr Bartlett – the lucky man! – has checked that all their underwear hasn't been altered and can be ripped off with no undue problems!" There was enthusiastic applause, wolf whistles and cheers.

Bartlett skirted round the developing mud pool and prepared to take his place ringside as referee and judge, together with two of his security staff. There was a good atmosphere developing and he began to relax. Both girls had seemed keyed up and ready to go when he had checked that under the plain shirts and fashionable, gypsy type skirts their underwear hadn't been tampered with. The black haired one had seemed the more docile and his palm still tingled with the memory of how her breasts had felt when he had tested her bra with more thoroughness than was strictly called for and her buttocks had been even better! The skimpy thong had only served to accentuate the bulge of her labia at the tops of her long – so long! – and shapely thighs. It had been all he could do to keep his hands off her.

He really hoped the fight would be good so he could invite their masters to join; and that would mean adding the sluts to Lewington's collection.

Bartlett took his seat as the MC was finally outlining the tenth round – ten circuits of the yard followed by a dash for one riding crop. After that it would be a free for all until one girl went down and stayed there.

"And now let's welcome our two furies! Vanessa and Rae!" The MC struck a pose pointing to the door of the barn and the two girls entered with their seconds beside them. Two more of Lewington House's security force kept between them at the door and as they walked to the ring, to prevent them ripping each other apart in the aisle.

There was a thunderous burst of applause and ribald cheers from the male audience together with appreciative whistles as the two camps made their way to the ring. Bartlett noticed that both Nigel and Paul kept a hand gripped tightly around their girl's upper arm. The girls themselves glared at each other until they had to break eye contact in order to duck through the ropes into the ring.

The atmosphere was suddenly so thick that it was almost choking, Bartlett thought, as a hush fell over the barn and the audience settled down tensely and waited for the fight to start.

CHAPTER TWENTY ONE

Vanessa dared a quick scan of the audience as she walked, her hips swaying enticingly beneath her pale turquoise skirt. There was a sick feeling in the pit of her stomach and her heart was racketing as if were about to detonate. She had been dreading this moment. She really hadn't been sure she was going to be able to go through with it. Somehow, what she thought of as the "farmyard" setting, coupled with the fact that she would have to fight in a real ring made it much more frightening than anything she had ever done before....worse even than when she had arranged her own gangbang! And it wasn't as if she was going to get thrashed by any men either. But just when she began to wish that she was somewhere.... anywhere else, she felt the stirring of her exhibitionist nature and knew she could draw on that. Once again she dared to check out the spectators – so many of them – and knowing that there were plenty of men who were going to be getting almighty erections as they watched her went some way to compensate for the lack of male use of her aroused, whip-hungry, fuck-ready body. And of course if she did well, it would lead to further nights of ecstasy with Maggie and their master. The trouble was that she had reached a time in her life when she was happier than ever before, happier than she had thought possible, and the truth of it was that she had been finding it hard to hate Rae as much she had done before.

But when she had walked out of the stable on trembling legs with Maggie's hand supporting her at her elbow and seen Rae Carroll, everything had slotted into place.

The blonde cow had actually sneered when she had seen Nigel and Maggie with her.

"All the usual suspects eh? Might have known you'd be involved Miss Huffer! Got your falsies on today have you? And Mr Pervy Pickett himself! The lousiest shag north of the Thames!"

Suddenly Vanessa had relaxed, the insults cascading from the bitch's mouth were just the tonic she needed. Behind her she heard Maggie cry out softly in distress on her master's behalf. Vanessa turned and smiled at her lover, her expression conveying both love and reassurance. There was no way she was going to lose. Not now.

Keeping a dignified silence but returning the blonde's hate-filled stare, and with Rae's face turning pink as she was humiliatingly hushed by her master, they walked into the barn and into the ring.

And now that she was actually in the ring, she trembled not with anxiety but animosity, a hatred that was almost strong enough to blot out everything else. Only vaguely did she hear the applause and now she hardly noticed the men at all. All she wanted was Rae Carroll's naked body, sprawled at her feet, eating dirt.

"Seconds out!" Bartlett called as he replaced the MC in the ring.

Maggie gave her arm one last encouraging squeeze, then Nigel took her by both upper arms and looked hard at her.

"Slaughter the bitch!" he whispered hoarsely and gave her a rare smile that lit up his face and her heart.

Maggie and Nigel went to take their seats on the front row and Bartlett called her to the centre of the ring. As arranged she took off her turquoise, high-heeled sandals and tossed them out of the ring. Then, with her skirt fluttering around her knees, she sauntered towards Rae, smiling as irritatingly as she could manage.

"The only way you're gonna walk out of this is if you cheat like you always have!" Rae yelled over the increasing roar of encouragement coming from the audience now that it seemed the entertainment was about to start at long last. Rae's face was so close Vanessa felt her spittle as she spat out her words. She lifted a hand and, playing to the crowd, wiped her cheek with a slow, exaggerated gesture that had the crowd laughing, and flicked the non-existent goo from her fingers.

"I beat you fair and square in the office, Rae. I'll do it again here!" Vanessa replied quietly, her full lips drawn back in an engaging smile.

Bartlett dived his arms between them as Rae seemed about to lunge straight at her. He could certainly feel the hatred as he stood between them and was overjoyed, he was sure now that he was about to get everything he had been promised.

"Back off both of you! Come out fighting at the bell!" he commanded and spread his arms apart, pushing them back. His hands made contact with their lace-clad mounds of soft breastmeat and it was only the sound of the bell for round one ringing that made him beat a hasty retreat.

***

Rae came at her so fast that Vanessa had no chance to defend herself and her head was wrenched back by a fist clenching in her hair while another slammed into her stomach. She screamed and tried to double over but was prevented by the scalp-ripping grip on her hair. The next thing she knew was that she was being dragged with her arms flailing towards one of the posts and before she could do anything to save herself her head banged numbingly hard against it. She felt Rae's grip loosen as she was let go and she staggered backwards in a daze. Rae relinquished her hold on the long strands of black hair she had pulled out and quick as a flash took full advantage and ripped open Vanessa's shirt, sending a spray of buttons flying everywhere and revealing her turquoise and black bra which fought to contain her breasts. The roar from the crowd penetrated even Vanessa's fuddled brain and belatedly she began to blink and clear her head and eyes but again Rae had the advantage. She had got behind her and wrenched the shirt down her back, impeding her arms. Furiously Vanessa tried to shake them free but felt Rae's hands on her bra strap, effortlessly slipping the catch. Instantly her breasts spilled free and she heard the hoots of delight from the audience as momentarily helpless, Vanessa's contest became one to free her trapped arms. But Rae wasn't about to wait and pushed her hard in the back and as Vanessa stumbled forwards, stuck her foot out and tripped her. She went crashing down face first and felt Rae's foot stamp down on her back.

"That's for tripping me up on the athletics track when we were sixteen!" she hissed in Vanessa ear, then raised her voice and she heard her crow to an appreciative audience,

"She usually goes down on her back and with less fuss than that!"

Humiliated by the laughter, Vanessa wriggled frantically to get away. But to no avail. She felt the zip on her skirt being undone. Suddenly all the incidents in her life where Rae had made her feel inadequate and belittled came pouring back into her mind. Using the memory of her ruined birthday party when Rae had got the other kids to gang up on her and pelt her with jelly as a spur, with a huge effort she wrenched her arms forwards and round, feeling

~ 187 ~

the ragged scrap of shirt ride up to her shoulders, allowing her to get her hands under her. Then with a roar of effort she reared up and sent her opponent staggering backwards. Regaining her feet, Vanessa threw off the shirt and then hurled her bra scornfully at the crowd. Her tits bounced as if with joy at their freedom and the crowd cheered. Then, half crouching and keeping her skirt up by pressing an elbow into her waist, she stalked forwards, muttering beneath her breath. "This one's for stealing my place on the Swimming Team!"

But Rae was still on a high and ran at her. Vanessa dodged and tripped her easily, grabbing at her and ripping her shirt open as she passed and then following her down into the dirt to lie on her back and rip the shirt down the back. With shaking fingers and such a feeling of triumph that she thought she would explode with joy, she fumbled the bra strap open and got a hand down between their hot, perspiring bodies to undo the zip on Rae's skirt; all before the blonde could throw her off and send her sprawling.

As the two tempestuous girls scrambled to their feet, briefly Vanessa saw herself as a gawky thirteen year old, crying because that spiteful little bitch Rae had stolen her boyfriend. Well, it was payback time! As she narrowed her eyes, Vanessa swept a hand beneath her hair and lifted it up to flick it back over her shoulder, kicked her own skirt away and then ran in while a bare-breasted Rae was still scrabbling to get rid of the tatters of clothing that hindered her. Her dusky pink skirt fell to her feet and Vanessa easily threw her down onto her back. Gleefully she lunged for the thong – all that stood between her and victory in the first round but Rae was too fast and rolled away in time and scrambled up. The two circled each other with only their thongs on, and the crowd quietened for a moment as the male audience took in the true splendour of the two girls' bodies. Both girls were covered in an attractive sheen of perspiration and both pairs of breasts wobbled in the most entrancing way. Such was the fury between them that neither girl seemed to recognise the erotic tingles that assailed their quivering insides, neither suspecting that their exertions were fuelling not only their hatred but their lust – it wasn't only the men who were aroused! Four nipples stuck out scandalously hard, like bullets. And unknown to the spectators, both cunts were seeping their juice and dampening the thongs.

Someone shouted. "Get on with it!"

Another shout went up. "Let's see her cunt!"

The crowd's noise and stamping were shaking loose the dust of years from the rafters and motes danced in the bars of sunlight that struck down from the holes in the roof and lit the two nearly naked beauties, their breasts heaving and swaying as they panted and moved, their long legs, sinewy and graceful, their buttocks, ripe, round and enticing.

It was almost too horny for the crowd to endure and for a moment Bartlett feared a riot would break out if the girls didn't get on with the action. Fortunately someone had had the sense to send in the champagne serving girls and already he could see some of them being put to use.

Vanessa went on the offensive again and ran in but her opponent was ready for her and grabbed her arms, using her own momentum to swing her round and send her careering backwards into the ropes. They were so loose that Vanessa almost went right over the top one but just managed to stop herself. Unfortunately it gave Rae time to dart in, ram her shoulder into Vanessa's chest and rip the fragile straps of her thong.

The bell rang and Rae paraded around the ring with her turquoise trophy, waving at the crowd and smirking at Vanessa. Standing watching her, Vanessa caught her lower lip with her teeth to stop it quivering. She felt the terrible heat of humiliation wash over her and knew she was blushing. All she wanted was for a big hole to open beneath her feet to swallow her up. It was one of the worst moments of her entire life because this time Rae had shamed her in front of the two most important people in her life, and every other humiliation she had heaped on her over their lives paled into insignificance. For once her pride in her physique didn't come to her rescue and she made pathetic attempts to cover herself, throwing one hand over her breasts and using the other to cover the hairless cunt that Nigel had so diligently shaved that morning – only fuelling the audience's scorn and support for Rae. Desperately she looked over to where Nigel and Maggie were hurrying towards her corner.

"It's okay!" Maggie said, as she gently stroked her perspiration-drenched face with a towel. "It's only the first round."

"Could've gone either way," Nigel said almost flippantly, and won her undying gratitude for his calmness.

"I'll get the bitch in the next one!" she panted as Maggie went on towelling her and Nigel sorted through their kit bag for the cerise and black lace-trimmed basque, black stockings and replacement thong. She felt much better for the shelter the garments gave her, she knew she looked stunning in a corset that cinched her waist and as Maggie smoothed the black stockings up her legs, she stood up straight and proud again. Maggie brushed her hair.

"Keep calm and think your way through this," Nigel advised her quietly as he massaged her shoulders just as Bartlett called the contestants into the centre of the ring again.

Maggie slipped black, high-heeled court shoes onto her feet and she stepped forwards, knowing she looked superb and quietly determined to take Rae Carroll down this time. Bartlett looked them over then, taking Rae's narrow wrist he closed a steel cuff around it. There was a jingling sound and then he did the same to Vanessa, closing the steel around her only slightly larger wrist. And the two girls found their left hands joined together by a yard long chain. For their right hands they were given eighteen inch straps of soft, pliable leather that Vanessa saw straightaway would leave very clear welts instantly.

"Marks will be awarded for clear, hard strikes on exposed skin and if either of you goes down before ten minutes are up your opponent will be awarded five points. At the end of ten minutes we will total the number of welts you are both carrying and announce the winner. Understand?" Bartlett explained.

Vanessa nodded, staring hard at her opponent who returned it with a confident grin. But Vanessa's thoughts were not on Rae; Nigel's words came back to her, and she thought also about what Bartlett had said – or rather hadn't said.

***

When the bell rang, Rae went straight onto the attack again, yanking hard on the chain to draw Vanessa in and try to get a strike in across her hip and buttock. Vanessa let herself be drawn forwards but danced away sideways when she saw the lash coming. It was a good move that left Rae off balance and Vanessa was able to swing in a clean lash across her buttocks.

It was an intoxicating feeling to be delivering the lash for once and even Vanessa had to admit that Rae's buttocks made a fine target. She wondered just how used to the lash Rae was as she managed another strike as Rae twisted and yelped, but fireed off a lash of her own, catching Vanessa across the fronts of the thighs. Then she was back on balance and the two of them slowly circled each other, though the court shoes made them less surefooted than before. But it was worth it, Vanessa conceded, for she knew they enhanced their legs and the crowd would be getting seriously hot as they watched two glamorous women whip each other for their fun. Except it wasn't for their fun, whatever the stupid bastards thought, Vanessa reminded herself as they continued to circle, it was for her dear Master and Maggie....and for the total annihilation of fucking, shit-stirring Rae sodding Carroll! And then with a grimace as she started her next move, she reminded herself, think it through.... She wrenched on the chain and Rae instinctively pulled back. And then Vanessa sprang forwards and shoulder charged her, sending her sprawling onto her back with her legs waving in the air. Giving her victim no time to recover, immediately she began to rain lashes down onto the squirming, basque-hindered body beneath her. Welts blossomed becomingly across the generous upper swells of her sweat-beaded breasts, one burst completely free of the half cup of her corset and Rae screamed as a stray lash caught her across the turgid nipple. She scrabbled madly as she tried to get her feet under her but Vanessa piled in lashes to her thighs and then, forsaking the scoring area of naked flesh, she tangled Rae's nylon clad ankles with her strap and Vanessa almost whooped with joy as she went down again. This time she managed to wriggle in a most tantalising way onto her front, squashing her tits beneath her, and Vanessa was able to enjoy lashing the shapely back and shoulders. She put the venom of all the years into each blow, yanking on the chain to stop her getting the left hand under her.

Eventually Rae rolled over and tried to swing her own lash but only caught Vanessa low on the thighs – not a scoring or a disabling area.

"You fucking cheat!" she screamed. "There should be a count when you're down!"

Vanessa paused, smiled grimly and savoured the moment. "I didn't hear the ref say that. You should have listened better!" Then she lifted the whip to continue the thrashing but Rae kicked out in desperation and managed to land an agonising blow to Vanessa's shin, giving herself just enough time to scramble up, dirty, tousled, one breast still naked, her stockings torn and looking for revenge.

Rae punched with her left hand and by luck connected with Vanessa's right breast, sending her reeling back to the end of the chain. And with her blonde hair flying, Rae followed her. Vanessa felt the first hot caress of the whip across her back and although she knew she was well in the lead, she knew she couldn't risk Rae getting the upper hand. No time to revel in the pain, she thought as she whirled around and used the chain to wrap around the blonde's chest, dragging her arm across with it as she stepped behind her and then lashed at the thighs as Rae spun. But Rae didn't attempt a lash at all, she swung her whole arm forwards using the handle of the whip as a club.

It caught Vanessa full across her mouth and as she stumbled back she discerned the iron taste of blood. She heard the gasp from the crowd as first blood was drawn. She had no way of knowing how that would count – she was damn sure it wouldn't be penalised! – there was only one thing to do.

She bent and turned away as if she was badly hurt but used the movement to drag the chain with all her strength. She felt Rae cannon into her back and in the same second jabbed her elbow backwards. "This is for Alex Mayfair!" To her delight she felt it sink into the gap between those long, athletic thighs and slam against the pubic bone and the softness of the labia.

Rae's agonised cry was drowned by the crowd's roar of delight. Vanessa was quick to seize on her victory and spun back and brought her knee up to add another jolt to Rae's groin. She jacknifed in shocked pain and Vanessa went back to scoring lashes across her back, aware of blood coursing over her chin. Rae charged sideways and took her across the fronts of her thighs and Vanessa found herself floored and taking savage lashes across her breasts. But still following her Master's advice she kept her head enough to yank on the chain again and bring Rae crashing down onto her.

***

At ringside, Bartlett was beside himself with delight. His faith in the venture had not been misplaced after all! Whichever one of them lost this fight, she was going to be desperate for a rematch and he could charge a fortune to stage it. Maybe even at The Lodge itself. He glanced over at John Carpenter who was following the action raptly with a broad smile on his face. Bartlett himself turned back and watched the two luscious, sweating, wriggling and thrashing bodies on the ground. Long, shapely thighs wrapped round other thighs in a tangle of female flesh, spiteful fingers clawed – so deliciously deeply – into welted buttocks, bountiful breasts shook and wobbled invitingly. The black haired one was bleeding from a cut lip and the blonde had a smear of blood across the top of one breast and it struck him that they were like opposite sides of the same being. He watched as the blonde somehow got to her feet and put the other one in a headlock from behind with one arm and lashed out with the other trying to score her opponent's thighs, but she was too fast and twisted free. Now they faced each other again on their feet, soaking hair falling over their lovely faces, their stockings torn, their breasts now irrevocably free of restraint.

The crowd was on its feet as one man, waving and cheering on their fancy. The girls came together again, ignoring the whips, they were just trying to punch the other one out. The hatred was almost tangible. He checked his watch, two minutes to go. The black haired one managed to throw the blonde across her hip and had the sense to use her whip again, making sure she stayed well ahead. To his surprise the blonde seemed beyond thought and fought with nails and fists, seeming not to care about the score on welts. And as fatigue finally cut in, they tottered together, breast to wobbling, heaving breast, feebly trying to get in just one more strike – or one more punch. Staggeringly they held each other up, their heads together and their hair falling over their opponent's shoulders. The crowd's noise reached a crescendo as the clock ran down and the blonde's supporters tried to encourage her to a last minute comeback.

CHAPTER TWENTY TWO

When the bell rang, Vanessa sank to her knees and beside her Rae collapsed as well. Both girls were trembling and set the chain between them jingling.

"Fucking have you next time!" Rae panted.

"I've been caned by better than you......and that's not hard!" Vanessa hissed back.

Rae tried to lunge for her again but just in time her master grabbed her and dragged her away as far as the chain would allow. Bartlett uncuffed them and at once Maggie was there to help her back to the corner where there was a welcome mouth wash. Gently and efficiently, Maggie towelled her down again while Bartlett made a cursory examination of the few welts Rae had managed to leave and declared Vanessa the winner of Round Two.

Vanessa looked over at Rae's corner and smiled happily as she carefully scooped her breasts back into her corset, straightened out her stockings and collected her thoughts before the next round.

A man carried a simple chair into the ring and then used a brush and some whitewash to make some marks on the floor of the ring, and when Bartlett called them into the centre he explained.

"The victim will lean over the back of the chair and put her feet there and there," he told them pointing to two squares behind the chair's back. "The caner will stand exactly there." He pointed to a line a little way behind the feet marks and off to one side. "Any movement of the feet back from that line will incur a penalty – so no run-ups. Any movement of the feet in front of that line will also incur a penalty. Any move to try and protect her backside by the victim will cost her the round, also any attempt to stand or dodge a lash."

He tossed a coin in the air and Vanessa was invited to call it. She went for heads and lost. She was going to take the first dose.

"But to even things up," Bartlett said. "If the eventual loser turns out to be the first girl to bend and take five, then she will have five extra strokes at the winner to see if she can force a draw."

Vanessa placed her feet carefully where instructed and then bent forwards over the back of the chair, with her hair hanging like a black silk curtain. Using one finger she hooked it back behind her ears then settled her hands into gripping the sides of the seat tightly. Playing to the crowd once more, with her old bravado she wriggled her bum as if inviting Rae to do her worst. As the crowd laughed delightedly, with her heart swelling she looked back over her shoulder to see Rae, now calmed down and back in her basque and stockings, toeing the line carefully and flexing the cane.

Vanessa turned her head back and bit her lip. There was no way this wasn't going to hurt and without a man doing it, it really would be pain without a shred of pleasure. She would just have to try a bit of mind over matter – pretend it was that hunk from the first row who was wielding it!

The bell rang again and Vanessa heard the hush that fell across the crowd. This was going to be slow, calm, devastating torment......with the added bonus for the onlookers of watching two superb arses slowly mark into scarlet and black infernos.

Whack!

The barn echoed to the sound of the strike and Vanessa hiccupped as she tried to contain the pain that clutched at her throat as a vicious fire scorched across both hinds.

Whack!

The second came almost immediately so that the escalation of pain was continuous. Vanessa bit more deeply into her lip and re-settled her hands just as the third came snapping in. Her head flew up and she tramped her feet a couple of times as she was blinded by agony. Her attempts at mind over matter were failing miserably in the wake of Rae's spite – there was no doubt that it was a sadistic cow behind it!

Whack!

Whack!

Rae let fly with two in quick succession.

Vanessa fought the urge to move with all her strength and in the end let out a shriek that silenced the crowd. It worked like a valve letting off steam, and somehow the agony in her bottom seemed to abate a little.

"First tranche complete," Bartlett announced. "You may rise and take the cane."

Vanessa stiffly uncurled her fingers and slowly struggled upright. She didn't dare rub at the tramlines she knew would be carved savagely across her soft hinds but sniffed back her tears, tossed her hair back in a defiant gesture and hobbled with all the dignity she could muster over to where Rae stood and snatched the cane from her.

Only when Bartlett was busy making sure that Rae bent over correctly did Vanessa succumb and with one hand reach behind her and rub frantically at the damage. She heard the cheers go up as the men watched her hand knead the deep cushions of sweetly rounded flesh. She wished that it had been one of them delivering the cane – and following up with a good hard cock!

But Bartlett was standing back and inviting her to retaliate, Vanessa sternly brought her thoughts back under control.

As much as she hated to admit it, the fucking cow really did look stunning. Her waist-constricting cerise corset, exactly the same as her own, made her hindquarters swell out spectacularly and the black lace framed her pale flesh as it followed the shapely contours. The smooth pillars of her thighs were caressed so perfectly by the hold up stockings. The gusset of her cerise-and-black thong curled so lovingly around the pouch of her cunt......
Vanessa wished it was Maggie. But before she could get back to the warm and sensual comfort of her lover, she had to dispatch this bitch.

She flicked the tip of her tongue over her dry lips and tried to steady her breathing She shifted her stance slightly, as she steadied herself for action. With the tip of her tongue just poking through her lips as if it could aid concentration, she took aim at the pale globes of Rae's buttocks and drew the cane back. And then back some more; held it, then launched herself as hard as she could.

She was shocked by how loud the report was and there was an immediate cheer from her supporters. She saw Rae's head snap up and her torso twist in agony. She fired in another, off her head with delight at being able to inflict so much pain on her arch enemy.

Rae's head sagged this time and her knees trembled. Vanessa snapped another lash home, putting as much weight as she dared – not wanting to risk stumbling over the line – into the stroke.

Rae screamed.

Vanessa grinned and struck again. Rae's shoulders were shaking. She was sobbing, Vanessa realised. She couldn't take it. With the first whiff of victory, Vanessa tried to make her final lash as devastating as possible, trying to finish this round off right here. The stroke crossed the earlier ones that were already blossoming into fully fledged tramlines but somehow, although she twitched and seemed on the point of begging for mercy, Rae survived and now Vanessa had to face the cane again.

Rae stood up and used the back of an elegant, pink-nailed hand to wipe her tears before she rounded on Vanessa and strode back to snatch the cane. The two women locked glances and Vanessa could read in her eyes all the spite and selfishness of the spoilt brat who had now been hurt and wanted revenge. Gripped by a sudden doubt Vanessa glanced across at Nigel and Maggie. Both were on their feet and watching anxiously. And that was all she needed; whatever else happened, she couldn't let them down!

Slowly and in the sure and certain expectation of extreme pain, Vanessa swayed her hips for the crowd as she walked to the chair and settled herself as the men required her to.....if only it was one of them holding the cane!

She looked out at the hunk in the first row again but now he had a naked girl kneeling in front of him and fellating him with rapid nodding movements of her head. His hands kneaded her breasts and he was smiling directly at her. For just a second she felt lust burn wetly in her belly, but then the cane arrived. Its fiery impact across skin where nerve endings had had time to fully engorge and bruise in the wake of the initial beating was blinding. Vanessa screamed at the top of her lungs and hurled her head up, screwing her eyes tight shut and channelling all her pain into her voice. But as the wave of agony swept over her, she became aware that there was an extra dimension. A sharp, hot spear point of agony persisted in her right buttock.

Whack!

The second devastating stroke broke across her brain, numbing it and reducing her scream to a strangled croak. Shattered, she felt reality slipping away.... she just wanted to close her eyes and sink into oblivion. But then she remembered Maggie and Nigel, and somehow she held on and felt again an extra bite. She wouldn't let the bitch defeat her! Risking a penalty she craned her head around and by twisting her spine was able to see that two deep, angry red craters had been gouged into the crown of her right cheek. Immediately she could see that blood would very shortly be drawn. She turned her head the other way and looked back at

Rae. The cow was smiling grimly and flexing the cane in readiness for the next strike.

Vanessa looked straight ahead and focussed on the men in the audience, she could see several other girls now, some were being shafted from behind, some were taking two up, some were frantically sucking at rock hard cocks! If only she could just get some cock, it would make everything so much more bearable…

Whack!

The third came within an ace of breaking her. The pain subsumed her entire body and seemed to shatter her brain, forcing her to think the unthinkable…..perhaps she should just accept defeat gracefully and yield….. It was a tidal wave of agony and in its midst was that extra dagger and as the pain peaked and then began to subside, Vanessa cottoned on to what was happening.

The devious bitch was not using the cane to deliver strokes with the side of the shaft cracking across both buttocks, she was laying them on deliberately short, so that the end of the cane was biting and cutting into her buttock and the tramlines already inscribed there. She fully intended to make her bleed freely in the hope that Nigel would retire her from the fight.

Well this was one time when it was not going to happen. Rae Carroll was not going to win here. Suddenly there was no question of any master, or of any audience. There was just her and Rae and a lifetime of her coming off second best. Well not now! Not here!

With a surge of joyous relief, Vanessa rose, screaming defiance. In what seemed to be one fluid movement that left no chance for redress she ran at the astonished Rae, snatched the cane, broke it over her knee and landed a punch on the blonde bitch's face that knocked her clean out of the ring.

CHAPTER TWENTY THREE

B artlett had been riveted by the caning contest, both girls had arses that just begged for the decoration that a cane could lay on. And the sight of those delicious mounds flattening and then swaying and quivering in the aftermath of a strike was the stuff of dreams. The crowd was greeting each impact with a cheer and living every second of each girl's pain. And there was pain... beautiful, bollock-boiling, genuine pain.

So wrapped up was he that when the blonde came hurtling backwards through the ropes and knocked his desk flying, he was tipped backwards onto the floor himself. He struggled up in the same moments as the blonde regained her feet and was in time to see the other girl dive through the ropes and cannon into the blonde, taking her screaming over the upturned table.

The crowd was on its feet, even some of the naked serving girls were screaming encouragement, everyone was riveted to the action as the two semi-naked bodies wrestled in the dirt until the black haired one stood up and with a growl of exasperation reached behind her and with surprising dexterity given her anger, unfastened the eyes on her basque and threw it away toward the crowd. While a knot of men squabbled over the discarded garment, the blonde wriggled away and climbed to her feet. All around them the audience were standing and yelling the contestants on, the blonde grabbed one of the lightweight folding chairs and flung it at the black haired one as she advanced. The crash of it hitting her mingled almost musically with her yell as she was thrown backwards into more rows of chairs. The blonde launched herself at her opponent. They rolled over and over scattering chairs and spectators as they went. The show had become one tangle of limbs and for a moment it was difficult to discern which set belonged to which girl. One of them squealed shrilly as the other squeezed and scratched her breast, and from where Bartlett stood it looked as though it was the black haired one on the receiving end. Without looking he reached out as one of his girls went past and he pushed her to her knees in front of him. She undid his flies with competent haste and as he looked around for their masters to signal there was no way he was stopping it, he felt the soft caress of lips and tongue on his urgent cock and then the clever little cave of her mouth stroked his length and it seemed fitting that a man should watch such a spectacle as this with his cock comfortably catered for.

He looked around for the two masters and found them standing in amongst the other spectators and urging their girls on, fists pumping the air.

The fight was now totally out of control – but it was all the better for that, he realised as he spotted John Carpenter himself on his feet cheering the girls on, his face red with shouting.

Turning his attention back to the fight he discovered it was going well beyond anything he could have hoped for, and was not unduly worried about the escalation of female ferocity, for it was unbelievably erotic! And to give them their due, he acknowledged as he saw that somehow they had both managed to drag themselves upright again, the girls were fearless! At his groin, the slut kneeling before him took him out of her mouth for a moment to lick the helm lovingly. He shuddered in delight.

Drinking in the raw sexuality of the two combatants, he was just in time to see the blonde one rush in with a strangled war-cry as her arm dived between the black haired one's thighs and, channelling her hatred into pure brawn she sent the girl flying through the air to crash into the rows of seats behind them. Chairs clattered and tumbled, and mixed in with the turmoil there was a pained, female cry that was underlined by the gasp from the crowd, surprised at the savagery of the impact. Bartlett found the eroticism of the scene too much, and felt his climax tear through him and spurt out into the tight but practised throat of the girl on her knees.

For a second the black haired one lay with her limbs submissively spread and her hair in total disarray, stunned in the middle of the chaos her landing had caused. From somewhere, a husky, male shout went up.

"Get up, you stupid fucking slut! I've got money on you!"

Meanwhile the blonde, to a bank of rousing cheers, took off her corset and tore off the remaining scraps of her stockings. She was an audacious little vixen, that one, Bartlett thought, kicking his girl away and fastening his trousers, she even had the nerve to hold her tits up towards the men cheering her on and flirt with them before swaying seductively over to where her winded opponent was only then picking herself up. But the blonde gave her no respite and, catching her off guard, she grabbed a fistful of long, black hair and used it to swing Vanessa round full circle before suddenly letting go, sending her careering into more rows of chairs. For the second time that day, Rae released the stray hairs she had pulled out while men leapt back to get out of the way as her exhausted rival's tantalising, nearly naked body tumbled and rolled.

It was more from luck than design that she managed to save herself and stagger upright, only to take the blonde's knee in between her legs. As Vanessa let out a shrill shriek of pain, Rae followed up with a headlock from behind as an almost crushed Vanessa crumpled down onto her knees. But Rae wasn't finished yet and, while she still had a tight hold of her opponent, her free hand clawed spitefully into Vanessa's luscious, hard-nippled and heaving breast. The onlookers were treated to a most amusing display of sensuality as the victim's sweat-sheened body twisted and wriggled frantically, until she finally shook herself clear and scrambled away and onto her feet again, while Rae savoured her victory and blew exaggerated air kisses to the crowd.

But even now the plucky girl, with black hair plastered to her face and blossoming bruises decorating her body, refused to give in and from somewhere she found the will to continue. Despite having been knocked around so much and probably feeling as if she'd been thumped in the cunt with a crowbar, she caught the blonde napping by going straight onto the attack. With a war-cry of her own, she bowled the blonde over and they both toppled through more chairs until they hit the straw bales. Then, with bits of straw sticking out of her black hair and one long piece poking out from the black lacy leg hole of her cerise thong, she was up first and grabbed one of the chairs. It folded itself as she picked it up and she swung it like a broad, flat club, hitting the bruised and battered blonde in the chest and making the crowd wince as the soft, ripe breasts were flattened by the metal. The blonde shrieked and rolled into a gangway between two banks of bales and tried to put some distance between her and her tormentor.

The black haired one laughed in delight at her opponent's distress. Bartlett watched as she plucked straw from her hair and then, as she drew the single straw slowly from where it had lodged in her thong, he noticed how she closed her thighs together as if with the sweet sensation of it, and he realised with a faintly salacious grin that the end was probably sticking in her cunt and she'd only noticed it when the straw stirred! The sheer wantonness of girls never ceased to amaze him, and this one was obviously a gloriously dirty bitch!

But by the time the black-haired one had walked to the gangway, the other girl had made it to the back wall of the barn and was armed.

**

Vanessa listened to the cheering from the crowd and accepted their adulation happily. After all, she had worked hard enough for it! She had no idea whether what she had done was going to be called cheating or not and anyway, she was beyond caring.

"Stick your fancy rules where the sun don't fucking shine!" she muttered with a snarl. She had waited a lifetime for the chance to get at the two-faced, empty-headed cow and in that highly charged atmosphere all that mattered was that she would beat Rae – and beat her any way she could. It had felt so good when the bitch had gone through the ropes, the look of shock still on her stupid face – and then it had felt so good to land on her.... and feel again the softness of a female body under her. Ah, that moment had been sweet, and if things had been different between them, maybe..... but no! She pushed the thought aside with a fierce vehemence. The stupid fucking tart had fought back! And now, as Vanessa stalked through the gap between the bales, with savage hunger pounding through her veins and a wild look in her eyes, she wiped her mouth and nose, both of them bloodied. She must look like a fucking vampire or something! she thought with a wry smile.

The crowd roared as Rae lunged at her with what was probably the handle of a pitchfork or something – a thick wooden rod about three feet long – which she swung in a vicious arc that hummed through the air and Vanessa just had time to draw in her stomach to avoid getting hurt. She stopped dead, shocked in her turn, for this was an escalation she hadn't anticipated. As her heart hammered she searched frantically for something to arm herself with in retaliation.

Rae charged in again, the staff held high and with surprising agility given her injuries so far, Vanessa ducked and dodged past her. Instinct took over and, in an echo of the athletics track, she lashed out with a foot as Rae hurtled past. But instead of tripping her up as before, it caught her behind a knee and the blonde stumbled. Seeing an advantage, she ran forwards but the staff swung up as if with a life of its own and caught her across the front of one thigh. Fuelled by anger she somehow managed to block out the pain for long enough to wrench the staff towards her. But primitive as that anger was, it didn't aid her in getting the pole away from Rae, on the contrary, the leggy blonde was able to use it to lever herself back onto her feet. And then the two of them found themselves at either end of the pole, clutching it as tightly as if their very lives depended on it and circling warily again.

All around them the crowd were cheering encouragement to their favourite girl. Vanessa felt she'd got the worst of the recent exchanges but as she glared along the wood at the dishevelled and snarling figure of her arch enemy, she realised that her fatigue had ebbed away and thankfully she now felt good and fresh. And the knowledge gave her the impetus she needed. Suddenly, she jerked the pole forwards and she was rewarded with a loud "ooomph!" as it dug into Rae's stomach. Almost at once there was a cheer from her supporters and Rae reeled away, doubled over in pain. Vanessa laughed aloud and, now in total possession of the rod, she swung it, and relished the sound as it smacked hard across Rae's buttocks. The audience erupted once more as Rae yelped, and twisting round to protect her bottom from further assault, she tripped backwards over the rusting hulk of a motorcycle standing abandoned by one wall.

The appreciative crowd was treated to the sight of Rae's long and shapely legs, widely parted and up-turned as she disappeared backwards over the petrol tank. Vanessa ran forwards and leaped up onto the ancient saddle.

She stood almost naked, victorious and proud, with her lovely legs spread and her hands on her hips, on top of the bike and the crowd howled and stamped their appreciation. Below her, Rae struggled to rise from a mess of cobwebs, burst feed sacks and bird droppings, and for once, despite Rae's presence, Vanessa knew that all the male lust in the room was directed firmly at her, because Rae was a nightmare coated in dust and grime, tottering upright and spitting out filth. Now she was revealed to everyone as the trashy alley cat Vanessa had always known lurked beneath the sweet façade. Vanessa bent forwards, moved her hands from her hips to her knees and stuck out her bottom in a blatant invitation as she wiggled it at the crowd.

The sparkle in her eyes and the note of triumph in her voice were impossible to miss as she asked Rae, "Want to give in now?"

The blonde just glared up at her through a matted curtain of once-blonde hair – and charged in again.

But this time Vanessa was ready and neatly jumped backwards out of harm's way. Rae cannoned into the bike and fell over it again, forwards this time, but her anger protected her... she was a fury unleashed. She rolled forwards even as she hit the ground and came up to grab the startled Vanessa by one arm, swing her round and send her crashing into the tractor, which stood alongside. Taken completely by surprise, it was reflex alone that raised Vanessa's arm to protect her face, but even so she was severely stunned and Rae's clawing fingers reached around and grabbed her traitorously-hard nipples, twisting them and wrenching them so cruelly that, had it been her master's fingers, she would have found it desperately sweet. But they were fucking Rae's fingertips and so produced nothing but agony. Vanessa screamed and, rendered thrillingly vulnerable she followed where the tormenting fingers led her. But common sense prevailed and in fevered desperation she tried to prise the fingers loose but Rae just increased the pain to stop her every time. That disloyal, unprincipled part of her being wanted to give in to the promised ecstasy that almost always came with nipple-torment, but the lucid part of her brain warned of complete and utter defeat if she were to let that sensual side of her take control..... and Vanessa knew she must not – could not – let that happen! She tried to retaliate and reached for Rae's nipples which, she noticed, were equally as hard as her own! But the blue-eyed girl just laughed and hollowed her chest so Vanessa couldn't make contact. Her own eyes began to swim with tears as the pain became sharper and sharper. Come on, Vee, she told herself, you've got to do something!

Gritting her teeth she took a deep breath and brought both her hands down in a chopping motion onto Rae's. For a moment her nipples exploded into white hot agony as blood pounded back into them but at least they were free and Vanessa was able to land a vengeful kick between Rae's spread legs as the blonde hesitated for a moment. Vanessa recognised an opportunity as Rae crouched down with her hands between her legs and, seizing the moment she darted in, caught the blonde by her hair and before she had really worked out what she intended to do next, she was dragging her as the winded girl stumbled along behind her, squealing like a pig in pain.

Suddenly Vanessa saw the barn door and for no particular reason headed toward it, then with a burst of wild and welcome energy she threw her opponent out into the yard, where she sprawled inelegantly on the cobbles.

The noise of chairs overturning inside as the men followed en masse came to her outside. Risking everything as a tidal wave of men spilled out, Vanessa closed in on her prey again and managed to drag Rae's thong down her long legs before she had recovered.

Now the men gathered round, and sensing their lust and her own victory, Vanessa stood up and paraded around the clearing as Rae had inside. Even those men who were backing Rae cheered at Vanessa's success as their eyes gorged on Rae's exposed and honey-dewed cunt.

But just as before, Vanessa took her eye off the ball and underestimated her opponent who scrambled up behind her and with one sharp yank, pulled her own thong down. Another cheer went up as the second cunt was revealed, but before it had died down or Vanessa had had chance to react, a sharp push in the back as the flimsy garment tangled round her knees had Vanessa down, painfully skinning her knees and palms. She tried to get up as fast as she could but Rae was there, aiming a kick at her breasts. Vanessa dodged back just enough and then helped Rae's foot on its way upwards. With a despairing scream Rae fell backwards. There was a loud and satisfying Splosh! as she toppled into the mud pool. It broke the blonde's fall but as Vanessa gained her own feet at last, Rae emerged a half red-brown, half flesh pink apparition, her face a mask of disgust.

Vanessa stood at the edge of the pool and joined in the crowd's laughter as Rae waded towards her. It never crossed her mind that she wouldn't give in at this utter humiliation.

But with a final, desperate lurch and lunge, Rae grabbed Vanessa's hair and pulled her shrieking, face down into the ooze. It was so cold it took Vanessa's breath away and it splattered into every nook and female crevice. She felt it squidge between her legs and freeze her labia and anus, she felt her abused nipples harden even further as the ooze closed over them. Mud splattered in all directions and Vanessa urgently pushed herself up by her splayed hands and gulped in air only for Rae to throw herself onto her and try to force her back down. But the mud meant she slid off and splashed back into the muck on Vanessa's other side. Reacting quickly, Vanessa tried to hold her down but her hands slid off as well. She tried to stand but her feet slid from under her and she landed heavily on her sore bottom, aware that she was now covered front and back, head to toe in thick red mud. She blinked rapidly and tried to wipe her mud-clogged eyes, but Rae, kneeling in front of her now, hurled a fistful of the wretched stuff at her and hit her in the mouth. As Vanessa sat choking and spluttering, spitting out the gooey stuff and close to tears, her opponent launched herself forwards. For the briefest of moments Vanessa felt the pressure of Rae's lavish breasts soft, slippery and yielding against own before their bodies slid apart in a strangely sensual way – as if they were both coated in massage oil or body lotion. But instead of letting the eroticism of the moment ambush her as she had done before, Vanessa reached out and snagged Rae's hair as she fell and pulled her down onto her. Except as their legs and arms entwined and thrashed, she realised that despite her best efforts, she was getting dangerously turned on. Rae's breasts thrust and rubbed enticingly against her own, her own thigh was seductively lodged in between Rae's and for a moment she felt the soft cushion of her cunt press against it. Rae's hands were all over her as she struggled to get a grip, but they slid off and erred into places like Vanessa's own crotch. God it was good! If things were different, she..... With a jolt Vanessa realised that for the crowd it must look as though the two humiliated, gleaming sluts were making out in full sight of everyone. The thought inspired her to one more effort to break the deadlock. She reached for a handful of muddied blonde hair, it was the only place she could grip but unfortunately Rae had had the same thought and she yelled as her own hair was pulled. Equally tenacious, without letting go both of them struggled up to their knees and with their free hands they began pummelling each other. Mud oozed between their fingers as they rubbed more of the filthy stuff into each other's faces.

It was tiring work however and soon they both had to take a break. Blinking furiously Vanessa realised that only a few feet away the yard opened into the welcoming grass of the meadow. Ignoring her opponent she began to crawl for it over the cobbles, the fact that she was naked and on hands on knees in front of a crowd of leering men, made her glad the mud hid the pearls of moisture that she knew were forming on her nether lips. Rae crawled after her, both girls too exhausted now to do anything other than get out of the cloying mud to rest.

**

Bartlett, like most of the other men was hoarse from shouting. More glasses of champagne had been handed out as the two sluts, mud-oiled and shining statues of erotic nudity hit, scratched and wrestled each other in the amusing and uniquely thrilling exhibition. Then they both seemed to understand they couldn't keep up the pace in the mud and, to catcalls, applause and whistles, crawled out. Quickly he grabbed another glass of champagne and drained it in one gulp before hurrying to the grass to see what they would do to each other next.

Nigel clenched his fingers in Maggie's cunt as she held her skirt up for him beside the mud pool. He hardly noticed how wet she was though, he was concentrating on Vanessa and was pleased at how well she was enduring. God! He was going to beat her until he found her limits once she'd recovered from this!

Paul took a glass of champagne from a passing girl's tray and gave it to Eve as she knelt in front of him, her spectacular breasts pillowed by the corset he had made her strip down to. He handed her the glass as he undid his flies.

"Suck me until I come and then make sure it all goes into that glass. After that you can drink it."

Eve looked up with grateful, shining eyes. "Thank you, Sir!"

Paul sighed with pleasure as her lips parted for him and he watched his other slave and her delicious – if treacherous – opponent.

Crawling made their hindquarters roll and sway superbly and their chocolate labia beckoned between the shining thighs. Heavy, chocolate melons swung ripely beneath their chests. Then as they cleared the mud by degrees they warily climbed to their feet and, slipping every now and then they made their way off the cobbles and onto the grass. Then they faced each other, bent over with hands on knees and breasts heaving delightfully.

"Give in yet?" the once-perfect-blonde asked.

"What do you think!" the once-black haired one replied.

For a moment there was nothing but distant bird song and the girls' breathing to break the silence. And then, as if some secret signal had passed between them, they charged together again. The blonde got a throw in and both girls tumbled into the soft, lush grass and rolled down the slope until the black haired one got the blonde in a headlock and brought them to a halt. The rolling had got rid of some of the mud but now they were patchworks of flesh pink and clay covered in stalks of grass. With her free hand the black haired one gripped the other's breast and squeezed so hard that Bartlett swore he saw white marks. The mud no longer being wet enough to make it slip.

Digging into fast depleting reserves, the blonde got her knee up and tried to give her opponent a dead leg but her victim twisted out of harm's way and shifted her grip from the breast to the nipple and applied the same, spiteful torment that she had suffered earlier. The blonde squealed and thrashed around desperately as the crowd, some of them bringing their drinks with them, began to follow the action into the meadow. The black haired one suddenly released her hold and as the blonde straightened up, the girl punched her. Like the blow in the caning round, it wasn't a girlie, round house, flailing blow it was much straighter and it caught the blonde bombshell full on one luscious tit – the same bruised mammary that had just been hurt – she backed off, twisted and fell. And then it was chaos as instantly the other was on her and again they rolled down the slope in a confusing tangle of arms and legs. The crowd cheered as they saw the black haired girl had her hand between the other's legs as if she were groping at her cunt!

Again they came to a stop, and as the crowd approached, Bartlett saw that just a few feet more would land the girls in the stream that flowed through the meadow. He looked around until he saw the two lads who had been judging with him and caught their eyes when they could tear them away from watching the black haired girl pinch and twist the purse of labial flesh between the blonde's thighs.

~ 210 ~

He cocked his head towards the water and saw them take his meaning and move to stand close to the water's edge.

***

Vanessa at last felt she was getting the upper hand. She could hear Rae's breathing getting noisier and she wasn't struggling as strongly as she had been. Even as Vanessa played with her cunt flesh, inflicting delicious pain on her by pinching and twisting, she was capable only of powder puff slaps and cuffs around Vanessa's head, which really didn't bother her at all. To be perfectly honest, Vanessa acknowledged with a lust-induced smile as she insinuated two jabbing fingers inside her pussy and fancied that the cunt-walls wrapped around them while she pressed her thumb hard against her engorged bud, the feel of having Rae's fabulously juicy quim at her mercy was so sweet that she could have taken anything and not lost her grip! She twirled her fingers sharply inside then withdrew them again and worked on the gloriously swollen labia once more, nipping them sharply between finger and thumb. Still locked in a sinuous knot of limbs, the girls twisted and scrambled as Vanessa shifted her grip on her opponent's cunt for a better hold and twisted it savagely, making her cry out.

"I just love this!" Vanessa whispered against Rae's shoulder as the girl arched her back in response to another savage twist, then she bent her head and bit at a nipple, holding it between her teeth just hard enough to let the bitch know that harder was always an option. She let the tip of her tongue flick the rubbery flesh of the trapped nipple and heard Rae gasp in shock. The bitch was enjoying it too! So much the better! Vanessa continued to flick until the girl moaned, her body tensed and then went slack. Then having distracted her she went for the hair again, loosened her other holds, untangled herself and as she righted herself, meshed the fingers of both hands in the dirty blonde hair as she dragged Rae Carroll to her feet with her. All of a sudden fatigue had cut in and Rae was beaten; she stood – her blue eyes almost shockingly bright as they looked out from her brown and green stained face beneath the mess of hair – staring at Vanessa as if daring her to do her worst but not fighting any more, her hands limp by her sides, her legs tantalisingly open and vulnerable. For a second Vanessa stared back, savouring the moment she had dreamed of for so many nights during her life. Then she braced her feet and roaring with effort she gathered the last of her own strength to drag Rae forwards and then swing her around full circle and propel her forwards again. The girl had no choice but to follow – or get her hair ripped out by the roots – and was sent screaming into the water.

It was surprisingly deep and Rae went under before resurfacing, choking and spluttering. There was something deeply erotic about the way the water cascaded off her breasts which now sported a rich embroidery of scratches and bruises. The recently tormented nipples were still standing hard and proud at their peaks with little droplets sparkling prettily, and her shapely thighs, smooth and gleaming flesh coloured again looked so invitingly soft. And her hair was blonde once more. Vanessa felt a catch in her throat and realised that she almost fancied her – for the split second it took to gather her breath – before she launched herself just once more. The warm wet body felt so right against hers as she bore it down to defeat and the water gurgled and thundered in her ears. This wasn't the time for niceties! She found Rae's hair once more and held on grimly. It seemed she had waited forever but at last it was payback time.

Suddenly, from out of nowhere, strong hands gripped Vanessa's arms and yanked her upwards, as she screamed in protest.

"Get off me! Let me at the fucking bitch!"

Other hands reached for Rae and then they were both back in daylight, standing up to mid thigh in freezing water with four big men from Lewington House security grinning at them.

One of them picked Vanessa up and hoisted her over his shoulder while he powered his way out of the water and set her down on the grass, behind her Rae was deposited in the same way, but she immediately collapsed to her hands and knees, gulping in huge breaths of air and periodically choking.

The man they called Bartlett appeared at Vanessa's side and took her arm, holding it up.

"The winner!" he said simply.

CHAPTER TWENTY FOUR

"Gentlemen, please!" Bartlett was astonished at the depth of the hostility that had arisen between the two slave owners. And here in the comfortable seclusion of his own private sitting room, it was woefully misplaced.

"His bitch cheated!" Paul Gregory was adamant.

"She most certainly did not!"

"Gentlemen! Gentlemen!"

Chained on either side of the imposing fireplace, the two girls at the centre of the furore were naked and hooded with their hair pulled back in ponytails and threaded through holes at the back. The one belonging to Paul Gregory was kneeling on the right, a long chain was clipped to the top of the hood and fixed to a ring in the high ceiling. Her head lolled to the side and her hands were linked together behind her back. Pickett's slut and the cause of all the trouble was chained by a different method to a ring in the floor that was set in the centre of the conversationally-arranged seating. Oblivious to their presence, she sat with legs spread, fingering her cunt.

"She cheated, Pickett!" Paul repeated his accusation yet again and with surprising venom. At his feet as he sat in the chair Eve, corseted and kneeling with her legs tucked beneath her and bound ankle and wrist, laid her head on his knee and whimpered caution. He patted her head to let her know he was aware of her concerns, then gripped her earlobe and twisted it viciously.

"No way!" Nigel replied hotly from the chair facing him. How could it all go so wrong? he wondered as he re-crossed his ankles that rested on a naked Maggie's back, shooting a look over at the cause of all the trouble – Vanessa! He'd flay the skin from her hide when he got her home, he decided as he saw his membership chances recede once more. He glanced at the other bitch and as he drank his malt whisky he couldn't help smiling to think that the silly girls didn't even know they were moored so close..... if they did they would rip each other apart again! In fact, neither was aware that the other was even in the same room. Shamed and subjugated – their submission and exploitation complete – they were pure eye candy he thought as he watched two sets of wonderfully besmirched tits rise and fall with their steady breathing. It gave him a warm glow to realise how much pain they had inflicted on each other and, whichever of them had won – surely Vanessa – it had been the most erotic thing he had ever seen. Vanessa was chained by her new belly button ring – Hah! Bet she'd never thought of that when she'd fitted it, he thought – and any sudden movement could lead to unfortunate and painful consequences. The wide, leather wrist cuffs looked so good against her skin. She was a vision of horniness that would have been totally anonymous had the men present not recognised her war-wounds. She was just a hooded body that awaited their pleasure. But the most erotic thing about it for Nigel was that she wouldn't know exactly whose pleasure she awaited, for she had had the hood fitted by one of the rubber-clad girls before being delivered naked and barefoot into the room, just as Rae had been some minutes later.

Bartlett had brought them here to reach an amicable agreement and award the prize money, their total withdrawal into privacy necessary due to the controversy of the outcome. Bartlett had generously offered non-members the use of Lewington girls in the convivial surroundings of the Veranda Bar, where everyone concerned would convene later for the official announcement. He was seated on a mahogany-framed settee –upholstered in pale gold fabric that was a real bother to clean after girls had leaked cunt juice over it and earned themselves a thrashing – he refilled his glass from the tray carried by Lush.

He used his foot to nudge Maggie aside and rose from the chair. With malt in hand, he went over to Vanessa to examine the hood in more detail. Made of soft, black leather the front was studded with silver-coloured metal and moulded attractively around the nose, with two convenient holes to ease the wearer's breathing.

"Anyone at home?" he said, rapping sharply on Vanessa's forehead. She flinched and immediately stopped frigging. Feeling more at ease now that the men laughed, Nigel asked, "Can she hear anything? It's very thin leather."

"The ears are padded on the inside," Bartlett assured him, "so she….they'll… hear nothing at all."

"And the gag?" Nigel pressed his fingers to the mouth area.

"Penis-shaped, fixed to the inside and fits….. probably uncomfortably…. down the throat."

Struck by the warm, tactile feel of the leather, Nigel ran his fingers firmly over eyes and nose, then down the side of the face and beneath the chin. As he brought his finger up the other side, he stroked beneath the nostrils and was taken aback by Vanessa's breath on his flesh, because for those few short, delightful seconds, he had almost forgotten that the wearer was a living, breathing person.

Rising from his seat, Paul approached Rae and studied her hood in the same way.

"I had the hoods made especially for Lewington House," Bartlett informed them. "Some masters prefer a snug fit to see the shape of the slave's face, as with your two, and the buckles at the back allow for the required effect."

Bartlett pointed out the small buckle in the centre of the forehead and a corresponding one at the back. This allowed for a strap with a central ring to be fixed in place so that, like Rae, the slave could be secured by the top of her head.

"May I?" Paul asked brusquely, his hand hovering over Vanessa's breast.

Nigel's look was frosty but nevertheless he didn't want to appear petty in front of Bartlett – the man was generosity itself when it came to sharing girls – and with a nod of consent he asked, "and may I?" as his hand reached for Rae's nether regions.

The two men spent the next few minutes examining the girls' charms. As Nigel rummaged in Rae's squelching cunt he remembered how she had come on to him in the office – how he had fucked her on the desk. Meanwhile, Paul was touching Vanessa for the first time, making her jerk on her chain and pull her belly-ring painfully as he took out his displeasure on her breast.

"Time for a little entertainment, Gentlemen?" Bartlett asked, then suggested, "Drag them closer to each other. Leave them chained and hooded, and let's see what happens."

Reluctantly, Paul released Vanessa's tit and instead grabbed her ponytail. Yanking her onto all fours he guided her closer to Rae, then released his hold and regained his seat. At the same time, Nigel jerked Rae's chain and encouraged her onto all fours also, drawing her toward Vanessa. Then he also returned to his seat.

Bartlett gave a harsh open-palmed Whack! across Lush's

bottom and sent her to the men to replenish their glasses while Eve and Maggie settled themselves as before.

***

Vanessa edged forward and in her dark, silent world was unaware of the men's amusement as she found her way blocked. She had no way of knowing, of course, that the obstacle was Rae. She lifted her head, sniffed and discerned the smell of leather just an inch or two from her nose. Tentatively, she lifted her chained hands and reached out exploringly. She made contact with soft, obviously female flesh and realised it was a tit! She would have smiled, had the horrid gag not obstructed her mouth and throat, for she was sure she had found her lover! Unaware of her mistake, of Rae's horror at the soft female touch, of the men's growing amusement and Maggie's fascinated consternation, she pressed on. Kneeling upright, she skimmed her fingers softly over the damaged, lavish cushions of flesh and, unable to draw her own hands apart because of the three inches or so of chain between the cuffs, gripped both tits and drew the figure closer. Then, as the watching men realised that Rae was submitting to whatever ordeal was being oh-so-gently forced upon her, Vanessa managed to pull her joined hands up between their bodies and hook them over Rae's head.

Convinced she held a hooded Maggie in her arms, Vanessa gently rubbed her own leather-encased head against Rae's, like a cat rubbing against its owner's leg. It was a gesture of pure delight as their lavish mounds squashed against each others. Soft and pliable, the twin sets of marred breastmeat quivered, warm and sensual, each girl aware of the other's heartbeat reverberating through the ripeness. Helpless to do anything but revel in the moment, Vanessa was comforted. It didn't matter that she had been accused of cheating after initially being awarded the win, didn't matter that fucking Rae Carroll was probably laughing her head off somewhere with glee, didn't matter that her beloved Master was probably displeased with her – he would get over it – she was with her lover at last! If only she could cover her wonderful body in kisses!

She felt hands pulling her backward, and her concern at once was for the chain between her hands that would surely hurt her

~ 216 ~

lover's neck as it was pulled tautly. She had no idea that it was Nigel who unfastened the mouthpiece and pulled out the stopple.

She gagged terribly as her reflexes kicked in at having the thing withdrawn! She had no idea that exactly the same thing was happening to Rae now that Paul had removed hers also.

"Shit! That was fucking murder!" she said, without knowing that Rae was talking too.

"That fucking hurt my neck!"

The men laughed as the girls failed to realise that neither of them could hear! Vanessa brought her hands back over Rae's head and eased their bodies apart enough for her to lower her head and find the turgid nipples. As she flicked her tongue joyously over them, her fingers alighted at last on the soft, hairless flesh between thighs that opened obligingly and at last found entry. Naturally she didn't hear Rae's soft murmuring, nor the men's lewd comments, just wondered why her lover didn't caress her back, until she realised that her hands were probably bound behind her. She felt the pressure on the top of her forehead as Rae put her own lips to the leather. Vanessa's fingers eased in and out, then built up to a rapid movement that had Rae's body tensing as she threw her head back. At once, Vanessa shuffled back and withdrew her fingers, skimming her hands upward until she found Rae's shoulders and gently eased her down. When she gauged that her 'lover' was in position, she stretched out on her stomach and fumbled blindly for the cunt that she knew was within her reach.

At last Vanessa's questing head found its prize. Feeling the pressure of Rae's legs on either side of her head, she clamped her lips over Rae's clitoris. Her tongue flicked it this way and that, then she nipped it gently between her teeth before sucking..... sucking..... sucking for all she was worth.....sucking.... until at last the recipient of her devotion convulsed and cried out her release.

Stunned into silence by the sheer eroticism of the moment, the men and their slaves gazed down at the intertwined bodies, the accompanying humour of the situation defusing the ill-feeling that had earlier poisoned the air.

Nigel bent down and hauled on Vanessa's chain hard enough to make her yelp and grope her way back to her position beside the fire. Paul likewise guided Rae back on her chain.

"Gentlemen," Bartlett said, breaking the silence. "We really should settle this. It is in all our interests that a further fight – at least one! – should take place. As referee I still say the declared result should stand. The blonde did most definitely use the cane in a way we hadn't intended. Nigel's slut merely reacted in such a way as to ensure that a good entertaining contest did take place. Had she not, blood would have been drawn in sufficient quantities to force a premature end to proceedings. But next time we'll word the rules more carefully so there can be no mistakes." He looked questioningly at the two men. Nigel nodded his assent immediately, Paul hesitated for a second and then nodded as well.

"Good! Let's shake on it as sportsmen."

Paul gave Nigel a wry grin as they shook hands. "They gave the punters good sport and that's all that matters," he said.

As they stood to leave, Bartlett said, "Nigel and Paul – welcome to the club! I propose we leave all four sluts here for the members to enjoy."

***

In the rich, leather scented prison of the hood, Vanessa licked her lips, savouring the taste of female sex. No one seemed to want her to do anything just now so she spread her legs once more and began to run her fingers up and down her crack, before settling down to a steady frictioning of her clitoris. In her mind's eye she replayed the final moments of victory over that bitch who had tormented her for so long.

She hoped her master would let her get at Rae Carroll again some day….. she'd wipe the floor with the stupid tart.

CONTACT

THE SILVER MOON
READER SERVICES

AT;

**Barrington Hall Publishing
Hexgreave Hall
Farnsfield
Nottinghamshire NG22 8LS
Tel: 01157 141616**

You'll find more of our superb novels of
erotic domination and submission and
there's a whole lot more, including special
offers and a magazine that's specially
written for our readers.